WE CAN'T SAVE YOU

WE CAN'T SAVE YOU

A TALE OF POLITICS, MURDER, AND MAINE

THOMAS E. RICKS

PEGASUS CRIME

NEW YORK LONDON

WE CAN'T SAVE YOU

Pegasus Crime is an imprint of
Pegasus Books, Ltd.
148 West 37th Street, 13th Floor
New York, NY 10018

Copyright © 2025 by Thomas E. Ricks

First Pegasus Books cloth edition June 2025

Interior design by Maria Fernandez

Map on page ix by Gene Thorp

Library of Congress Cataloging-in-Publication Data is available.

ISBN: 978-1-63936-907-2

10 9 8 7 6 5 4 3 2 1

Printed in the United States of America
Distributed by Simon & Schuster
www.pegasusbooks.com

For my family: Mary Kay, Chris, Eva, Molly,
Mohammad, Sofie, June, and Violet

CAST OF CHARACTERS

Ryan Tapia: FBI agent based in Bangor, Maine

Solidarity Harrison: high-end fish marketer with emerging political ambitions

Al Castillo: Republican nominee for governor of Maine

Paul Soco: member of the Malpense Indian tribe

Captain Renny Sanpeer: police chief on the main Malpense Indian Reservation

James Reveur: member of the Quivive tribe

Rock: becomes chief of security for the March to the Future

Mook: member of march who becomes the unofficial spokesman for the march

Other members of the march: Seaweeds, Red, Trout, Distant Thunder, Blood, Moosecollar, Lonesome Whale, King Turtle, Tallfellow, Daylights, Big Duck, Pigtoe, and Gutter

Jimmy Love: FBI resident agent in Portland, Maine

Bob Bulster: Love's boss in Boston

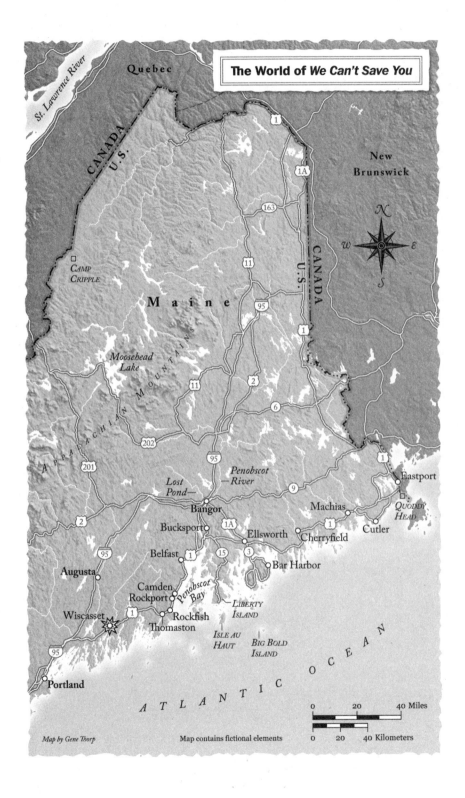

Quebec

St. Lawrence River

The World of We Can't Save You

New Brunswick

CANADA
U.S.

1

1A

163

CANADA
U.S.

11

95

1

□ CAMP CRIPPLE

Maine

N
W E
S

Moosehead Lake

11

2

6

APPALACHIAN MOUNTAINS

202

95

1

201

Lost Pond

Penobscot River

9

Eastport

□ QUODDY HEAD

2

Bangor

Machias

Cutler

Bucksport

1A

Ellsworth

Cherryfield

1

Belfast

1

15

3

Bar Harbor

Augusta

Camden
Rockport

Penobscot Bay

Wiscasset

1

Rockfish
Thomaston

LIBERTY ISLAND

ISLE AU HAUT

BIG BOLD ISLAND

95

Portland

ATLANTIC OCEAN

Map by Gene Thorp

Map contains fictional elements

0   20   40 Miles

0   20   40 Kilometers

PROLOGUE
"CAMP CRIPPLE"

MAINE, FEBRUARY 1945

It was a hell of a place to locate a prisoner of war camp, deep in the mountains of northwestern Maine, hard up against the Canadian border. During World War II, the Americans treated most of their German prisoners decently—quite well, in fact—feeding them good meat and healthy vegetables and even a ration of beer. The captive soldiers cut wood in Colorado, reaped wheat in Kansas, and picked potatoes in eastern Maine. They were paid for their labor and had military shops called PXs in each camp where they could buy soap, toothpaste, candy, and tobacco, all of a quality that had not been seen in German stores for years. In turn, most German prisoners were cooperative. By war's end, some even would be ready to marry local American girls and settle down.

But by late 1944, it became clear that there was a problem in several camps—a lethal one. Germans who were true believers in both Nazism and the inevitability of an Axis victory had estab-lished an enforcement system that punished prisoners who reported on the Nazi power structure inside the prison camps. This system also was used to attack those merely suspected of being on the verge of turning, resulting often in the targeting of onetime leftists, Poles, Czechs, and other foreigners who had been swept up into the Wehrmacht. In several camps, prisoners died of "suicides" that looked suspicious.

With the passage of time, and the lack of American retaliation, the Nazi enforcers became more brazen. One informant was found hanging at dawn in front of the camp commander's office, no place for a quiet suicide. Another who had complained to prison authorities about these enforcers was found with his throat cut and his genitals mutilated. A prisoner in the disciplinary camp at Camp Rupert, Idaho, was discovered by the Nazi officers to be of Jewish background. He was found crucified behind the latrines.

That was the last straw. At that point the US Army rounded up all prisoners listed in their files as hardcore Nazis, as well as the senior German officer in all camps where murders had occurred, and shipped them by train and truck over muddy logging roads deep into the backwoods of Maine. The weak jokes among Army officials was that this would be "The Fritz Ritz," "supercamp for uberchumps," "the nastiest Nazis." The location had been picked mainly for its inaccessibility, but also because it sat below a hillside spring that each hour dependably delivered hundreds of gallons of clean, clear water.

In a nod to northern Maine's heavily Franco-American population, the official name for the place was Camp Lafayette, but because of the unusual way the Pentagon staffed the place, it soon became known within the Army as "Camp Cripple." Every single US Army officer running the camp, it became apparent upon meeting them, had been seriously wounded fighting the Germans. The camp commandant, Colonel John "Whistling Jack"

Allen, had been hit twice, once in each world war. In the first one, he had been a lieutenant in the infantry when a bullet hit one side of his face, knocked out a few teeth, and exited through the other cheek. Thereafter, when he yelled in drunken anger, some air would whistle through the small hole in his right cheek. It whistled a lot. Early in the American entry into World War II, Allen was commanding a regiment in Tunisia when his Jeep hit a landmine. He was thrown almost completely clear, but the edge of the overturning vehicle landed on his left ankle and crushed the entire foot.

The wounds of his executive officer, Major Robert "Walking Bob" Walker, were less evident. During fighting at Anzio, in Italy, he had been hit in the spine and back of the head by grenade shrapnel, leaving him with headaches and back pain that made it nearly impossible to get restful sleep. At the POW camp this led to a neat division of responsibilities—he avoided Colonel Allen by sleeping most of the day, then sat smoking at his desk until dusk, and finally walked the camp perimeter much of the night, which he had found eased the pain, especially when he stirred a little morphine into his whiskey.

The inmates of this camp deep in the big north woods remained quiet during the clear, crisp days of fall of 1944, and into the winter. Every morning at prisoner formation they eyed the poster-sized map of Europe hanging on the wall in front of the commandant's office. It had two pieces of red yarn, each held in place by several thumbtacks. The one on the left depicted the location of the Allied advance through France and into Germany. The one on the right showed the progress of Soviet forces in the East. Each morning when the prisoners gathered, they would discuss the map. The two lines of yarn were edging toward each other. The prisoners would shake their heads and mutter, "Russkies." By early 1945 it was evident that there was no way Germany would win, or even arrive at a conditional surrender with the West that would preserve some portion of German power.

In those cold months in 1945, the prisoners began to recognize that defeat was inevitable. Some of them, especially those whose roles in the killings were widely known, grew worried. They once had been confident they would eventually go home to be decorated for their loyalty while being held prisoner, but now began to fear that when peace came, they would be held accountable for the murders they had planned and overseen. And so they began to plot some kind of breakout. They had no hope of making it to Germany or Europe. Rather, they aimed to simply get out of the camp and disappear into Canada, where their records would not be so well known.

They had calculated by the comings and goings of trucks and their sightings of airplanes that their camp was only a short hike from the international border with Quebec. They had even heard and seen workmen heading up there to erect a gate and reinforce barbed wire fences. They knew there were a handful of guards posted at that new gate, but figured that battle-hardened Germans could overcome the kinds of soldiers posted deep in the woods, who either would be invalids or boys. They also had noticed that the regular guards went on leave on the weekends, with their posts filled by clerks, cooks, and drivers barely trained for combat.

They also had what they considered good luck. The sloppiness and indiscipline of American workers no longer surprised them—in previous weeks they had collected a wrench and a hacksaw left lying around by workmen. On a recent evening, one of the workers had left behind a pair of wire cutters while eating dinner at the camp. That night they grabbed and concealed the tool.

A few days later, on a cold and cloudy Saturday night in February, when it was overcast, with a steady snow falling that would cover their tracks, sixteen of them, the hardest of the lot, waited in the latrine that had been built a bit distant from the barracks to keep away flies and odors. They lifted a cover from a hole already cut in the boards of the back wall and sent out a man with the cutters, low-crawling on his knees and elbows, to open a passage in the barbed wire. It took an agonizingly long time—he was wearing socks as mittens, which made his cutting awkward. But after twenty minutes of his efforts, they slipped out quietly. They angled through the woods to the path leading up the ridge to the US–Canada gate. There were, in fact, no soldiers present at the gate, which again made them praise their luck. There was no way to cut open the thick wood and metal grating of the gate, so they began to climb it, dropping down into the "no-man's-land" between the American and Canadian fences.

Just a hundred yards away from that gate, Major Walker lay in the woods in a sleeping bag burrowed under the snow. An American soldier on his left had an electrical latching switch laid out in front of him, his hand waiting just in front of its n-shaped handle. On Walker's right, another soldier waited with a detonator linked by wire to a series of mines they had placed in the no-man's-land between the fences.

When the last of the escapees was hanging on the American fence and the first were getting to the top of the Canadian, Walker slapped the soldier on his left on the back and said, "Juice, now." The fences electrified, giving off long blue arcs that snapped into the cold night air. Men began flying backwards off them into the area between the two fences, their bones making cracking sounds as they hit the frozen earth. A moment later, Walker slapped the soldier on his right and said, "Detonate, now." Snow and soil erupted for a hundred feet in either direction along the no-man's-land. Walker and the two soldiers themselves put their heads down and their arms over them as their bodies were pummeled by a quick and heavy rain of wood, dirt, arms, and legs.

In the morning a burial party collected the frozen corpses, counting a total of fifteen torsos. The camp's commanders had known that sixteen were planning on escaping, which is one reason they had turned a blind eye to the hole cut in the back of the latrine and also arranged for the wire cutters to be left in plain sight. The search-and-burial party found a blood track into the woods and followed it about a thousand feet, where they discovered the last corpse, partly chewed on by wolves or coyotes.

The usual Army policies were followed in reporting the deaths and giving the bodies a decent burial. All sixteen were buried under grave markers that looked like the standard Army issue. These were a slab of cement with a curved top, except for one small and very different feature: Instead of Christian crosses, each gravestone bore a German "Iron Cross" with a swastika at its center. And there they stayed in the cold, cold ground of the remote Maine woods, undisturbed for many decades.

PART I

COASTS

1
RYAN TAPIA'S HOUSE, LOST POND, MAINE

PRESENT DAY

Ryan Tapia, a thirty-three-year-old FBI agent assigned to the Bureau's remotest post in the northeast, in Bangor, Maine, lay in bed with his lover, Solidarity Harrison, a high-end seafood merchant from the coastal town of Rockfish.

She was on her side, her left hand supporting her head, her long brown hair strewn about, her right hand resting on his stomach. They were not talking about anything in particular, just enjoying post-sex chatting, contented and resting. Ryan found himself focused on a freckle high on her chest, just above the location of her heart. He loved that mark, romantically thinking of it as containing her essence. Ryan usually was not sentimental or questioning of life but today was in a contemplative mood. "Thing is," he told her, "this is the first relationship I've been in where I know the woman is smarter than I am, much smarter."

Solid didn't dispute the comparison. She looked at him, thinking for a moment, her high forehead slightly furrowed, and finally asked, "Does that scare you?"

"You know it doesn't," he said. "I like it. But it's harder than I thought it would be."

She considered that. "You called me 'the woman'? It's funny you don't call me your girlfriend."

He studied her face for signs of irritation. He didn't see any. "Solid, you're wonderful. You're my lover. You're a special friend. You mean a lot to me. But one thing I wouldn't call you is 'girlfriend.'"

"Why?"

"It wouldn't be accurate. You're no girl." This was a reference to her being fifteen years older than him.

She seemed to take that on board. "Why does my intelligence worry you?" she said.

"I always feel like you're a step ahead of me."

"That's not necessarily bad."

"It is if I get left behind," he said.

"What's bothering you?" she asked.

He thought a moment, and then told her. "I dreamed last night that we were up in Baxter Park, hiking, and you turned to me and said, 'I'm going to climb this mountain, but you can't.'"

"What do you think that meant?" she asked.

"I think I'm realizing that we're on different tracks in life. I know who I am, who I am going to be. I'm a foot soldier in federal law enforcement. Got it. I'm alright with that. In fact, I like it. It's comforting to know who I am."

"But?" She sounded slightly worried.

"But it isn't where you're at. You're still climbing, ascending in life. There's a restless energy in you. You always have one foot in the moment, the other stepping into the future. Who knows where you are going. I sure don't. You could wind up a big CEO, or going into politics."

Solid's face fell. For the first time in their relationship, now several months old, Solid appeared genuinely at a loss. Almost scared. She got up from the bed, threw a blanket around her shoulders. He thought her body looked terrific, but she felt she was too old to be seen while standing up naked. "Either lying down bare or standing up covered, that's what you get," she had stated. She paced back and forth.

He watched her. He hadn't meant to upset her. "Solid, I didn't mean—" he began.

"Please be quiet, just give me a few minutes," she said softly. She continued to walk the bedroom. She was in one of her most intense, concentrated moods, he could tell. He could see that the small squiggly temporal vein on the right side of her forehead was pulsing.

Eventually she spoke. "First of all, Ryan, you are smarter than you think," she said. "You may not articulate it, but you sense a lot."

He waited. He was not sure where this was going. He had learned to focus and try to keep up with her. That's what he was trying to tell her, that it was an effort, but one he didn't mind. But sometimes it added a dose of uncertainty that he found perplexing.

When she turned again, he saw that her eyes had welled up. "Ryan, I don't know how you sensed it, but you are right. I haven't told a soul, but I am considering running for Congress."

He sat up in bed. "Solid, that's great."

She held her crossed arms tight against herself. "I don't know. We'll see. And remember, you may not always be the person you think you are now. Sometimes we don't get to choose how and when we change." This indeed was something Ryan knew all too well. One truck driver not paying attention and blinded by the rising California sun had killed his family and blown apart his old life in that state. The eventual settlement the construction company had paid of $4 million meant nothing to him. He almost resented the money. He had deposited it in a bank and rarely thought about it.

2
A MAN DROPS IN

It was a fine spring morning, cloudless and calm. The waters of the Gulf of Maine were ideal for spearing flounder, so "Peeled Paul" Soco was slowly rowing in the shallows just west of Big Bold Island, where he had lived alone as a hermit for two full years. He was moving along at just more than a drift, peering over the gunwales, searching the sandy bottom for the telltale signs of flounder—that is, a slight oval bump in the sand and a curious fish eye watching for worms and minnows to eat.

Paul noted just such a bump on the ocean floor, a good-sized flounder at least eighteen inches long. He raised his three-pronged spear and prepared to jab it into the water. As he did, an insistent chainsaw-like sound came buzzing across the surface of the water. Paul looked up in irritation. He assumed it was a boat. He didn't like unwanted visitors. Tall and lithe, with a sharp, narrow face, Paul's aspect tended to deter people from landing. Still, visitors had become a problem since he had been publicized as the "Indian hermit of Big Bold Island" in the wake of a murder case in which he had been called as a witness a year earlier.

He especially didn't like his fishing interrupted. He cherished his time alone on the island, even though global overheating was changing it in ways that worried him. Last year the crab population had collapsed. This year he was seeing fewer lobsters.

He looked in the direction of the unwanted noise and saw that it was not a watercraft but a small plane coming at him, very low, maybe one hundred feet above the water. It had spotted him. The buzzsaw sound of its single propeller grew louder as the plane came closer. It dropped a bit lower, then circled above his dory, its left wing dipped downward. Paul watched it, now growing worried. Something was up.

The left door of the aircraft opened. The plane dipped that wing even lower, and a body dropped out the open door. Even at that height, it was clear that this was not a live person—there was no struggle, no scream, no arm moving to resist. It looked to Paul as if it were coming straight down at him. He leaned on the spear to push his dory a few feet to the right. Still, the stiff body hit the water close enough that the impact splashed him. It disappeared down into the shallow water, then bobbed back up. The plane wheeled and headed to the west, the direction it had come from.

Paul rowed the dory over to the corpse. It was a man who looked about twenty-five to thirty years old, he thought. It was hard to tell because the guy, now stiff and gray-skinned, clearly had been dead for a day or two. To Paul's eye, he looked kind of Native American, but not one from Maine. Somehow his jaw looked longer, and the hairline a bit higher, than Paul's family, friends, and neighbors on the reservation where he had grown up.

But the most striking thing about this corpse was a yellow wig nailed to the skull. What was that about? Paul looped a stern line around the corpse's neck and rowed back to his island. He didn't want to touch the body, so he pulled on the rope and dragged it up the flat rocks to the edge of the woods. As he did, he saw that a screwdriver handle protruded from the dead man's chest, just above his heart. To keep off the crows and badgers, he covered the man with a spare tarp he'd found on shore one morning after a storm, then put a line of rocks on either side of it.

Then he sat down next to it. "Talk to me, man," he said to the covered corpse. Who was it? Why was it dropped dangerously close to him? And what was with that wig?—clearly added by someone else after this man's premature death.

He got back in the dory and rowed a mile or two north to where he knew he could get a weak cell signal. He dialed Ryan Tapia, an FBI agent he had met during that murder case, and told him about the body dropping in.

Ryan's first question was jurisdictional: "Did the body hit the water, or your island?"

"What does it matter?" Paul asked.

"In the water, it's a case for Maine. On the island, which belongs to your tribe, it might be a case for the tribe. But that airplane complicates things. If the flight's interstate, then it's on my plate."

The next morning, Ryan came out to the island, driven in a National Park Service boat by "the Stoned Ranger," as the marijuana-puffing officer from Acadia National Park was known. There was a third man in the big Boston Whaler. Ryan hopped off the boat onto the beach and said, "I brought Lieutenant D'Agostino, the state trooper in charge of their homicide work."

Tapia and D'Agostino took photographs. "Doesn't look like anyone on our missing persons list," D'Agostino said, checking his heavy-duty laptop.

"What's with the yellow wig?" Ryan asked. "Mean anything to either of you?"

"Not off the top of my head," D'Agostino said, and laughed at his own joke. Paul Soco simply shook his head. That wig, and the two roofing nails holding it onto the man's skull, creeped him out.

D'Agostino knelt next to the corpse and inked the ends of its fingers. "It's surprisingly difficult to take the prints of a stiff," he observed to Ryan and Paul. "They lack flexibility. Almost unco-operative, like."

3
THE RETURN OF THE NATIVE AMERICAN

Two days later Paul was rowing to the other side of his little island when he saw a Boston Whaler adrift. He went to it and saw a dead body lying in it. This time he recognized the guy. It was Tinker Paradis, a Malpense Indian who sometimes crewed on swordfish boats, but when he got lonesome for his people came back to fish out of Malpense Island. His wrists were slashed, and his hunting knife lay next to him, covered in blood. Next to the knife was an empty bottle of Fireball Cinnamon Whisky.

He called Ryan again. "I think this is a sign."

"Of what?"

"Two dead Indians in four days? Something is telling me it's time for me to leave this island."

"Because you're next?"

"No, because my people are dying. The vibe is bad. The climate is screwy. There's something wrong. Badly wrong."

"What are you going to do about it?"

That question surprised Paul. He thought Ryan understood Native Americans better than that. "Go to them, of course." That afternoon he packed up. In the morning, he awoke with an even stronger feeling that it was time to leave his island home. His two years on it had served their purpose. He had done penance for unintentionally causing the death of his father, and in the process of living alone, surviving on his own, and being truly isolated, he had become a new person. He had reconnected to nature and given himself a new start in life. Now it was time to repay that debt to nature, he felt. The question was: How?

He put out his uneaten food as a treat for the island's deer and birds. He rowed his dory the few miles east to Malpense Island. There he hitched a ride on a fishing boat taking a haul to the mainland, and then hitchhiked his way toward his tribe's main reservation, on the very eastern edge of Maine.

Homecomings rarely go as expected. By mid-afternoon Paul had been dropped off on the highway that crossed the Malpense reservation on its way south to Eastport. He walked on a gravel road a few minutes to his family's old mobile home. He stopped out front and gazed at it. The place looked different, felt odd. Someone had left a child's plastic car in the front yard. He turned the knob. It was locked. That was strange—his family had never done that. He knocked. A woman came to the door. Clearly a Malpense, but he didn't recognize her. "Can I help you?" she said softly.

"I don't know," he said. He was puzzled. "Who are you?"

She stared at this stranger. "I think you should go," she said, and closed the door.

Paul walked back down the steps to the street. The tribal police chief, Renny Sanpeer, rolled up in his official pickup truck, with its door depicting the tribe's official emblem, a three-pronged fishing spear and hunting arrow crossed with each other. "I just heard you were back on the res," the big-bellied policeman said.

"Hey, Renny," Paul replied. "News travels fast." He gestured with his thumb over his shoulder. "What's up with my house?"

"With your father dead and you out on the island, it was unoccupied for more than eighteen months, so we put in a family that needed shelter. That's the tribal way. Anyway, they're related to you—your mother's cousin from Calais."

"I never knew her," Paul said. "And it's my house."

"In fact, it's your family's house—and she's part of your family. It stands on tribal soil. All the land is common to the tribe, you know that. 'We don't own it, we just care for it and it cares for us,' you've heard all that stuff." He was quoting one of the basic principles of the tribe.

Paul sagged. This was not the homecoming he had dreamed about.

"Hop in," Sanpeer said. "I'll give you a ride." He knew that the reservation's sober house, intentionally built large, had two bedrooms that were unoccupied. All Paul needed was one of them, and the company there wouldn't be bad. The others in the house would be pleased to have him there—Paul Soco had become kind of a legend, the Indian who lived alone on a remote sea island through two Maine winters without asking for any help.

"You're thinner," Sanpeer assessed. "Gone real OG Indian, huh?"

"So they say," Paul said. He glanced at Sanpeer's stomach, bulging over his holster belt. "You could try it."

As they drove slowly across the reservation, Sanpeer scanned the streets out of habit while he asked Paul questions out of a pressing need to figure out what his presence portended. "Are you planning to run for chief?" he asked. "If so, between you and me, you've got my full support."

Tribal politics, Paul thought. The gaming is incessant. He had forgotten about that. And it was beginning instantly. He didn't even have a place to lay his head yet and a powerful official was sucking up to him.

"I got no intention of doing that," Paul said. "Not quite the hermit lifestyle, you know?"

"Well, what are you going to do?" Sanpeer asked. Paul detected a slightly less friendly tone now. It was as if Sanpeer had switched from feeling the need to polish him up to taking an opportunity to put him in his place. In fact, Sanpeer was not being as calculating as that. Paul's unexpected presence simply made the policeman nervous. Paul had built a powerful reputation as a "big spirit," and that could make life difficult for someone entrusted to oversee law and order. Sanpeer's job was to maintain the equilibrium of the place, and Paul's roiling presence could upset that in a number of ways.

"I have some ideas," Paul said.

Now the policeman became downright Anglo in his directness. He stopped scanning, braked the pickup truck, and looked directly at Paul. "Are you here to make trouble?" he said.

"Not for you," Paul said. "And if I do, it will be good trouble."

A frown crossed the man's face. "I don't know I like the sound of that. Is it going to upset the Elders?"

Paul wanted to reassure him. "I think you and I both know that anything that makes tomorrow different from yesterday is going to bug them. 'Do nothing, say nothing, everyone's happy,'" he said, citing the line with which people mocked the Elders—but only behind their backs. They were still powerful, both in spiritual terms and in the hard numbers of the budget, which the tribal council had to submit to them for approval.

"Yep," Sanpeer said.

"But before I do anything, I'll talk to you, okay?" This was Paul's olive branch.

That calmed down the police chief a bit. As Paul had discerned, the main thing the police chief wanted was not to be surprised. If he could tell the Elders and the state police what was coming down the pike, that bolstered his standing. A good police chief maintained a steady awareness of what was happening on his turf and kept his overseers informed.

Sanpeer parked and walked Paul into the sober house. Paul, carrying only his little rucksack, was greeted with smiles, Sanpeer a bit less so. At one time or another, the police chief had arrested every single one of the eight people living there, even the house's supervisor. Generally speaking, no one likes to wake up in a drunk tank. At the same time, everyone knew that Renny took pride in serving up a good breakfast in the jailhouse, in part because he ate the same meal. On Saturday and Sunday mornings, after the traditional hard-drinking nights, he cooked up eggs, sausage, bacon, and cornbread, and put them on the table with big pitchers of strong coffee and cold orange juice. It was a meal almost worth getting blind drunk for.

Sanpeer walked alone back out to his truck. Well, he thought to himself, it could be worse. At least, he thought, Soco's not a casino whore, like some other young up-and-coming Indians he knew.

4
THE RISE AND FALL OF JIMMY LOVE

R yan Tapia, the sole occupant of the Bangor suboffice of the FBI, was having a difficult time figuring out his new boss in the FBI's office in Portland. Jimmy Love had been a young star, made head of the Bureau's Miami office by the age of thirty-eight. He had been going places.

But some people change in midlife. A lot. One morning shortly after he turned forty years old, Jimmy Love was at an FBI farewell party for a retiring agent. These were always well-attended events, in part because the Bureau's "retirees" tended to go on to second careers in corporate security and could be good contacts down the road, either for information or for jobs. But Jimmy found the entire evening disorienting. He stood and wondered to himself: What had this man retiring done with his life? What did it matter? When people spoke to Jimmy that evening, he sometimes found it difficult to understand them. Their words washed over him like outpourings of meaningless mush.

In the morning, he awakened in the same dysphoric mood. It was as if a switch inside his head that had been "on" for forty energetic years had suddenly clicked to "off." He doubted everything in his life, everything he had done. His achievements seemed empty, his work a fool's errand. He once had found each day promising drama; now the day stretched before him in an end-less mist of gray boredom. He sat that morning at his breakfast table for hours, sipping a cold coffee, and pondered: What did it matter if he nabbed one more accountant who was illegally moving untaxed money to offshore havens? There would always be another. And more Medicare fraud doctors. And more dishonest lawyers whose hands were sticky with clients' assets. And more scammers in the swampy Gulf coast towns ripping off seniors with "surefire" financial instruments. As he thought about it, the years to come seemed a waste of breath, as did the years behind.

When he finally stood up, dressed, and walked to his car, instead of driving north then east into the office, where he usually was the first one in, he turned south and headed toward Coconut Grove, with no particular destination in mind. He spent most of the late morning strolling the wharves of marinas, looking at boats and watching the ponderous gray pelicans. He drank three martinis with his waterfront lunch of blackened redfish and rice.

That afternoon, on a boozy whim, he wrote a check for $90,000 for a thirty-two-foot Century powerboat. Thereafter he was on it every weekend when the weather was good. Sometimes he would motor out to the Gulf Stream, turn off the engine, and just drift, admiring the blue water, gazing back at the office buildings lining Brickell Avenue visible to the distant west. Sucker traps, those glassy high-rises now seemed to him. He got into fishing, even installing a gas grill overhanging the stern so that he could sear fresh-caught fillets of pompano and grouper. He once had spent hours online studying how to track down financial fraud; now his screen time was devoted mainly to where the big fish were biting. He named his boat "The Field," so when people phoned he could jokingly say he was "in the field," as if he were out investigating something. But it stopped being a joke, especially for subordinate agents who began wondering what had happened to their boss, once a genuine Bureau firebreather but now an insouciant angler.

He even began to take the boat out on weekdays. At first, he would tell himself that he needed to think over a particularly knotty office problem. But eventually he stopped trying to pretend. He was working half time and getting away with it. Life was good. Behind the back of the special agent in charge, they began calling him "Breaker," because when anyone called him when he was on the boat, he would say, "Hey, you're breaking up, send me an email." He began dating an English teacher from the Ransom Everglades school who got him into reading Irish poetry. With her encouragement, he let his hair grow long, far longer than was usual for an FBI agent, especially one in charge of an important office.

All went well that fall and winter, until one pretty Friday in late February. Over breakfast he checked the forecast and saw that the weather promised to be perfect—77 degrees and brilliantly sunny. And the fishing was good. The blues were running in the Gulf Stream. How could he resist a day on the boat? He pulled in three big hogfish. After he laid each one atop the ice in the cooler, he took out a cold can of beer to celebrate the catch. The third Heineken persuaded him to cut the engine and take a nap. He turned off his phone and radio, went below, lay down in the side berth and closed his eyes. The gentle waves of the Stream rocked him into a deep sleep.

Unfortunately for Jimmy Love's career, he had gone below at precisely the same moment that the president, on a whim, ended a lunch at the White House with the director of the FBI by inviting the man to join him on Air Force One for a flight down to Miami that afternoon. The president wanted to get a sense of the director's private views on some national security issues, and perhaps also to be alerted to any inside skinny the FBI had on some of his likely opponents in the next election. They had a grand time on the flight, with the director feeding him some tidbits about one senator's penchant for triangular sex. The president was perplexed. "I don't get it," he confessed. "Sex between two people is complex enough. What's the fun of making it more complicated?"

"Well," the director said with a shrug, "most guys play checkers, he's into chess."

"Check and mate!" the president punned weakly.

The director laughed boisterously. "Good one, sir!" The president liked that. Some people who hold power are uneasy with obvious suck-ups, but to this president, such oleaginous behavior reassured him that all was right with his world.

After Air Force One landed in Miami, the president bid the director goodbye on the tarmac and strode to his waiting limousine. Sycophants often require obeisance in turn. The director looked around the area for his local agent in charge, who under usual protocol would be waiting planeside to learn the director's plans and wishes for the weekend. Instead he saw someone who clearly was FBI but whom he didn't know. The man hesitated a moment before saying, "Hello, sir. How was your flight?"

"Who are you?"

"Wilson, number three in Miami. The office deputy is on vacation."

"And the SAC—Jimmy Love, right?" persisted the director.

"Uh, we've been unable to locate him, sir," the man said.

The director took that on board. A special agent in charge gone AWOL?

In fact, by this point Jimmy was only a few miles to the south, at his boat's marina in the Grove. He had berthed it and happily strolled over for an early dinner at the marina's high-end joint. He ordered a Caesar salad and a martini. When his second martini arrived, he idly turned on his phone to catch up on the day. There were, he saw to his chagrin, some thirty-two emails, sixteen texts, and forty-eight voicemails, all from his office. There also were two messages from his ex-wife. A sampling gave him the gist of them all—he had fucked up.

And so began, by the skin of his teeth, the next, much humbler phase of Jimmy's new career, as the sole occupant of the FBI's branch in Portland, Maine, a sub-office of the Bureau's Boston office. He only managed to eke out that demotion, rather than a termination, by putting on an abject display of shame the following morning, showing up at the director's cabana on Key Biscayne with cold champagne, flanked by two younger agents carrying three-dozen shucked oysters on ice and a bouquet of roses—the last a peculiar FBI tradition dating back to the glory days of J. Edgar Hoover and Clyde Tolson. The director's parting words to him were, "And get a fucking haircut."

Thereafter he became known as a cautionary tale in Bureau circles. After two or three drinks, someone at a social gathering of agents would say, "Did you hear about old Jimmy Love? Whoa!"

And someone else would respond, "Yeah, what the hell happened to him?" And they would philosophize about the hazards of the job, especially as one aged.

Sometimes during the dark gray days of the Maine winter, Jimmy would think back to that day of wine and roses. He missed the Century boat. Not much else.

"I feel like I am in a witness protection program up here," Love said to Ryan on their first meeting. Ryan suspected that Love, with his leathery, lined face but still trim build, was that most unusual of men in civilian life, an alcoholic who worked out regularly and was—aside from his liver, which was also getting a workout—in pretty good physical shape.

In their second conversation, two weeks later, Love added, "I don't think you really need to call me so much. Maybe just email. No worries. No one really cares what we do up here, you know?" He was getting into sailing.

Ryan wasn't sure where he stood with Jimmy Love. But having the Bureau's most notorious fuckup as his immediate supervisor made him uneasy.

5
PAUL SOCO'S MEETING WITH JOHN OF TIDES

The old man had long gone blind and couldn't walk, but still loved being outdoors. So when Paul Soco went to see him, he asked that they go outside. His name was John of Tides. At the age of eighty-eight, he was the senior member of the tribal Elders. His daughter wrapped a wool blanket around him and pushed the wheelchair down the ramp, where she handed it over to Paul. "Head for the beach," John ordered, pointing eastward.

They rolled along in silence. John sniffed the air and listened for a moment. "Mid-ebb," he said. Paul was impressed. Most anyone who lived near the sea knew that high tide and low tide smelled different, but to catch the tide at the middle, and to know it was going out, that impressed him. "How can you tell?" he asked.

"Easy enough," John of Tides said slowly. Paul had to lean forward to hear his words. "I can smell seaweed, but not the sea muck that's farther out—and that means the tide is about half."

"And how did you know it was on the ebb?"

"Well, I knew the high was about three hours ago. But also, as we sit here, I can hear the terns and gulls. They are eating as they follow the tide out, trying to catch the worms and snails as they are exposed by the fall of the water. You don't hear that when the tide is flowing in."

At the beach, Paul stood next to him and shared why he had decided to leave his hermit life on the island. After all his years, getting to know the rhythms of the land and water, he was attuned to the changes, and it was now time for action. He wanted to organize what he thought of as "The High Tide Movement." The idea was that with climate change accelerating, it was time for their people to pay serious attention to preparatory steps. It was of particular interest to them, the Malpense, because the tribe lived in low land adjoining the sea. Paul's notion was to stop traffic on the state highway that crossed the reservation for an hour every day during the daylight high tide. "It's our land, and we are recognized as a nation under the treaty with Maine," he said. Where it all would lead, he didn't know. His initial thought was that global overheating violated the treaties between the Indians and the British that had been signed in colonial times. In those documents, both sides had pledged to care for the land and the creatures that lived on it. Exactly how his protests would play out would have to be seen. He wanted to signal that it was time to take a different approach.

John, as attuned to the state of the ocean as Paul was, and probably even more so, was sympathetic. "I like your attitude, young Paul Soco," he said. "Things are heating up too much around here. Oysters this year started growing earlier and faster than I've ever known. Lobster shells are getting thinner cuz of acidity in the ocean. We've had fog blow in from the north, which is just wrong. Lakes are warming up. Insect mix is changing. Storms are getting more intense. I've heard birds I've never heard before—like a crested caracara from Mexico. I would have liked to be able to see that bird. Like an eagle, my daughter said. I've heard of barracuda being caught about one hundred miles offshore, and they've never been found this far north before." He paused for a moment, then said, "Anyway, something's going haywire."

Old John held up a bony index finger that trembled in the air. "Now, the other Elders, they're not gonna like it," he said. "Stopping traffic, getting in the Anglos' faces, that makes some of them nervous. I can't make any promises. But I'll sound them out. We need to do something before it is too late. I can do my part here. And I think you are a good person to lead the way out there."

That was all Paul wanted. As they were rolling back to his house, Paul asked how the unusual family name was developed. "Well, as you know, tides are real important hereabouts, with the twenty-foot variation," John said. "I am told that my great-great-grandfather wasn't real smart about a lot of things, didn't speak well, but he was totally attuned to the tides here. He could tell you when the highs and lows would be a week, or a month, or even a year ahead. Also when the king tides would come in, always good to know." Those were the huge tides, created by the alignment of the moon and the sun, that added an extra two or three feet on top of the area's regular twenty-foot rise.

"When's the next king tide here?" Paul asked.

"About five Sundays from now, mid-July, right around noon. Gonna be a whopper. Maybe twenty-three foot. Even twenty-six, if the wind is from the south. We call that big summer one the Lobster Tide, because the lobsters ride the tides in from the deep ocean around then, as the coastal water warms up to where they like it."

"Will the water come up across the causeway?"

"Pretty sure it will."

Paul filed that away.

"I have one final thought for you, Paul Soco," the old man said.

"Yes?"

"It's not going to be easy. You've been alone, living a hermit's life. Now you are going to be putting yourself out there, breaking your routine, asking people to follow you."

"I hear you," Paul said. He had been worrying about this but hadn't articulated his concern in the way that John of Tides just had.

"I'm glad you're doing this," John of Tides said as his daughter helped him back inside. Then he pulled the blanket tighter and shut his eyelids over his whitened eyes.

6

THE WORLDVIEW OF PHYLLIS AMES

R yan called Lt. D'Agostino at the state police. "Who would you consider the most imaginative drug investigator in Maine?"

"Funny you should ask," D'Agostino said without hesitation. "I was just talking to her. Phyllis Ames, down in Kittery. Maine Drug Enforcement. Consistently impressive. Always interested in what's going on out in the field. Gets the job done with a minimum of fuss, too." D'Agostino gave him a cell number.

Ryan called Ames, told her D'Agostino sent him, and said, "Do you know anyone who would drop a dead body out of a plane on a guy who was fishing offshore?"

"Not really," said Ames.

Ryan figured it was another dead end. But Ames asked Ryan to tell her about the case. "Airplane. And maybe newcomers. That combination gets my spidey sense tingling," she said.

"How come?"

"Well, you know, I-95 used to be a total pipeline for narcotics coming into Maine. As the state's lead drug agent in Kittery, I'm kind of the gatekeeper for interstate traffic coming in. We knew that tons were being brought in every year, and that we were only getting a fraction. But that changed in the last couple of years."

"How?"

"We put the hurt on that traffic up the turnpike. Basically, we used artificial intelligence to do fast searches of digitized car registration information. You know those tollbooth counters where you don't slow down?"

"Yeah, E-ZPass."

"Well, with a federal grant we reprogrammed them to read every license plate coming over the Piscataqua River Bridge and into the state. Superfast, without any human intervention, the AI sees who those plates are registered to, and then checks those names for previous convictions. If a guy has been busted for narcotics, his car becomes a yellow dot on the maps displayed on the laptops we have in the state trooper cars. If a guy had narcotics and weapons convictions, he gets a red dot. And if he's ever attacked a law enforcement official, he gets a red dot with a black slash across it, warning the guys not to try to handle it alone. Our guys are in unmarked cars sitting on the side of the road about four miles to the north of the bridge. Bottom line, our success rate went way up."

"So where are we now?"

"You know the game. You squeeze the water balloon in one place, the water moves to another part of it. So the smarter guys started looking at different methods. Using different roads. Even boats running up the coast. And now, I guess, some airplanes."

"Have you come across any dealers around here using a single-engine Cessna?"

"No, but I have your number."

7
SOLID'S CHOICE

S olid had not been completely candid with Ryan when she revealed to him that she was thinking of running for Congress. There was something else that she couldn't tell him yet, a major move she had in mind. For over a year, she had been quietly talking to a major Japanese seafood distributor, Fuji Fruit of the Sea, about a joint venture. But she couldn't see a way to make such a partnership work, mainly because they were such a big firm and would dwarf her operation. Eventually she proposed that she sell her entire company to them. Fuji was enticed by the national nature of her operation. They figured they could turn a profit on it in the United States and could probably replicate it in Japan, South Korea, and even perhaps a few big Chinese cities. In just a few conversations and one meeting in New York City, they had settled on $8.5 million, and she was about to accept it. Looking ahead, she'd have money but no job, and a noncompete agreement that would keep her out of seafood work elsewhere for three years.

What to do with her life? She was not interested in yachting, partly because all that yachters seemed to talk about was boating gear and seaside restaurants. She didn't care about the former subject, and they didn't know anything interesting about the latter. Nature? She liked to hike but not every day. Volunteering? She'd had her fill of the nonprofit world in the past—too many meddlers who thought that, because they were working for free, they didn't need to act professionally or follow governance rules. And she needed a major new challenge, something to absorb her restless energy. She figured she had at least one more big leap to make in life.

With the sale to Fuji underway, she made an appointment to visit the chairman of the county Democratic party. He was the president of a small local bank. She knew him well, having gone to the University of Maine at Orono a year after him, and then having helpfully answered his fundraising requests for years. Invitations to her receptions for Democratic candidates were actually sought out, because she would hire a local chef and let him or her play with a variety of top-quality lobsters, oysters, clams, mussels, and tuna. It was a treat both for the cooks and the partygoers. More than a few favorite dishes at local restaurants had made their debut at her gatherings, such as the lobster tail and fiddleheads in Pernod cream sauce served over buttered couscous.

The banker leaned back in his big office chair and heard her out. Her pitch was that she understood that running in the inherently conservative second congressional district of Maine, which covered the northern and eastern parts of the state, would be an uphill climb. But she had money, had connections across the state, and believed the Republican incumbent was weak. And she hadn't heard of any new Democratic challengers considering a run. One worry—her father farmed marijuana, and she wasn't sure how that would play with some voters.

His genial response surprised her. "Don't run for Congress. You can't win in the second district," he said. "In the general, at best you'd take 48 percent. More likely, with your vulnerabilities, probably 43."

"What do you mean, my 'vulnerabilities'?" she asked, a bit miffed.

"Three that I can see right off the bat: female, sort of gay, Harvard Law," he ticked off quickly. He leaned forward and held up a hand. "Hear me out. I have an idea. Those are weaknesses in a district race—but in a statewide one, conversely, they would become strengths."

That interested her. It was a different direction, one she hadn't considered.

"Look at it this way," he said. "You're a woman, and that hurts you with conservative men in the second district. But statewide, it will increase female turnout, which breaks Democratic. Also, you're gay, or were. Hurts in the second district, but helps down in Portland, where there are ten times as many votes. You're a Harvard-trained lawyer, and that would be used against you in the district, but it will impress voters from the Portland suburbs down to Kittery. Again, lots of votes there.

"On the plus side: You're a Mainer, born and raised, that counts a lot, I think more these days than in the past. The post-COVID emigrants are stepping on a lot of toes at town meetings, talking too much about the way they did it back home before they moved up here. Being a real Mainer, not some from-away COVID-come-lately, will neutralize some of the anti-Harvard feeling farther north. And of course you went to Orono, too, and we'd all be proud of that. The alumni will come out for you and, more importantly, mobilize the vote for you—a lot of them around the state are the backbone types—judges, principals, selectmen, town managers, librarians, other local officials. That'll help you out especially in the little towns inland. At the very least, they'll get you a turnout on the campaign trail, give you the chance to be heard.

"Finally, you're known and trusted in the seafood business, which will get you a second hearing from a good chunk of lobstermen who normally vote conservative by reflex. Show them you really understand their concerns and fears, and some of them will vote for you."

"So what does that add up to?"

"It means this: don't run for Congress, not in the second district. Instead, run for governor. With term limits, it's coming open, so you have a good shot, if you can win the primary." He wrote down the name of a political consultant in Brunswick who had managed several statewide campaigns.

She left his office with a feeling of quiet satisfaction. She was on her way. It wouldn't be easy. After all, between primaries and general elections, the majority of people who stood for office went down in defeat. But she welcomed the challenge. She needed it to feel fully alive.

For a fee of $2,500, the consultant interviewed her for several hours, asking questions about her past and present, from education to business to personal relationships. Three days later the consultant emailed a memo to her. Most of it told her much the same things that the county chair had. The consultant dismissed her concern about her father—"no one cares about marijuana anymore." But he warned that she had one big vulnerability. And it was something she hadn't foreseen: her FBI boyfriend. "That hurts you with the gay vote, because it looks like you've switched teams. He's also an out-of-stater, which undercuts you with the hardcore Mainers. And he's an FBI man, so in the eyes of the Portland liberals, you're sleeping with a fascist." He added, "Fix that problem, and I'll run a winning campaign for you."

The memo concluded, "Call me when you finish reading this."

Over the phone, he had a pricing plan on offer. "I'll do the primary just for expenses, with no fee. That's all on incentive. If you win the Democratic nomination—and I think you have a good shot at that—then I run your general election campaign for $25,000 a month. And if you win the race, I get a $100,000 bonus. Or if you fire me, which happens more than people realize."

"That's a lot to think about." And it was. But she was a fast thinker. A minute later she accepted his offer. They began to plan for her announcement. They would aim to do it early, to deter other challengers. Because she was an unknown, the smaller the field the better. That afternoon she mailed him a check for $10,000 to cover his initial expenses. It was nice having money. She didn't focus on what the consultant had recommended about Ryan until that evening.

8
FINGERPRINTS

Two weeks after the body splashed down next to Paul Soco, Lieutenant D'Agostino called Ryan. "When I was in school, the nuns would tell us that 'good things come to those who wait,'" he began. He clearly was in a happy mood. "I think we caught a break," he explained.

"Whattaya got?" Ryan replied, intrigued.

"Fingerprints on the body that came out of the plane. Just popped up in the national register. They belong to one Casper Ottaway, who applied two months ago to be a clerk in the New Hampshire Department of Corrections. The prints only were downloaded three days ago."

"Interesting," Ryan said. That could make the death of Casper Ottaway an interstate matter. And investigating corruption in local law enforcement sometimes was an FBI mission. This case was shaping up as a Bureau matter, at least in part.

He dove into it. Ottaway, it developed, had a criminal record, not in New Hampshire but in far northern New York, not far from the Canadian border. He had been busted three times on drug misdemeanors—once in Watertown, twice in Plattsburgh.

The third arrest had been for felony distribution; the charge had been reduced on the condition that he become sober and remain so. That had all happened three years ago.

Ryan put in a call to the head of the Narcotics Enforcement team at the New York State Police regional headquarters in Plattsburgh. "I remember Ottaway," the officer told him. "Sorry to hear he's dead. He's actually a nice guy. After that last bust, a few years back, he cleaned up his act. When he got out of rehab, he came to visit me. He told me he was interested in law enforcement. I said that if he took courses on that at SUNY Plattsburgh, by the time he was finished, and stayed clean, he might be eligible in some jurisdictions."

"Did he?"

"Stay clean, you mean?"

"Yeah," Ryan said.

"You never know. But with this guy, pretty sure he did. He actually became a kind of local crusader. Held meetings on the Mohawk Reservation up near the border. He was originally from near there."

"He's an Indian?" Ryan said.

"Well, we say 'Native American' now," the Plattsburgh officer said. "But yeah, the Akwesasne branch of the Mohawks. He went on the tribal radio station, gave anti-drug talks, got some of the district chiefs to run some small-time dealers out of town. I think that may have pissed them off, naturally.

"Anyway, before the Plattsburgh guys could do anything, I heard he met a girl from New Hampshire, got serious about her, and moved there. Good for him, given that some of his old Plattsburgh buddies may have been riled with him."

"So how does he wind up dead in Maine?"

"My guess? The Plattsburgh dealers put out the word."

33

"Why?"

"They're bigger than you might think, because of their proximity to Canada. And they have the ability to bring in narcotics three ways—land, air, and Lake Champlain. In recent years, they've been expanding on the east side of the lake, mainly Burlington. And once you're over there, it's just a jump down Interstate 89 to the big New Hampshire mill towns, like Manchester and Portsmouth, where they got more junkies than you'd think. So my guess is they run into him in New Hampshire, maybe hear he's going to become some kind of police, and decide they need him out of the way. After all, he knows them all. He could help the law in New Hampshire roll them up pretty fast. So they told their buddies in Manchester that Ottoway was dangerous for them and to take care of the problem."

Ryan called the police in Nashua, New Hampshire. "Yeah, we know him," the duty sergeant told him. "We have his application on file. He also applied to the department of corrections. We thought he'd be good. But he disappeared on us. That happens."

9
PAUL'S FIRST PROTEST

Late on the morning of the second Sunday in June, Paul and two fellow residents of the sober house were ready to go. No one in the house still possessed a usable vehicle, so one of the residents called a friend, who in turn brought a friend who owned one.

On the highway, which was the sole road through the reservation and into the end-of-the-highway town of Eastport, Paul put on the truck's flashers when he came to where the pavement narrowed down to a causeway across the tidal flats. He parked it sideways. The others hopped out and placed two lines of orange traffic cones on either side of the truck. Behind the cones, they stood holding big hand-painted signs stating:

TIDE IS HIGH PROTEST

A black Ford 150 stopped, driven by a middle-aged white male Mainer heading for Eastport.

"What's up?"

Paul explained what they were doing.

"How long?"

"One hour."

"Fuck that," the man said. "I'd be late for church." He swung the truck off the highway. It rolled a few feet, and, in slow motion, sank up to its hubcaps. He hadn't known that the sand there was deceptive, just a thin layer covering a bed of seaweed three feet deep, pushed there by the big tides twice a day. The man revved the engine and the wheels sunk deeper.

"We'll pull you out when our hour is up," Paul shouted to the man. The man gave him the finger, turned off the truck, and closed his eyes.

Traffic backed up, about thirty cars, trucks, and pickups on either side of their little roadblock. At precisely sixty minutes, Paul and his comrades threw the cones and signs in the back of the friend's pickup. They ran out two chains from trucks to pull the angry man's truck out of the muck. Other drivers filed by, some glaring, others puzzled.

A state policeman rolled up in his patrol vehicle. "What's going on?" he asked.

"Nothing," said one of the protesters.

❖

That afternoon the Elders held an informal meeting about Paul's protest. "I kind of like having someone stand up for us," John of Tides said. "At least he is trying to do something."

The Elders were uneasy but agreed to hold back from judgment. At the end of the meeting they summoned Sanpeer, the police chief. The youngest of the Elders delivered their conclusion. "We think you should be neutral with this demonstration stuff," he said. "Don't facilitate it, but don't stop it, either. Just observe it."

"That's going to be hell to explain to the state police," Sanpeer muttered under his breath.

Most of the Elders didn't hear that complaint, but the one who was speaking, sitting closest to him, caught it. "And do they pay your salary, or do we?" the younger Elder asked the police chief.

Sanpeer got the message. Tribal loyalties, and his paycheck, took priority over any solidarity Sanpeer might feel with his colleagues in law enforcement.

10
SOLID'S FAREWELL

It was Saturday afternoon, so Solid, as she often did, drove up to Lost Pond to visit Ryan. She brought a bottle of Sancerre and two cooked lobsters on ice. She sat down on his back porch. "I've been learning a lot about politics," she began. "A lot." Her gray-green eyes stared into his.

"Oh?" Ryan wasn't sure where this was going.

"Not all of it good," she said.

Now he was worried.

She related how the county chairman had advised her to consider running for governor. And how he had sent her to a consultant.

"And what did that guy say?"

"That I have one big liability," she said. She sipped her glass of wine and gazed over the rim straight at him. "You." Her eyes were steady.

"Me?" He was puzzled. "Why me? What did I do?"

"Yes. He said the gay vote doesn't like that I'm seeing a man, the liberals don't like that you're an FBI agent, the Mainers don't like that you're an out-of-stater."

"So what are you going to do?" he asked. He suspected he knew the answer.

"Ryan, I'm sorry," she said.

He was right. He had known Solid could be calculating, even predatory. She had a bit of an animal appetite to her, but he enjoyed it. Sex and conversation with her sometimes was like two wolves playing. But sometimes you don't see a real bite coming. He said nothing.

She took advantage of his silence to offer the thoughts she had rehearsed on the drive up from the coast. "Here's how I see it," she said. "Our paths crossed at the right time. We were both in transition. We've enjoyed each other's company, and we were good with each other."

"But you're leaving me because a political consultant told you to. That's pretty cold."

"Yes," she said. "He also said that people want to see a stable couple."

"Well, you certainly have the makings of a successful politician," he said. It came out a little more bitterly than he intended, but at the same time, he wasn't exactly sorry.

"Don't be that way," she parried, but seemed to take the barb gracefully. "In a few years, when you get married to some pretty younger woman, the governor will attend your wedding—that is, if you invite me."

They sat in silence for several minutes.

Solid spoke again. "To be honest, I liked us. I enjoyed our time together, but I always kind of missed Dorothy." Dorothy had been her partner before their breakup a year earlier. "And ours was a temporary thing, couldn't be more than that. I think Dorothy could be permanent, if she and I both work on it."

She stood. "Ryan, we had a good time," she said. She leaned down to kiss him on the cheek and left.

So that was that, he thought after she was gone. He always had known it would end. But he was still surprised when it did. He picked up the green half-empty bottle of white wine by the neck and hurled it out into Lost Pond. He sat and watched it bob out there until dark. A kingfisher studied him from a branch, its big black head intense and brooding.

11

AN OBSERVER AT PAUL'S SECOND PROTEST

A week after the first one, Paul staged his second blockage of the highway. It had been underway for about half an hour when two state police cars appeared, sirens blaring and light racks pulsing. From the second emerged the commander of the Eastern District himself. He strode up and put his hands on hips. He nodded over to Renny Sanpeer, the tribal police chief, who stood on the side of the road, arms hanging by his side, just observing the situation and feeling a bit helpless.

"You're gonna have to move this roadblock," the commander said to Paul Soco. "It's illegal."

"Officer, I am afraid you are standing on tribal land," Paul said. "That means you have no jurisdiction here."

"This"—the officer pointed downward—"is a state highway," he said, but with a little less authority in his voice. This was going to be more complex than he had realized.

"It's the state's asphalt," Paul said softly. "But it's the tribe's land. And the treaty came before the highway. You want to move the asphalt, be my guest."

The trooper looked for support across at Sanpeer. "Renny, you want to chip in here?"

"Commander, I'm sorry, but he's right on that," Sanpeer said thinly. Paul thought Sanpeer sounded a little too apologetic.

Today the traffic was heavier. It backed up for a quarter mile. People were honking their truck horns. No vehicles were going in and, worse for the isolated town of Eastport, no lobsters were being trucked out.

"I'll get back to you," the trooper said, and retreated to his car. He was still there a few minutes later when Paul declared the protest ended for the day.

This time about twenty members of the tribe had joined the demonstration. A Malpense named Rock, for his block-like face, quiet and stolid, had stepped up as a kind of record-keeper, using a yellow legal pad to collect the contact information of participants. He had been an enlisted military intelligence specialist in the Army, and was notable for his ability to collect and organize information.

But the person who caught Paul's attention on this day was a man who watched the demonstration but did not join it. He clearly looked Indian—tall, copper-skinned, moon-faced, with a shaven head. Not quite frowning, but serious. He stood on the side of the road with his arms crossed and just observed, intently. He had the calm intensity of a good hunter. Paul wondered who he was.

❖

That night, the mayor of Eastport and the town's police chief came to a meeting with the Elders. Usually they didn't have much time for the local Indians. Now they were hat in hand, asking for the Elders to help them out. The Elders listened politely.

12

A SECOND OBSERVER AT THE THIRD PROTEST

Ryan's life suddenly was a lot emptier. He threw himself into his work. With nothing else much to do, he was working on a Sunday morning in his office in the basement of the federal building in Bangor. Only one other person was there, an older, gray-haired National Guard soldier doing his weekend duty. Ryan had seen the man around as a state patrol officer, where he was chief of the patrol's intelligence office, but hadn't realized the guy also was in the Guard.

"What do you think of this Indian protest that's closing the road into Eastport?" the state patrol officer asked him.

"I don't know much about it," Ryan said. "Is it interesting?"

"Kinda," the officer said. "Dunno why, but I think it could get bigger."

"Why?"

"I've never seen anything like it before. I'd heard of something like it happening, briefly, with the Maine tribes in the sixties. But this time the protest is about global warming, and that's new."

"Might be worth a look," Ryan said. "Care to show it to me?"

"Sure," said the officer and got up from his desk. Ryan noted his wrinkled uniform and bushy moustache. He introduced himself as Merrill Bouchard, Maine National Guard Chief Warrant Officer 5. He smelled of cigarette smoke and bad coffee. The little corner of the basement where he had been working was designated—with a bit of stretching—as a SCIF, or "Sensitive Compartmented Information Facility."

On their drive to the southeastern corner of Maine, Bouchard explained what had pulled him into the office that weekend day. CWO5 was an obscure rank, and he liked it that way. Commanders and officers came and went in the Guard, but this old soldier effectively was the Maine National Guard's one-man intelligence office, having been in that position for fifteen years. He literally knew where the bodies were buried, some of them being the thwarted German escapees from the spring of 1945. He was in the office because whenever the CIA wanted to use Camp Cripple, that extremely remote and obscure location just under three miles from the border with Quebec, they were required to notify him, both for legal reasons and to ensure that no one would bother the Agency officers when they were at the camp. "I get a message that there's a classified notification waiting for me in the SCIF," which he pronounced as "skiff." "I have to come in the office to actually open it," he explained. "Talk about spooky, spies and ghosts, got them both up there at that border camp."

"In my experience, the Agency isn't so polite about working and playing with others," Ryan noted mildly.

"Oh, with this site, they have no choice, they have to be," Bouchard said breezily. "First, when they fly in, they don't say they're CIA. They ID themselves to air controllers as a National Guard flight, and use the transponder the same way. So they have to inform us so we can go along with the cover story if we are asked.

Second, the funny thing about Camp Cripple is it actually is the property of the state."

"But it's a CIA base?"

"It is," Bouchard said. "But it belongs to us. The Agency kind of likes it that way, keeping it off their books. It originally was a World War Two POW camp. After the war it just kind of was there, falling apart, but the CIA began to use it during the fifties for the quiet movement of people sometimes, getting them into Canada and maybe onto a train in Montreal or a ship in Quebec City. Also, you could use it for clandestine meetings, like one they did in 1969 with a Soviet foreign minister, just zipping him in across the border from a diplomatic visit in Ottawa. Dunno what they told him, or showed him. Something to do with Lin Biao, I'm told. The story I've heard is that after that sit-down the Russkies took a different approach with China. Another time, in the nineties, a top North Korean diplomat who defected to a French freighter in Vietnam, they brought the ship into Quebec, then hustled him in across the border at the camp. He had spent months on that ship, keeping himself busy by writing down recipes and planning a restaurant. He now runs a great Korean barbeque place in Houston, by the way.

"But," Bouchard continued, "Camp Cripple really took off after 9/11. That brought the age of universal surveillance. As a result, it got very hard to move people through airports or other border gateways without them being photographed and data-crawlers able to locate individual images. And now you got that AI stuff. Even if you controlled the systems, they could be hacked."

"Well, isn't that why they use American military bases for renditions?" Ryan asked, referring to the CIA's practice of abducting wanted terrorists and bringing them to remote spots such as Guam and Guantanamo for interrogation.

"That used to work. But even military bases aren't information-secure anymore, cuz of the dumbass information techs in their twenties, like Snowden and that kid in the Massachusetts Air Guard, the Gen Z types who keep leaking classified stuff, sharing it on social media.

"And even if you control all that, there's the problem of cell phones everywhere. People just get seen and randomly photographed. A defector might just be in the background while on vacation at Disney World—but an AI machine in Shanghai might be able to identify that person and geolocate them. And then ID their family members. And that could be bad. Gets real hard to hide people.

"So it turns out that this little corner of Vacationland is almost unique in our part of the world. It is about the one place in the entire United States where you can move people across an international border with confidence that the act won't be recorded. It's a pretty cool asset. In the last few years, they've done maybe five or six missions a year there, plus a few rehearsals and training iterations. And as a bonus, there's no cell phone reception in the area, so the bad guys can't ping your phone to locate you."

They stopped for fried haddock sandwiches and genuine onion rings at a roadside stand in Machias. It was pleasantly surprising, Ryan thought to himself, how one guy who had been sitting in the basement of the federal building in Bangor, Maine, on a quiet Sunday morning could have such a unique perspective on the world.

They arrived at the Tide Is High demonstration, parked on the side of the road, and walked down the shoulder to where a group of about twenty-five Indians stood behind their signs. The old National Guard officer stood and smoked. Ryan walked around, listening to conversations.

When he got to the actual blockage, Ryan saw the man leading it, standing behind the big black-and-white TIDE IS HIGH sign.

"Paul?" he said. "I hadn't realized that you were involved in this."

Paul Soco looked at him somberly. "I told you my people needed me. I decided this is the way." Then his face darkened. "Why are you here?"

"I just came down because I was curious. Wanted to see these Indian protests for myself. You're making some waves."

"So you're investigating us, Agent Tapia?" Paul asked, suddenly more formal.

"No, but I need to know what you're doing. In case I get asked." He looked around, made sure no one was close enough to hear, and said, "I also need to talk to you about that body that got dropped out of the airplane. I've been meaning to call you."

Paul did not look reassured. "Not now," he said. "Gotta go."

"You be careful, okay?" Ryan said to Paul's turning back. He didn't know why. Maybe it was that "sense" of his that Solid had talked about. But he was worried. Not about Paul. For Paul.

After dropping Bouchard off at the Bangor office, Ryan headed home while meditating on Paul. He felt he had just been given the cold shoulder and didn't know why. When he first got to Maine a few years back, he wouldn't have even noticed that brusque treatment, let alone cared about it. Back then, he had been emotionally wounded and shy of confrontation. He had asked to be posted to Maine because he needed to get as far as possible from California. His wife, two children, and their dog had all been killed in San Diego in a car accident, crushed by a construction truck laden with dirt. The driver simply had missed the red light in the glare of the sun.

Now, as Ryan recovered, he was beginning to feel less inclined to go with the flow, to defer to others. He also had been thinking about what Solid Harrison had said to him, that he wasn't analytically brilliant, but more than most people, he had an unusual ability to sense, generally nonverbally, what was going on around him. He would feel a tingle, a need to pause and reconsider. He picked up on small signals.

And he realized, whether because of age or experience, he was becoming less tolerant of bureaucratic bullshit. The FBI had such a strong culture that it expected all its agents to get in line without being told to. He was less inclined to do that nowadays. He decided to tell his boss exactly what he thought of the situation with the Indians. That night he typed out on his laptop a report to Jimmy Love, his boss in Portland. "Something may be happening with the Native American tribes in Maine," it began. "I think the Bureau should pay attention. This is a chance for us to do right by Indigenous Americans, as the Bureau has not always done in the past. I think we could work with them in a spirit of friendship, especially in deconfliction and de-escalation of tensions." He recounted his history with Paul Soco—encountering the hermit out on a remote island in the Gulf of Maine and using what Paul had told him to crack the case of a murdered lobsterman on Liberty Island. He noted that Paul had become a figure of admiration in the Indian community, someone who might rise in the tribal leadership, even become a statewide figure.

He wrote 750 words and read it over. He was pleased. In the past, cautious Ryan would have slept on it and reread the report over morning coffee before sending it. Not the emerging new Ryan. He finished it, put in Jimmy Love's email address and, on a whim, added the email address of Bob Bulster, the special agent over-seeing the regional office in Boston. He hit Send and went to bed.

In the morning he was awakened at 7 by a ringing on his cell. He saw that it was Bulster in Boston. This was either very good or very bad. "Agent Tapia, I'm sitting here with your memo," Bulster began. "Frankly, you can hold hands with these Indians and sing 'Kumbaya' if you like, for all I care. But we need real intel here, not warm and fuzzies. I need to know things, real things. Like: Who are they? What are their weaknesses? Criminal records? In my own quick research I see that one of them, Soco, has a violent past. You neglected to mention that. Who else? Other criminal associations? Drug use? How do they communicate? What are their plans?"

Bulster continued. "I've reviewed your personnel file," he began. "I think we can get your career back on track."

Ryan thought to himself, *I wasn't aware it was off track.*

"That dead lobsterman case, I don't know why the Bureau is even getting involved in local homicides," Bulster said.

"Well, sir, that was a problem of jurisdiction, and it wound up on my plate," Ryan said.

"Okay, but try to stay out of local problems from now on. We're a national agency, not pinch hitters for Barney Fife."

He made it seem like Ryan taking on the Ricky Cutts case had been a foul-up. Ryan believed it actually had been a rather adept piece of investigation in difficult circumstances.

"I look forward to your next report," Bulster said, and hung up.

❖

Next, Bulster called Jimmy Love, who answered on the first ring. "Jimmy, I think your man up in Bangor is on thin ice. He wants to make nice with the Indian protesters."

"And?" said Love.

"On the one hand, it's a good way to get up close to these protesters, see what is happening. On the other, he's kind of soft-headed."

"How do you think we should play it, sir?" Love asked.

"You have to keep on it, and let me know if he starts wandering into goo-goo territory," he said. "Give him enough rope. If he screws up, we cut him loose. We're not a day care center for wayward agents." Then he added, to drive home the point, "Despite the presence in my area of you and Tapia." Bulster hung up.

Love stared at his phone. He told himself that he was not going to expend any personal influence saving Ryan Tapia. Not that he had any to spare.

13

A CONVERSATION WITH PAUL SOCO

Ryan finally got around to calling Paul Soco. "Does the name Casper Ottaway mean anything to you?"

"No." He paused. "Should it?"

"It's the guy who got dropped near your boat."

"What do you know about him?" Paul asked. Ryan filled him in on the background information he'd developed on drug dealers in Plattsburgh, New York, and Manchester, New Hampshire.

Paul pondered all that. "I've never come across the Plattsburgh guys. But the meth dealers down in Manchester, I know they heard about the comment I made in the paper. Remember when the Bangor paper profiled me as 'the hermit of Big Bold Island?' Story got picked up by papers across New England, I think."

"I do."

"In that article, the reporter had asked me about people who sell dope to Indians. I had said, 'They're just doing Custer's work for him.' I got some hate mail for that one, including one postmarked Manchester, New Hampshire. Told me to mind my own business."

"Yeah. But I don't get it."

"Remember the Indian nickname for Custer?"

"No," Ryan admitted, "I don't."

"Yellow Hair."

"So they kill Ottaway because he might get in the way in New Hampshire, and then nail a blond wig to the poor guy's head and drop his body on you?"

"I think they contracted the work out to the Manchester guys you're talking about. And those guys were pissed at me. So they used Ottaway's corpse as a message to me."

"That's weird."

"Well, those meth guys think in pretty twisted ways. They have these endless amphetamine conversations, going down rat holes, cooking up conspiracy theories. They might have thought the Indian tribes were turning against them. Or they just didn't like it that some Indians are standing up for themselves."

"Yeah, about that—" Ryan began.

Paul interrupted. "Gotta go. Got another demonstration tomorrow."

Ryan thought over the call. He felt a quiet sense of dread for Paul but didn't know why.

14
THE RECURRING DREAM OF JAMES REVEUR

The tall, round-faced Indian also was present at that third demonstration. Again he just stood silently, taking it all in.

His name was James Reveur. He was a young member of the small and mostly unrecognized Quivive tribe. He was emerging from a transitional phase in his life. He had grown up on both sides of the Maine–Quebec border, and in fact held triple citizenship—American, Canadian, and Quivive. As a child he was questioning, curious, even querulous. The slow pace and mindless discipline of school had bored him.

After graduating from high school in Ashland, Maine, he was hired by a contractor in the Maine woods as a tree cutter. He found the work hot, hard, and destructive, downing trees with chattering chainsaws and hauling the wood with draggers to big diesel trucks. It was a world of smoke, noise, and mud. The incessant shaking of the saws left his wrists feeling numb at the end of each day. He wore the required ear protection, but still felt he was hurting his hearing. In the evenings he escaped into clouds of marijuana and television. He was nearly comatose with boredom.

After one night of channel surfing, he realized as he clicked off the television that he could not remember what he had been watching for the previous several hours. That scared him. He felt like his life was evaporating.

The next morning he quit his job as a cutter and enrolled at the University of Maine at Fort Kent. There he came alive. He took an array of courses in literature and philosophy. The more he read, the more he felt that after years of working at destroying part of nature, he now needed to understand how to live in it better.

He consumed the texts. All he did was read, work, and sleep. He bussed tables at a diner during the week, and pulled night shifts at the Circle K on weekends. Books and jobs replaced dope, TV, and pretty much everything else in his life. When he had spare time he walked in the forest and meditated on what he read. He went to his professors to ask questions, and they in turn suggested more books. Along the way, he memorized dozens of poems he liked. He received an A in every one of the eight courses he took. During his second semester, one professor took him aside and told him he needed a bigger challenge and more time to study.

James saw the logic and transferred to McGill University, in Montreal. There, he received two scholarships that eased the financial pressure. One was a reward for his grades at Fort Kent, while the second was a Red Oak scholarship for Indigenous students from Canada. For pocket money, he still worked three days a week at a Starbucks on the campus. When a labor activist tried to unionize the coffee shop, James listened long and hard. He was impressed by how much preparatory work went into the organizing effort, such as finding people who were interested and training them in organizing. Most of all, he learned how to hold a meeting. The organizer, a smart kid from Vermont, talked to participants before the session to find out what they expected from it. He moved the meeting along, keeping it on track, opening it up for people to speak but not letting them hijack it. By the end of each meeting, the organizer had a clear set of results, with assignments and commitments.

James missed the life and community of his tribe, but nevertheless did well—at least for his first year there. He threw himself into his studies, churning through the ancient Greek philosophers. Studying them, along with the Greek tragedians in literature courses, was invigorating.

But in his second year, he began to slow a bit, after encountering Montesquieu, Hume, Adam Smith, and the other philosophers of the French and Scottish Enlightenments. Their visions of the Earth as a great machine with a fire at its center reminded him of his destructive work in the woods. When he learned that James Watt's steam engine had been inspired in part by the philosophical geology work of James Hutton, he felt he had seen the light, and it was not a good one: There was a direct line from modern Western philosophy's Enlightenment to the Industrial Revolution and then to the possible destruction of human life on Earth. Indeed, he sensed that in every course he took, he was being instructed to celebrate the thinkers who had begun the process of slowly but surely getting on the path of burning the Earth's atmosphere. Doubt overtook him, wrapping itself around his shoulders like a dirty old blanket. He began to see the Industrial Revolution as a great anomaly, a three-hundred-year-long aberration that was overheating the planet and that the Earth itself would find ways to stop, even if it meant the end of the human race.

That was followed by a second recognition: That same post-Enlightenment period, from about 1800 to today, had been the worst in the history of his people. He took a class in North American history and was struck by how it was a catalog of Indigenous people being pounded by Europeans, who took the land, brought epidemics, wiped out herds of game, built dams that damaged the ecosystems of fruitful rivers, and enslaved and killed Indigenous people at every step. The industrial era basically had been hell on earth for Indians, he concluded.

He came away wondering if, as the industrial era waned, destroyed by its own machines that heated the Earth's air and water, Indigenous peoples might rise again.

As he dwelled on these thoughts, his work slid and his grades declined precipitously. He skipped most of his classes and instead sat and read every day in the philosophy section of the library, looking for other paths. He tried some religious mystics, but he was not interested in Christianity, which felt entirely alien to him. The exception was a pile of books he read on the history of the first monasteries in Europe, which for reasons he did not understand resonated with him. The early monasteries had been established in remote locations, away from the chaos and wealth of the cities, which attracted Viking raiders and other violent actors.

One day he was in the philosophy section when he overheard a graduate student at the next table telling an undergraduate about "an Indian named Gandhi," a "great man who had insight into what was wrong with the western way of life," the student said. This intrigued James. He had never heard of this Indian. And he was eager to read critiques of the industrialized capitalism of the modern West. So much about it seemed wrong to him, contrary to the ways of nature. But he needed to read more to flesh out that thought.

James asked the graduate student for the spelling of this Indian's name and then walked across the room to find the man's writings. He soon realized that Gandhi was a South Asian Indian, not a First People or Native American. Within the hour, James read Gandhi's assertion that, "A civilization is to be judged by its treatment of minorities." He spoke it aloud. Then he underlined it, forgetting that the book belonged to the university library, not to him.

At first he was puzzled by Gandhi's insistence on taking a non-violent approach. It didn't make sense to him until he realized that the power structure was fluent in violence but flummoxed by other approaches. It reassured him when he read Gandhi's explanation that nonviolence should not be considered passive, that it "does not mean meek submission to the will of the evil-doer, but it means the pitting of one's whole soul against the will of the tyrant." That seemed to James to be the beginning of a possible way of resistance.

He was captivated. He spent most of the rest of that month in the McGill library, reading every word by Gandhi that he could find. On the day he finished the last of those books, a collection of Gandhi's newspaper essays, he stood, walked back to his room, packed his rucksack, and hitchhiked home. He was no longer interested in climbing the career ladders of the white world. He wanted to go somewhere, and he needed to be someone different.

Back in Maine, he dove back into the life of hunting and fishing, living on the land. At night he read more books, increasingly turning to those about Native American/First Peoples history, and next about global heating. He wondered why there had not been more reaction from the tribes to all that. For relaxation he read twentieth-century poetry, especially works that dwelled on smoke and fog, or portrayed the evening sky laid out "like a patient etherized upon a table."

One night that spring he dreamed of a man of The People—that is, an Indigenous person—who could ride two horses at once. The next night he dreamed of it again, with more horses appearing. By the end of the spring, he was having dreams in which this Indian man was riding thirty-seven horses at once through a clear, cold night sky. James lay in bed in the morning, pondering this recurring vision. What did it mean?

He decided to find out. He hitchhiked to four reservations in Maine and Quebec where he had friends. He was searching for leaders, or at least people with a potential for taking political action. He attended many meetings, and he found many possible followers for a leader, some of them bursting with energy and interest. But he saw no one that evoked the dream. Frustrated by this fruitless search, he found it hard to get out of bed in the morning.

He was back at home on the Quivira land when a friend asked him if he had read about the Tide Is High demonstration down on the Maine coast. He hadn't. What he heard caught his attention: Indians talking about climate change, and taking a different, more confrontational course. He borrowed a car from a cousin and drove down across Maine to see it. He sensed something was going on, but he wasn't sure what. After seeing the demonstration, he had the dream again, and this time the horse leading the stampede had Paul's narrow face and searching black eyes.

He drove down again the following Sunday to see the next demonstration. Again, he just stood and watched. At the end of this one, Paul walked over to him and asked, "Can I help you?" What he really meant, of course, was, *Who are you and why are you staring at us?*

James ignored the implied meaning and took him literally. "Yes, I think you can," he said. There was something about this man that made James think he was a living version of Gandhi's approach. He hadn't sensed this with anyone else. But this guy seemed to have it.

"I'm Paul Soco," Paul said. "You are?"

"Me? I'm no one. But I'm an admirer of yours. My name is James Reveur. I'm a Quivira." He assumed that Paul would have heard of them, despite their small size—there were just about one hundred of them left.

"From up on the border?"

"Yep."

"What brings you here?"

James said, "I heard about your demonstrations, looked them up on Insta, and wanted to come see. You're all over Indian TikTok." He did not mention his dreams. He had learned that getting to that sort of thing early on made some people, even Indians, think he was odd.

"Well, what do you think?" Paul asked. Knowing that he was a novice at political action, he tried to remain open to criticism and commentary.

"You're onto something," James said simply. His arms were still folded across his chest.

Paul sensed only a partial endorsement. "But?"

"But I think you are still near the beginning of it. That's not a bad thing."

"Hell, we just got started. What do you think is beginning?"

"I don't know," James said. "But I think you already are on the second step of a different path."

"What was the first?"

"Your time out on that island."

Paul was intrigued. "You heard about that?"

"Every young Indian in Maine knows about that. They tell stories about you. I heard one about you sharing a fish with a weasel one night, and a bear came in and said, 'That's my salmon' and tried to take it. You and the weasel taught him manners."

Paul invited James to come back to the sober house for Sunday dinner. The supervisor placed a big bowl of steamed lobsters on the table. James, who had been so cool and distant, was at a loss. Having grown up on the northern border, hundreds of miles from the ocean, he had never seen a cooked lobster before, let alone eaten one. Staring at the bright red shellfish, his face froze in panic. The others around the table cracked up. "Maine Indian not knowing how to eat lobster, man, I have seen everything now," one said. Rock laughed. It was the first time Paul had seen a smile cross that big, thoughtful face of Rock's, with his long, square jaw, heavy cheekbones, and broad nose.

Later that afternoon, James told Paul about his recurring dream of an Indian riding thirty-seven horses. "I think you are that man," he said to Paul.

"Why me?"

"I can see an aura above your head. Kind of a yellow haze, like sunlight."

Paul's cautious face showed that he was not pleased by that idea. "That doesn't sound good to me."

"It might not be," Reveur said. "It just means you are different, special, maybe singled out for a particular role."

"I'm not ready to be an angel. I'd rather be me. I'm still finding out who that is."

"I hear you. I will keep your words in my ear," Reveur said after a moment. He had a habit when he was listening intently of cupping his right hand behind his ear, a hunter's move. He did that now. "But we don't get to pick our destinies. We interact with the world, and do the best we can."

That night, John of Tides's daughter called to ask Paul to come over. "My father wants to see you," she said.

The blind old man had a message. "The Elders want you to stop," he said. "They feel you have made your point. And the Anglos down in Eastport are getting irritated."

Paul agreed to end the Tide Is High demos. He went back and told James and the others in the sober house.

"So what's next?" James asked. They talked some more. They agreed to come together as a group after hunting season. "I met some people during my reservation visits who will be interested," James said.

All they needed, James thought, was a leader. And he believed he had found one.

15
SOLID'S TALK WITH RENEE CASTILLO

S olid proved to be a natural campaigner, moving constantly across the state and connecting in both towns and cities. Her leading opponent in the Democratic primary was Len Bousier, an investment banker who was from Massachusetts but for several years had lived in Kittery, down near the New Hampshire border. He poured his fortune into his campaign, outspending her 3-to-1, mainly on television commercials. For all that, his stiff manner never quite clicked with the voters, and he was unable to convey a sense of what he stood for. Solid, running as a tough, independent Mainer, won the Democratic Party nomination, collecting 46 percent of the vote. Her motto was "Hard choices need fresh voices." Bousier took 42, and didn't win a county north of Damariscotta. The remaining votes split among a socialist candidate (9 percent) and the candidate of the Maine Secession Society, who did surprisingly well, resonating with the lefty libertarians, and collecting 3 percent of the total.

Al Castillo, the Republican whom she would now face in the general election, was a two-term state senator who had run unopposed for his party's nomination. He owned a string of mid-scale Italian restaurants in Maine with the name "Big Al's." They were a cut above pizza and sub joints, and suitable for a date night, but not hugely expensive. Half the time, diners ordered the pizza anyway. But at his places they ordered beer and wine, too, which accounted for most of his profits. His television commercials for the restaurants had made him a statewide celebrity. They were personable, with him standing out front, opening his arms, and inviting people to come down and eat with "Big Al, the Mainer's pal." He didn't come off as particularly smart, but that could be a political asset. He was a person you'd feel comfortable having a beer with. With the Republican nomination in hand, he appeared unstoppable, fresh and rested, with a big war chest that he hadn't had to crack open for a primary campaign. His major donors had been business-people who disliked regulation, especially child labor laws. He also did well with the anti-vaccine crowd, and, inexplicably, car dealers.

Despite having to spend in the primary, there was a real benefit to that first round for Solid: it allowed her to define herself. By the time it was over, a majority of Mainers likely to vote told polling organizations that they felt they knew who she was.

With the Democratic nomination in hand, Solid took some needed downtime. She was at home, sleeping late after months of breakfast meetings, morning coffees, lunch speeches, and pre-dinner receptions, catching her breath before planning began for the general election five months later. She was in bed when she got a phone call from Lizotte LaPierre, a woman who said she worked with Al Castillo's wife at an Augusta real estate agency. "Solid, you may not remember me," she began. "I was at a fundraiser for Jared Golden at your house a few years ago." She said that Castillo's wife was very unhappy and appeared willing to talk about it. She could arrange a meeting.

Solid had to be in Augusta for dinner that night, so said she could come up a bit earlier. At four in the afternoon she arrived at the real estate office. Lizotte LaPierre took her through to the conference room, usually used for signing closing papers on houses. Solid wondered if this was some kind of political offer coming from Castillo's camp. If so, she thought to herself, she should have brought the consultant as a witness and advisor. But when Solid saw a small, black-haired woman sniffling and holding a crumpled tissue to her nose, she knew that this meeting must be about something else. This woman seemed to be carrying the weight of the world on her shoulders, leaning forward and staring down at the conference table.

"Mrs. Castillo?" Solid said, extending her hand.

Mrs. Castillo raised her gaze. She didn't stand. "I don't think I should even be here," she said. But she reached up and shook Solid's hand. "You're taller than I expected," she said.

Solid turned to look at Lizotte, who said, "Renee, tell her what you told me."

Renee Castillo's gaze shifted back and forth between the two women. She began crying. She burped, and said, "Excuse me, I've got anxiety."

"How can I help you?" Solid said, and she meant it. "You seem to have some trouble."

Renee Castillo clenched her fists together. She cried out, "He hit me."

Solid's brain went on full alert, almost like a fire alarm was clanging. She shifted to lawyer mode. "When?"

"Last December," Mrs. Castillo said. "We had been at a Christmas party down the street. I don't know how many drinks he had there. He was pretty full of himself that night, about how he was going to announce his candidacy after the new year and he was gonna win big.

"When we got home he didn't stop. We were sitting at the kitchen table. He was going on and on about the campaign plans, and he was still drinking pretty heavily. Slurring his words. Waving his arms a bit.

"I got sick of it. The bastard had never talked to me about it. Acted like it had nothing to do with me. The same way he did when he was fucking one of the waitresses when we were young.

"Finally I said, 'Al, did you even have the grace to ask me if I wanted you to run?' He waved his hand, 'Of course you wanted it. First lady of the state. Live in the governor's mansion.' I was fuming."

"I get that," Solid said.

Renee Castillo continued. "So I said, 'Okay, listen to me now. I. Don't. Want. You. To. Do. It. Have you got that?' Can you hear me in there through all the whiskey?' I think I was shouting a bit.

"Then I got up to leave the room. I said, 'Good night. Sleep on the damn couch.' I wanted to close my eyes and leave all this. He stood up and was blocking my way. He yelled, right in my face, 'I am running, I am, we are, you got that?'

"I asked him to move out of my way. He wouldn't. He kept talking, saying I never gave him credit for all his work. I'd heard that all before, I call it the 'Poor Al' act. So I turned to go out the back door. I was gonna walk around to the front. He grabbed my shoulder, probably harder than he meant to. It spinned me around. I was facing him. I pushed both my hands against his chest. He staggered a bit. And then his fist swung into my face. It just came up at me—I didn't see it coming. Loosened a tooth." Her hand went up to her left cheek at the memory.

"In the morning, he was all sorry, apologetic. It had been an accident, he said. He would make it up to me. He said nobody from either of our families had ever amounted to anything, and this was 'our big chance' to be someone. He was pleading, making all sorts of promises. Big vacations. Take me for a cruise after the election was over.

"I could hardly listen to him. I took the day off from work, drove down to the coast. Walked along a beach where the tides had cleaned off the snow and ice. Just myself and my thoughts. Sat in a Dunkin's a long time alone.

"When I got home there was, of course, a giant bouquet of roses on the living room table. Red, yellow, and white, maybe a dozen of each. I chucked them in the trash. He followed me around the house. He pleaded. He cajoled. He got one of my oldest friends, Jeanie, to call me and ask me to listen to him. 'Al says you're having second thoughts, but, Renee, it is too late for that,' Jeanie said to me. And he talked and talked to me. It wore me down."

She shrugged. "I gave in. I shouldn't have. I was tired. To him, the issue wasn't that he hit me, it was that he had to get me to agree to his running."

Solid waited a few beats. Mrs. Castillo seemed to be finished with her story. "Renee, may I ask you a few questions?" Solid said.

Mrs. Castillo looked up at her. "I guess so."

"Did you report this to the police?"

"No, it never occurred to me."

Solid gazed out the window at the leaves on the maples, still carrying some of their spring green, then turned back to Renee Castillo's eyes. "It's June now. This happened in December. Why did you wait?"

Renee Castillo nodded. "That's right. I bit my tongue."

"What changed lately?" Solid asked. She was curious, but she also needed to understand the circumstance of Renee Castillo's revelation.

"You mean to make me talk to you? I can tell you that," she said, almost shaking. "It was one word. The other night, when you won the primary? We were watching. Al had kind of expected Bousier to win." She looked down at the conference table. "When the PBS station said you had got the Democratic nomination, Al whooped, almost like a war cry. I stared at him, didn't understand. 'I'm gonna beat that cunt,' he said. 'That stuck-up cunt.' That's what he said." She glanced at Solid. "Sorry about the language."

"And?"

"And I thought, this is the guy who hit me. Now he's talking about you like that. I hated it."

"So what did you do?"

"Nothing. But the next day, I was at work, Lizotte saw me crying, just looking out the window. And she said I should tell someone. She said, 'Should a person who acts and talks like that be at the top of the state?'"

"And so?"

"Lizotte asked could she call you and ask you to come to see me, and I said she could," Renee Castillo said. She contemplated Solid. "You seem like a nice person. I don't think you're stuck up."

Solid had one more crucial question. "What do you think I should do with what you've told me?" she asked.

"I don't know," Renee said. "Whatever you like. I'm not into politics. Never was. I told Al that." She rose to leave. Solid walked her silently to the parking lot and shook her hand. Then Solid walked back to the conference room. Lizotte LaPierre was still there, and she poked an index finger at her iPhone. "I just emailed that whole conversation to you," she said. Her phone had been recording the entire time.

Solid felt up in the air, which didn't happen often. She needed to think. She went to her Prius and postponed the dinner in Augusta, pleading fatigue. She drove down to the parking lot of the Quarry Tap Room and sat in her car there, listening to the recording twice. She played it a third time on the drive back to Rockfish.

16
PAUL DOESN'T PROTEST

In early July, on the fourth Sunday after his protests began, Paul Soco brought a lawn chair to the side of the highway, well away from the asphalt. He was alone, and propped up next to him, one of the TIDE IS HIGH signs. He sat and waited, watching the water level on both sides of the causeway. He had his eye particularly on a little green-gray salt-tolerant evergreen bush about eighteen inches tall, out in the middle of the mud flats. The high tide usually stopped just short of it.

It was a quiet, calm morning, with absolutely no wind. Because there were no waves, he was able to actually see the line of water moving up, creeping ever so slowly but steadily. The patient eye was rewarded. It was going to be a huge tide, perhaps even bigger than John of Tides had expected.

At 11:30, the tide passed the bush. At 11:40, it wetted the asphalt. Ten minutes later, the waters from both sides of the road met. Soon there was an inch of standing water on the road, and it was deepening steadily. Some cars rolled through carefully. After a gap in the traffic, a big gray Chevy Silverado 2500 roared in at about forty miles an hour. Its bumper pushed out a bow wave that went rippling over the sides of the road, rocking Paul a bit in his chair. The truck's tires began planing and lost traction. The vehicle turned sideways, slid off the side of the road and into the seaweed. There it stopped, up to the top of its tires in water. Paul looked over to the little bush. It was entirely under water.

Two state trooper cars came howling down the wrong side of the highway. The vehicles stopped at acute angles to the side of the road. Four officers jumped out of the cars. They were in an aggressive mode, prepared to arrest demonstrators. The lead one stood arms akimbo, fingers touching the handcuffs on his service belt. After all, they had been briefed just a day earlier that the Indians had agreed to stop these protests. The Malpense Elders had conveyed their solemn promise. And now it appeared to be happening again, with traffic stopped on the highway.

The troopers stood and surveyed the scene. It was evident that there was no roadblock, just seawater covering the road, now peaking at about eleven inches deep. They turned to Paul, sitting in his lawn chair, well off the road. They were puzzled. "I'm not protesting," Paul said mildly. "I'm just observing."

It was a marvelous bit of theater. "Today, the sea is doing the protesting," Paul explained to the troopers.

And so the state police found themselves doing what they had come to stop the Indians from doing: putting up lines of orange traffic cones to stop traffic. Two took off their shoes and socks, rolled up the ends of their gray nylon pants, and waded through the tide-covered highway to the far side, carrying cones for there.

"Water should start coming down soon," Paul shouted helpfully.

17
SOLID VS. CASTILLO

The next day, Solid Harrison was asked at a campaign appearance in Kennebunk about the Tide Is High protests. "I share their concerns," she said. "We need to do more than we have about global overheating—the term they use for climate change, I think accurately. I think we can learn from listening to them. And I applaud their use of nonviolent tactics."

That move helped her across much of the state, but hurt her a bit in Washington County, where the demonstrations had cut off Eastport. Aside from that, she was faring well downstate, and doing better than expected in the more conservative but less populated north and east. Her college French came in handy when campaigning in mill towns and up in Aroostook County. She wouldn't win them, but she would cut down on her opponent's numbers in those places, and that was important.

❖

Castillo ran a respectable campaign, but by mid-October was still more or less tied with her in the polls. He had been wary of debating Solid, but finally, under pressure from several editorial pages of state newspapers and also the League of Women Voters, and looking for a boost that would put him over the top, he agreed to one to be held on October 28, just a week before election day. He was like a prizefighter when it came to confrontation, he figured, while she was a political amateur. A good early pop might even knock her out of contention. On top of that, he won the pre-debate coin toss. He chose to go first.

Ryan drove to the bar at the hotel at the Bangor airport to watch the debate. He wanted to see how others reacted to it. It was quiet, with just a handful of travelers waiting around for the airport's infrequent flights to New York, Philadelphia, Washington, and Chicago.

"Mr. Castillo?" began the moderator. He was a gravelly-voiced, white-haired old man who wrote editorials for the Bangor newspaper. His real love was composing essays about hunting and fishing, which actually were far better observed, and more widely read, than his wheezy political musings, which tended to be based on a starry-eyed nostalgia for the Kennedy administration. He was more reliable on casting for trout than he was on foreign and domestic policy.

Castillo came out roaring. His advisors had agreed with him that he should seek to land a knockout blow at the start. Push her off-balance and keep her there. He was big and loud, his salt-and-pepper hair well-oiled and combed with a deep part, his arms waving to command the attention of everyone out there. "My opponent, who is she?" he shouted. "Maybe a lesbian, or maybe not. Okay by me either way, but make up your mind, okay?" There were a few light laughs out there in the auditorium. He drew energy from that.

"Maybe she's a real Mainer, or maybe she's a Boston lawyer," he said, barking out the last two words with evident contempt. "Search me." He lifted his hands flat together, in the gesture that means what-you-gonnna-do?

"And talk about her friends! She hangs out with some weird types, I gotta tell you. One of her buddies is an Indian chief who killed his father. He's the guy who was sticking it to the folks in Eastport with his demonstrations. And her ex-boyfriend has a few ghosts in his past, too. But she's been hot-bunking it, you know? Now she's switched teams again, gone back to having a girlfriend. Don't get me wrong, I respect either way. But you got to wonder if she's switching around just to get more votes. I mean, she's gay, she's straight, she's gay. Talk about flip-flops!

"Now her current girlfriend, well, she spends a lot of time around dead people, too. And Miss Harrison's father, he's some kind of dope dealer. And this woman's been getting millions of dollars from the Japanese. Makes you wonder who she's really working for, doesn't it?

"In sum: Geronimo, Japs, and dope dealers! Quite a combo." He grinned across the stage at Solid, then turned to face the closest camera, with the red light on top of it indicating it was the one whose images were being broadcast.

It was time for his big pitch. "Maine, you know me," he said, smiling and spreading his arms wide as if to embrace the camera. "I'm Al, your pal. You've eaten at my table. You don't know her." He pointed an index finger at her and kept his arm extended. "Trust me on this."

❖

Solid stood quietly. She shifted her feet.

"Ms. Harrison, your response," the tired-looking moderator said. The underpowered public TV lighting made him look even older than his age.

Solid said nothing. She shifted her gaze toward her hands on the podium. She was dressed in a simple black suit with a doubled string of pearls. Her hair was tied back, almost severely. In her outfit, she had tried to evoke the seriousness and stature of Margaret Chase Smith, Maine's legendary twentieth-century senator. She had succeeded.

"Ms. Harrison?" the moderator repeated.

Nothing. She saw the audience staring at her probably wondering if she had been frozen by Castillo's flailing attack. She was, after all, a newcomer to politics.

"Ms. Harrison, do you wish to use your time?" the moderator asked.

She looked up at the moderator. In a low, even voice that was in marked contrast to Castillo's shouting, she said, "Sir, I want to offer my time to Mister Castillo. To give him a chance to apologize."

Castillo laughed. "Not gonna happen, lady!" The triumphant grin on his face said that this debate was going even better than he expected. He looked around happily.

Solid's jaw tightened. "Mister Castillo, I am giving you an opportunity to apologize."

Castillo waved his hand across his face in smirking dismissal. "Or else, what?"

Solid nodded. "Okay, then. You had your chance." She drew herself up into prosecutorial mode. "Mister Castillo, do you have an anger management problem?"

The smirk on his face said, This is the best you got? "Gimme a break," he said, lifting his chin. "Yes, you're right: I'm a passionate man. I care about Maine, and about its people. Sometimes I get loud. If that's a crime, well, hey, lock me up." He held out his hands together as if offering them to handcuffs.

"Mister Castillo, I will be more specific. Do you hit women?"

Castillo quickly looked over at her. As he did he seemed to blanch a hit, wondering where this was going. "Don't know what you're talking about," he said quickly. Too quickly. She had planted a seed of doubt in him. He was wondering: What did she have? A shadow crossed his face. She couldn't have *that*, he thought.

Solid slowed down, enunciating her words carefully and clearly. "Okay, Mister Castillo, I will be even more specific." She paused, knowing that he and everyone else listening was waiting for what came next. Slowly, clearly, she said, "Sir, have you hit your wife in the last year?"

Uh-oh, he thought. She had *that*. He stared at her, seeming to actually see her for the first time that evening—or to begin to assess who his opponent really was. The realization was growing in the pit of his stomach that he had committed that most dangerous mistake in politics and war—he had underestimated his foe.

She persisted on the point, again more specific. "Hit her in the face, in your home?"

He shook his head slightly. All he could think was, How does she know this? His mind was stuck on that. Renee wouldn't talk to her, would she? But this woman seems so confident, it couldn't just be third-party hearsay.

The calculation hit him: My wife blabbed to my opponent.

The next thought: When I get home tonight, I'll fucking kill her. But at the same moment he realized that none of these thoughts would help him get back into the debate. He needed to focus.

Meanwhile, while he was pondering all this, Solid's voice was hammering away at him with details. Her words seemed to float over him. It took him a moment to comprehend them, to grasp where she was going. She had the goods. He tried to understand as she spoke: "Last December, in your home? After a Christmas party? When you'd had a few? Mister Castillo, are you listening?" Her voice seemed very far away, almost echoing over a chasm between them.

At hearing the specifics of the time and place of his offense, he appeared as if he himself had been struck. His eyes grew large. But he was still trying to fight back. He took a deep breath and waded back into the brawl. "These are wild assertions," he scowled. "Irresponsible. Gutter politics." He turned to the moderator. "Are you going to allow this?" The Bangor editorialist sat impassively. He had never liked politicians, and didn't mind seeing one going down in flames.

Solid took her iPhone out of her jacket pocket and held it up to the camera. "If I am wrong, then you won't mind if I play for the audience a recent recording." She had it cued to begin where Mrs. Castillo said, "He hit me." But she didn't push the play button.

Castillo was staring at her but speaking to the moderator. "I am asking for a brief pause in this debate. I am not feeling well." He turned and walked behind a curtain to the backstage area.

Solid stood at her podium. The lead camera pulled back to show her and the other podium empty. Commentators who were on hand to provide post-debate analysis were pulled onto the air to fill the empty time. One, a reporter from Portland, went on about how unprecedented this was, a memorable evening in the state's political history. Another, from the *Moosehead Lake Steamboat Express*, was blunter: "With every minute that passes, he's losing another few thousand votes." Yes, they agreed, the next few minutes would be critical.

In the hotel bar, conversations stopped and heads swung toward the television. "Shit just got real," the bartender said in new admiration of Solid. "Looks like Al brought a knife to a gunfight." He walked over and turned up the volume.

After seven long minutes, Castillo reemerged from behind the green curtain. He had washed his face at some point and so removed the pancake makeup that is so essential to making people appear normal under the glare of harsh studio spotlights. Now his face was fish-belly pallid as he stood before his podium.

"I have a statement I wish to read," he began, holding a white piece of paper in front of him. It rustled a little as his right hand trembled. He pressed his left hand down on it to quiet it. A trickle of sweat ran down the right side of his whitened face and then leaped to his shirt collar. "At one point last year, when I was feeling, uh, depressed, I drank too much one evening. When my wife pointed this out to me, we had a, well, altercation. During this discussion, she may have interpreted what happened when I reached out as hitting her. Whatever may have happened, that was not my intention. Since that time, I have received counseling. I ask tonight that my entire life not be judged on the basis of a few bad moments that I deeply regret."

He looked up. "I am not an abuser of women. I respect women, and I ask the women of Maine, each and every one of you, to go to the polls and vote for me this coming Tuesday." He turned and left the stage.

Solid stood and waited. The moderator finally said, "Ms. Harrison, unless you have a closing statement, I think this debate is concluded."

Solid had spent days considering what she would do if it came to this. "I don't have a formal conclusion," Solid responded. "But I do have something I want to say."

She stared directly into the camera a few feet in front of her. "This is not a happy moment, for me or for Maine. I feel sorry for that man. I do. My heart goes out to him. And even more to his wife."

She leaned forward, as she had learned to do in making a final assertion in a courtroom argument. "But at this moment, as this debate ends, I think even more than I did before it began that I am the better candidate to lead the government of this state, to work better for you. You deserve quiet, competent leadership. I will deliver that. I don't think that is Mister Castillo's strength. And so I am asking every Mainer, every man and woman watching this, to vote for me."

A few days later Solid won the statewide vote 56 to 44, which amounted to a landslide in a state that tended to split its vote narrowly.

In her inaugural address two months later, she mentioned Paul's demonstrations. "It is clear that we need to do more and need to do different in dealing with the overheating of the planet. You can argue about what is causing it, but you can't say it isn't happening. I have followed the Tide Is High protests with interest. I salute those who are challenging us to work harder and smarter on this pressing problem."

18
A MEMORANDUM TO LOVE, AND LOVE'S RESPONSE

S purred on by Solid's win, Ryan wrote an impassioned report
to his supervisors. "These protesters are not violent," it began.
"Their concerns are genuine. Their movement is new and different."
Thus, he went on to argue,

> Those three aspects suggest to me that there is an
> opportunity here for the Bureau to deal with Native
> American protests differently than we have in the past.
> I believe we should follow the example of the new gov-
> ernor of Maine, who has reached out to the protesters
> with the hand of friendship. Here, perhaps, we could
> serve not as a threatening presence, but as a connection
> to the larger world.
>
> Historically speaking, there is no reason for the
> Bureau to take an antagonistic stance, except that we
> have reflexively done so in the past with social activists.

And on it went, for several hundred words.

In his office in Portland, Jimmy Love read the whole thing, and then dialed Bulster down in Boston. "Tapia's going native," he reported. "Next thing I expect is him to show up in a headband and breechcloth."

Jimmy Love was upset. He didn't need this kind of trouble from Ryan. Jimmy's plan was to serve three more years, until he could retire. He had zero interest in leading the Bureau in a new direction. Indeed, his assessment was that realistically, the Bureau would come down hard on anyone who tried that sort of thing. And so he began to cover his ass. It was time to distance himself from Ryan. He began composing a memo for the record: "Agent TAPIA's warm feelings for the Indian protesters in Maine are, to say the least, ill-advised," he began, using his most Hooverian rhetoric. "Indeed, at times he seems unaware that he is employed by the national domestic intelligence agency, not a publicity office for activists."

Ryan drove down to Augusta for his monthly appointment with his grief counselor, Dot Williams, a large and intelligent woman. He had learned that she missed nothing and was especially adept at catching the things left unsaid. She asked him what he was thinking these days about his family, now dead these three years.

"What have you kept from them?" she asked.

"You mean, as mementoes?"

"Yeah."

"Not much. My wife's wedding ring. The favorite toys of the children—Marta's brown bear and Pablo's wooden train."

"Anything else?"

"Why do you ask?"

"Humor me."

"Well, the dog's collar. And his water buffalo horn, for some reason. He'd chew on it when he was anxious, like if he was left at home alone when we went out for an evening."

"Where are they now?"

"In a box in the closet."

"I'd like to make a suggestion."

"Okay."

"Take them out. Make a little altar of them. Talk to them—the ring, the bear, the train, the buffalo horn."

"Why?"

"Because I think you are ready. And because, if you can, it is healthier to commune with our ghosts than it is to try to ignore them."

"I'm not ignoring them. I think about them every day."

"Then why are they in a closet?" She let the question hang in the air.

Ryan thought it over. "Okay," he conceded. "What kind of altar?"

"Whatever you like. Some people add it to the top of their dresser, or in a corner of the kitchen, with a piece of velvet or silk, maybe a candle."

"Why that?"

"The church knows something. You light it when you need to talk, when you want to signal that a spirit is present. You can blow it out when you're finished talking. And maybe their spirits are chilly, would like the warmth. They might be lonely."

"But they're all together—my wife, the kids, the dog. Why would they be lonely?"

"Because they were ripped untimely from this life. None of them was finished here."

"Me, too."

"And that's why you're here, meeting with me, to try to find a way forward through this senseless loss. That suddenness, that's the source of pain."

"Okay. I'll do it," he agreed, and stood to go.

Once home he made an altar in the corner of the kitchen, next to the coffee machine. It made sense—he could talk to them when he was waking, perhaps with a dream about them still clinging in wisps to his head. And there was a lovely view of the pond from that spot, too. He could stand there with the altar to the past and the view of the present while he waited for his coffee to brew.

19
PLANNING FOR THE MARCH BEGINS

In December, with the deer hunting season concluded and the resulting meat either smoked or frozen, Paul and James prepared for their first meeting to discuss where their little movement should go next.

Paul had noticed that it took a while to draw out James, who had thoughts but wanted to hear and understand what was being said before he spoke. That tendency made him a great listener and questioner.

"What are we thinking of doing?" Paul asked him one day as they walked the streets of the reservation. "What do we tell people when they ask?"

"Current solutions aren't working. The Earth is on fire."

"What makes us experts?" Paul asked.

"We're not. But we do have the advantage of a different perspective. We're not Anglos. It is Anglo culture that lit the fire. Don't expect that same culture to put it out."

"So, in other words, 'sustainability' isn't the answer."

"Yep. All that sustainability crap, that's just a way of avoiding the necessary major fixes," James said.

"Then what is our answer?"

"We're thinking of an action to find out. More protests. Maybe a march."

"What you are saying, I think, is that each action creates the next action—but we don't know what that will be, where this will lead."

"Yes," said James. "We do our best, as you did with the Tide Is High. That led us to this talk of a march down the coast. And the energy of that action, whether positive or negative, will lead to the next."

"I see what you mean," Paul said. "We know more than we think. The old ways may have answers for questions we've barely started to ask. For example, John of Tides knows a whole lot about how the ocean is changing."

❖

Paul and James, expecting no more than twenty attendees, had planned to hold the first meeting in the living room of the sober house. But even before ten o'clock in the morning, when it was scheduled to begin, that room was full, with standees spilling into the kitchen and front hall. More were outside, smoking. James's calls to his contacts on the reservations had been more fruitful than expected, with the people he invited talking to others, and small convoys coming down from several reservations.

John of Tides had been invited to begin the session with a prayer. He suggested that to accommodate the unexpectedly large turnout, they ask to borrow the tribal council house. After he made two calls, the group, now numbering forty-seven, walked over there, someone rolling John in his wheelchair at their front.

Then John spoke. His voice was feeble, so James Reveur, standing next to his wheelchair, repeated each of his phrases in a booming voice. "We are the people of the land between the sun and the water," John began.

"WE ARE THE PEOPLE . . ." James boomed, shouting over the heads of the crowd so those in back could hear.

"Everything comes from the sun. Everything goes back to the land and the water."

"EVERYTHING . . ." James repeated.

"The land does not belong to us," John said. "We belong to the land. We are gathered here today to try to help our people and other people take better care of the land."

"THE LAND DOES NOT . . ."

"We do this more for our descendants than for us. If we succeed, they will thank us. If we fail, they at least will know we tried."

"WE DO THIS . . ."

And then Paul stood. "Thank you, Elder," he began. He turned to the group. "James and I have been talking. We don't think we have all the answers. What we have is ideas and questions. And I know a lot of you do, too. So I thought we'd begin by having a conversation to build a foundation. No rules, no conclusions, just trying to figure out where we are."

"First things first," James said, reaching back to the lessons he had learned from the Starbucks organizer in Montreal. "First, who are we?" It was a classic strategic move: Begin with self-definition. Only when you figure out who you are can you begin to figure out your goals. That leads to what to do, and next to how to do it. He pointed to a teenager standing in the back. "Your thoughts?"

"We're a bunch of pissed-off Indians," the kid said.

"Yes, we sure are," said James. "And why?"

"Because of the land and water getting fucked up," another kid in the back said. "The climate shit you fellows have been protesting."

"Yes. Tell me more."

That led to several hours of discussions. What people were seeing. How they felt about it. What might be done. Paul and James let it ramble, but emphasized the points of agreement that emerged. People needed to try on ideas, think through them, see how they fit. In the process, they began to feel less like a collection of individuals and more like people who understood and sympathized with each other—that is, a genuine group.

James: "Like John of Tides said, it's not the land that belongs to us. We belong to the land. We live with it, on it, work with it, preserve it. We don't consume it. And we don't burn it."

Paul: "But that's not what this country is built on."

James: "Damn straight. This country was built on the theft of land from us, on the stolen labor of Black people held captive, and yes, on the idea of freedom, for some people, but rarely for all."

By midafternoon, they had hammered out a motto: *We belong to the land*.

Paul: "So what does that point to?"

James: "I think a march through the land, to declare our loyalty to it."

"Why?"

"It's a natural next step. It's a warning. And maybe a plea. We're saying, 'We have to live differently.' What is the basic ingredient of a march? Steps."

"And what if, after we march, they say, 'Get lost'?" asked an older man, sitting down in front.

"That might be the answer we're searching for. Really. We can say, 'Okay, we tried. And now we will go in a different direction.'"

"Meaning?" said Paul.

"We would leave them behind, we will separate. You know how the Ghost Dance was supposedly the last chance for the American Indian in the nineteenth century?"

"Yeah, I've read about that," Paul said.

"So," James said, "maybe our march will be the last chance for Anglo culture to stop burning the world."

"But why a march?" asked one of the Malpense.

"Because," James said, "overheating is ruining our world. We don't know where our march will lead us. But just by doing it, we are saying to people, and especially our own people, that we shouldn't follow the Anglos over the cliff. This is a chance, maybe the last chance, for Indians to take a different path from that. The march may show us the beginning of the path. We don't know exactly where that will lead. But we know we want a different path than the one the industrialized world is on. They are burning up the world."

"I like that phrase," Paul said. "So it's a march against the Worldburners."

"Yes. Precisely."

Next came the question of the makeup of the march. "Who marches?" James asked.

"Just Indians," another Quivive said. Several members of that tribe had followed James to the meeting. There were nods of agreement around the room.

"Just Maine Indians or any Indians?" asked another participant. "I ask because I'm a Wampanoag."

"From down in Massachusetts, near Rhode Island?" Paul asked.

"Exactly."

"I say, welcome, brother. Any dissents?" Paul said. He looked around the room.

There were none. Indeed, someone else shouted out a casual greeting, "Wamps inna house!"

"But what if Anglos want to join?" a kid from Old Town asked.

"It's a free country," Paul said. "They can tag along behind. But they are not part of our march. And they don't camp with us."

"What about Pretendians?" asked someone in the back. This was the disparaging term they all knew and used for Anglos who were wannabe Native Americans.

"That's worst of all," Paul said. "My sense of this group is that we need to keep it real. Has to be enrolled in a tribe, or with a credible reason for why not. None of these guys who say, 'My moms said my grandpa was one-third Cherokee.' We've all heard that nonsense." Nods all around. "And none of these fly-by-night tribes that are recognized by states, but not by the federal government."

"Why is Indian purity so important?" asked another participant who was a student in Machias. "It's not like we're a bunch of natural-born genius experts."

"Well," said Paul, "you know more than you think. And the march we are contemplating is about the relationship between people and nature. We want to reset the frame. We want human beings to see nature as something we are part of, not as something to be consumed. 'Sustainability' is a lie, because nine-tenths plunder and one-tenth preservation is not what we want. The Indian part of that, the thing that we've inherited as part of our culture, is that with nature it is not just a physical relationship, it is also spiritual."

James shook his head. "Paul is being too polite, as usual," James said. "Let me put a sharper point on what he just said: Anglo culture is burning the world. It is hard enough dealing with Anglo culture—you've all experienced that—without having Anglos inside the tent. Especially Anglos pretending to be Indians, getting all fuzzy thinking."

So ended the day. They agreed to meet again two months later for the first round of broad-stroke planning. In the interim, they would begin the hard work of preparation. A march was like an iceberg—only a small part of it was visible. The submerged part was getting ready. The logistics alone were mind-boggling: Daily food, water, shelter for a group of unknown size that would decide each day where it would march and how far. But that really was the least of it. What the marchers would need most, Paul and James had come to know in their bones, was a sense of cohesion, of mutual trust and understanding. And that came from working together, planning together, and talking together.

That evening, walking out along the highway, Paul noticed that the little salt-tolerant bush was dead, its needles turned brown. Apparently it could live with salt water on its roots, but not when it was entirely under water.

Over breakfast the next day, Paul said, "You know, they accepted us as their leaders. But we never really talked about how that works."

"What do you mean?" James asked.

"How do we divide our roles? People will ask who is the leader, you or me?"

James: "I think we are a two-headed organization. You are the *today*, interpreting where we are. And I'm the *tomorrow*, looking at where we're going."

Paul: "Your job sounds like more fun."

James, grimly: "Only someone who hasn't imagined tomorrow could say that."

Paul, with a grin: "Well played, sir."

James: "I'm deadly fucking serious."

Paul, still lightly: "Only a 'tomorrow' could not see the humor here."

James nodded. "I think we have a partnership."

Paul reached across the table and shook James's hand. "It's a deal," he said.

James: "What do we do if we have a disagreement, a serious one?"

Paul: "That tells us to put off the decision. That way, it will straddle the present and the future. But let's agree now: We don't move forward without consensus."

James nodded in agreement.

❖

James spent his evenings over the next six weeks studying. He began with looking at how members of the civil rights movement of the 1960s had applied Gandhi, focusing on the work of James Lawson and James Bevel in Nashville. He also read every interview he could find with Bayard Rustin, the mastermind of the landmark 1963 civil rights march in Washington, DC. Then he turned to the essays of James Baldwin, whom he began to consider the American version of Voltaire.

20
RYAN AT THE ALTAR

Ryan awoke and turned on the coffee machine. While he waited for it to brew, he lit the candle at the little altar and sat in the chair next to it. He stared at the yellow flame, close enough to it to feel its warmth on his left cheek. "I've been thinking about my relationship with the FBI," he said aloud to the wedding ring, the stuffed bear, the wooden train engine, and the dog's chew horn. "I'm not sure I have a future there."

Why? his dead wife's question hung in the bright morning air.

Ryan thought about that, and eventually said aloud, "I feel like I am diverging from it. Like what I think is right is not what my bosses think. If it comes down to doing the right thing or being loyal to the institution, I am going to do what I think is right."

That's a lonely road.

"Yeah, I know. But better to be on a lonely road than a dead-end path."

We'll be with you.

"That's what makes me able to do it." He finished the coffee and blew out the candle. "Thanks."

21
THE SECOND PLANNING MEETING FOR THE MARCH

Two months later, the group came together again. This time more than sixty people attended.

"Last meeting we talked about who we are and what we want to do," Paul began. "We are Indians planning a march to protest the burning of the world and trying to reframe our relationship with nature. We will spend a good part of the summer walking down the Maine coast. To the extent possible, we will hunt and fish to feed ourselves."

"So the question now is," James continued, "how do we do that? What kind of organization do we want to be to try to reach those goals? What kind of tactics do we use? The essence of a good march or demonstration is preparation. Today we will discuss how and where we march. Next time, we'll talk about training for the march. Often the success of an action is determined by these preparatory steps. Some of that is anticipating problems and some of it is figuring out how to respond to problems and where to find help when needed."

They decided that day to focus their march on large lots of land owned by out-of-staters, especially those along the coast and where the housing had been standing vacant. Basically, they wanted to stay each night on the land of big summer mansions on the coast. Rock volunteered to research properties that fit that bill. Another committee would assemble a roster of public lands they could use when private properties were sparse. "But only state lands," Paul admonished. "No national parks, no lands under the administration of the Interior Department, like federal wildlife management areas. We don't want to tangle with the federal authorities, at least not in this march. The state is going to be a lot friendlier."

22
SESSION THREE: TRAINING

They met again in April. James began this third gathering with a talk on nonviolence, telling the story of how he came across "this Indian named Gandhi." "I think he charts the course well. Basically, we use aggressive, confrontational nonviolence. It isn't passive. We stand our ground, we don't back down, but we don't hit."

"Why?" asked the young Malpense woman who went by the name Seaweeds. "That's not natural, going all passive resistance."

"It isn't passive," James insisted. "It is the opposite. When you do it right, you crackle with directed, intense energy. It is highly disciplined. And it puts the other side on the back foot."

"How?" Seaweeds persisted. James respected that.

"Because power speaks the language of violence. Fluently. Money is just distilled power. We don't have money, and we don't have power. If we don't speak their language, the opposition won't know what to do with us."

There was skepticism, but a willingness to at least try it.

"Most of all," James continued, "any violence from us gives them an excuse to shut us down. If we have the self-discipline to avoid that, we win."

"Also," Paul added, "that means you keep an eye out for provocateurs, people who might want to undermine us by maybe throwing a chunk of asphalt at a statie, or slugging a loudmouth bystander." He asked if anyone had anything to add.

An Indian lawyer who now practiced in Portland reported that he had lined up twenty-five colleagues who were willing to defend the marchers pro bono if they were arrested.

An older Indian from Presque Isle volunteered to run the two support trucks. One would carry all their backpacks, tents, and sleeping bags. A second would go out and get water and food each day and then they would prepare an evening meal. In the morning they would lay out breakfast foods, as well as the makings of lunches.

Later, over lunch, Paul asked Seaweeds how she acquired her nickname. She said, "You know our language puts 'S' on the end of Anglo words, like 'pizzas'?"

"Yeah," he said. "That's how we do plural nouns."

"So when I went to an Anglo school and said things like, 'Pass the spaghettis,' kids noticed. And at the beach, when I said 'seaweeds,' the name stuck."

That afternoon they broke up into training groups of four. James had written scripts for them. In each group, two would play the marchers, two would play the other side. Then they would switch roles and do it again.

- Marchers vs. mob
- Marchers vs. state policeman who said they couldn't march here
- Marchers meeting a friendly reporter—and learning still to be wary
- Marchers meeting an openly hostile reporter

Paul walked over to watch a marcher talking to someone playing the role of a landowner.

"My ancestors owned this land," the marcher said.

"But I own it now," the other responded.

"Really? Do you take care of it?"

"I have people for that."

"Can an absentee owner take care of land they don't see or know?"

"The land is in good shape. And I need you to leave."

"Okay, we will be gone soon, probably in the morning, and you will hardly know we were here. We respect the land."

Seaweeds distributed leaflets with a statement she had drawn up on her laptop. It was a kind of catechism for the march.

What are we about?

About finding a new path.

Where does it lead?

We don't know. But we have hopes. We know what it leads away from: The destructive anti-natural ways of the Worldburners. We believe they are on the road to catastrophe. We are looking for a way to live after the coming disaster. We believe our ancestors had many of the answers.

Are you anti-city?

Yes, we are. Cities destroy villages. Our ancestors called one of the white leaders "destroyers of villages." It was about the worst thing you could call someone. They would not even discuss a treaty with him.

But you favor villages?

Yes. Cities are about growth. Villages are about culture, about old ways. When you want to expand, trade, get new things, you want a city. When you want to hunker down and survive, stay out of the way of major destruction, the village will save you. Any experienced biologist can tell you that the smaller and simpler an organism, the better the chance it has of surviving a catastrophic event.

That evening the group came together for a feast of halibut and cod. After they ate, Rock briefed them on the planned march route. He had a projector for the map on his laptop. The march would begin in early July at the easternmost point in Maine, the lighthouse at Quoddy. From there it took them through the relative wilds of Washington County, and next into the wealthy crust from Bar Harbor down toward Portland. Every night they would sleep either on state land—parks, wildlife preserves and such—or on unoccupied estates owned by wealthy people from out-of-state. Rock's team had identified over one hundred properties within ten miles of the coast that were larger than five acres, had been on the market for several months, and had asking prices of more than $4 million. The goal always was to publicize their concerns while avoiding alienating locals, Anglo or Native, especially potential supporters.

"And what do we do at the end of the march?" someone asked.

"Something will turn up," James said. "The energy of the march will create something."

"You're surprisingly optimistic for a shaman," Paul teased.

James looked at him, more somber than ever. "No, I actually worry about what will turn up. And how we handle it. There will be a lot of loose energy crackling in the air, positive and negative, and we shouldn't think we can control it. But we can try to work with it."

On that foreboding note, the meeting ended.

PART II

THE MARCH

23

DAWN AT QUODDY HEAD

JULY 5: THE MARCH BEGINS

I n early July, before the march began, the Portland lawyer notified the state police and the governor's office of the plan to stage
a march, and asked for a permit to parade on Route 1. Someone
from the governor's office called back, saying she was interested
and would like to learn more. The lawyer invited the new governor
to come visit the march at her convenience.

At dawn on July 5, they convened just before sunrise at Quoddy
Head State Park, the easternmost point of the United States. Paul
was surprised that after their big meetings, only twenty-two people
showed up. James counseled him not to worry. "People gonna hold
back, want to see how it goes," he said.

They faced the point where the sun would rise up out of the gray
Atlantic. When the sky turned yellow and pink, marking the beginning of the new day, James stated to the group, "We are in the
presence of the Light. We will now pray."

He turned toward the sun and, in a loud, even voice, said, "On
this day, following the American observance, we declare our own

independence from a world that is burning. We find ourselves called together from different homes and campfires to be companions on the journey of life. We confess that we don't fully understand where we are going. But we know we will move forward in a spirit of love and faith.

"We will be gone for a long time, grandmothers and grandfathers. Do not worry about it. We know that fixing the world is a task for many generations. We can only hope to begin that journey."

He turned back to face the group. "Let's go," he said.

They pulled on their daypacks and began to walk out of the park and up Boot Cove Road. The two pickup trucks followed.

"Hold up," said one marcher, eyeing the trucks as they moved out on the gravel road. "How can a march like ours rely on gasoline-powered vehicles? Isn't that what we're protesting?"

"Good question," James said. "Bothers me, too. We're gonna change, but we can't do it all at once. I think of it this way: Instead of driving twenty-two trucks, we've combined our loads and are using just two. Got to crawl before we walk or run."

At first, Maine and the rest of the world remained blissfully ignorant of the march. Even those who saw them didn't think much. "There's a bunch of Indians walking on the side of the County Road," a plumber observed outside Whiting during a cell phone call back to the office.

"So what?" his boss responded. "At least they're not blocking the road to Eastport. Probably having a picnic."

The first day's destination was a swath of unnamed "Maine Public Reserve," a big chunk of land owned by the state and open to use, but lacking any amenities. They put up their tents and built a campfire next to a pond in the woods. While others cooked, Paul and James, leading by example, dug a sewage trench.

24
MARCH DAY 2

JULY 6: SELF-DEFINITION

At dawn, a moose stood knee deep at the far side of the pond, half-obscured by mists. "I think that's a good portent," James said. "Moose is keeping an eye on us."

Paul and James lifted a bag of lime from the second pickup truck. They pulled it to the sewage trench, cut open the bag, and spread the contents along the trench. Paul spaded soil over it, while James brought piles of pine needles to finish off the job. Some of the marchers watched them.

"These guys aren't fooling around," observed one who for the march had taken the name Lonesome Whale.

"If you're gonna be in the march, you're gonna have to dig trenches for shit," responded one who had dubbed himself Distant Thunder. Taking on new names was a long-standing Indian tradition—one might be given a name as an infant, then take on a new one when becoming a hunter, and a third when getting married or going on a war party. So it was here.

The marchers assembled in the morning fog. Paul introduced the marchers to a new aspect of the routine. Each morning, he said, he or James would select a marcher to address the group just before they set off. In part, this was a way of helping bring to the surface potential leaders and others with skills. But even more, it served to focus the entire group, as everyone came to realize that no one could know if they would be the person picked to speak that morning. Paul's ground rules were simple: Speak about something that is related to the march yesterday or today. And keep it to one minute or less.

This morning, to set the example, Paul pointed at James, who stood up, took in his audience, and said, "Good morning. This is what I was thinking about as we walked yesterday: By marching, we are redefining ourselves, or at least trying to. The question we are trying to address is, where does the future lie for human beings? For me, I define myself as a human within nature. Today I want to think about how to live out that definition."

They hit the road, a small band moving in the thick white fog of the upper Maine coast. They passed through the little town of Cutler, a huddle of modest white houses overlooking a narrow harbor dotted with lobster boats. Almost no one noticed them. There were just twenty of them, two having decided after a night on the ground that they really were not cut out for this life.

"Some effect we're having," Paul said.

"Early days, Paul, early days," James said. "Like I said this morning, it begins with changing yourself. We're still learning how to do this. I'm glad not to have audiences."

They camped that night on the heath above East Machias. It was quiet, still, and beautiful. But it also was buggy as hell, featuring not just mosquitoes but also black flies, deer flies, and no-see-ums.

25
MARCH DAY 3

JULY 7: A PREMONITION

This morning, Paul selected one of the younger members of the march to say a few words. The kid, who had long black eyebrows, almost a complete line from each side of his eyes, nearly meeting above the bridge of his nose, stood up and said, "I'm Pigtoe. I hate these bugs. Let's go." At first Paul thought that picking the kid had been a mistake. But as he walked, the more he thought about it, the more he realized the kid had captured the mood perfectly. Not every day was going to be profound. One of the lessons of the march was that it was hard to see what was in front of your eyes. Today, that happened to be bugs.

That morning, they came to Route 1 for the first time. Paul looked down at the asphalt of the two-lane highway and stopped walking. He had a grimace on his mosquito-bitten face, as if he had been struck by a twinge of pain. He crouched down on one knee to study the asphalt. He touched it with his right hand, feeling its texture.

"You okay?" James asked.

Paul turned his face toward the sky. After a long silence, he said, "James, is this the road to the future, or to my death?"

James said, "We are all on the road to death. The question is, what do we do along the way?"

Paul: "I just have an eerie feeling."

James: "That's part of what makes you special." He stared above Paul's head. He thought he saw Paul's yellow aura flickering, concentrating, a bit darker, tending more toward orange. He would have to keep an eye on that. On the other hand, he thought, only he could see it. They walked in silence.

A local police officer appeared. He parked on the shoulder of the road in front of them, his lights flashing. Paul thought he couldn't have been more than twenty-five years old.

"What are you guys?"

"Indians on a demonstration march," Paul said.

"You got a permit?" the trooper said.

"We've applied for one," Paul said. "And we've invited the governor to visit us at some point."

"You want an escort through Machias?"

"If you like," said Paul. "But please, no siren—we don't want to disturb people unnecessarily."

The police car led them into the town. People waved to them, not unkindly. They detected no hostility. On the west side of town, they cut southwest on a back road to Roque Bluffs State Park.

As they walked, three local Indians, all Malpense, fell in and walked with them. Paul went back to say hello. Two said they were brothers. "This is our cousin, Trout," one said.

Trout said he was into Indian poetry. Paul asked him to pick one to recite the next morning.

They made camp that afternoon on the long crescent of beach in the state park. A ranger walked over to meet them. "There's no camping here," he said.

"This is a demonstration. An expression of our rights under the First Amendment."

The ranger rolled his eyes. "First time I've heard that one. You all Indians?"

"Yep."

"What are you protesting?"

"Climate change. Abuse of the land. Burning up the Earth."

"I hear you," the park ranger said. "Don't disagree with you, either. And I don't want trouble. Clean it up and leave in the morning?"

"You bet."

"No guns, no violence?"

"Yes, sir."

"Have a good night." He turned and left.

And they did. The park had portable toilets, so no sewage trench was needed.

26
MARCH DAY 4

JULY 8: THE PRESIDENT COMMENTS

James and a few others of the hardier sort began their day with a
bracing plunge in the ocean, still below 50 degrees this early in
the year. They stood shivering by the morning campfire and sipped
scalding hot tea loaded with sugar. It was a powerful way to start
the day. While seawater and goose bumps still covered their skin,
they each had a core of warmth and energy in their stomachs.

When they assembled, Paul pointed to Trout. The young Malpense stood up and chanted:

> *There was never a time*
> *When we were not here*
> *Hunting the bear and the moose*
> *Egrigna*

Then, without looking around, the young man starting marching.
He struck James as a natural leader. "What does 'egrigna' mean?"
James asked him as they walked.

"I can't tell you," Trout said.

"How come?"

"Cuz I don't know. We really don't know what the word means. All we know is that our ancestors used it a lot in their songs. Probably something like 'amen.' So I want to keep it alive until we somehow recover the meaning."

"I think we will," James said.

They headed west through Columbia Falls and Harrington, a remote area with many blueberry fields and evergreen forests, but very few wealthy landowners.

❖

In his truck, Ryan drove toward Columbia Falls. He had heard on Maine NPR news that the march would pass through there that day. He also heard on that newscast that in Washington, at the end of a cabinet meeting, President Maloney had taken a few questions. A reporter from the *Boston Globe*, casting about for a regional angle, asked the president what he thought of the Indians marching on the Maine coast.

"I don't know what is going on up there, but I am keeping an eye on it," President Maloney responded. "I worry about these Indians just marching around, camping anywhere they want, no respect for property rights. If human-caused climate change even were real, how is trespassing going to stop it?" Later that day, he joked in his office, "Hell, we're the ones taking the country back, not them." His press secretary made sure Fox News heard about that line.

Late that afternoon, reporters began to appear in the path of the marchers. By 4 P.M. there were about seven following the march. Each one wanted to interview Paul and James. "There's a grocery store parking lot up ahead, half mile on the right," Rock advised, having checked the route ahead on his laptop. "You could hold a press conference there."

So they did. Paul stood in the lot. "I'm Paul Soco, S-O-C-O, and this is my co-leader on this march, James Reveur, R-E-V-E-U-R. We're both Maine Indians."

James, next to him, said: "To begin, several of you have asked, What is this march? In short, it is a journey to our holy places. They are not on the far side of the world, they are right here."

Reporter: "What are they?"

Paul: "They are all around. Mountains, lakes, cliffs, the ocean. But I wanna give a shout-out to springs in particular—that is the Earth offering clean, cool, pure water, the essence of life."

Bangor Press Citizen reporter: "Where is this march going?"

James: "We don't know. If you find out, please tell us."

The reporters chuckled.

Paul: "Where do *you* think we are going?"

Bangor reporter: "Me? I have no idea. Not my job, you know?"

James: "The Buddha might say that answer is the beginning of wisdom. For my part, I think we are looking at the end of old ways and the beginning of new ones. We are on a hunt, pursuing a path to the unknown world. And you and your colleagues have somehow obtained front-row seats on that journey. What could be more interesting?"

The *Washington Post* reporter had heard enough. This was a press conference, not a mystical powwow with some self-appointed backwoods shamans. She thought to herself, What's the lead? That is, I need to write a story soon, so how should it begin? What's the major point? She wasn't going to write a story that began, *Native American marchers seek to redefine their relationship with the natural world*. When in doubt, when flailing for a lead, turn to politics. That was always a reliable fallback, especially for the *Post*, where all subjects from baseball to desserts were somehow political. She said, "That's all very well, chief—"

Paul interrupted. "Please, neither of us has the honor to hold that title."

"Okay," the *Post* reporter said. "How does your march save, say, that pine tree over there?" She nodded at the green trees on the edge of the parking lot. An Australian shepherd dog lay in the shade of one tree, attentively watching the unusual gathering of people at the press conference.

Paul said, "Well, first of all, it's a spruce, so I guess the place to begin is with knowledge."

Some of the other reporters chuckled. The woman from the *Post* reformulated her question and made it more pointed: "Where do you, as leaders of this march, think you are leading your followers?"

Paul and James looked at each other, partly to see who would answer, and partly to see if they were on the same page. Both said, "Into the future."

"That's where we are walking each day," Paul added. "As far as we can, into the future. Care to join us?"

Post: "Thanks for the invitation, but President Maloney said that the march won't do anything to help your cause."

That was enough for James, who said, "The president holds power, but what does he *know*? He is the product of a doomed way of life. He has a big voice that, as we say in my tribe, can blow all the hairs off my head. But is it a wise voice? He is presiding over the funeral of a system based on fire and destruction, from the steam engine to the automobile to the nuclear bomb.

"As I see it, we face three questions: First, how long will this global funeral last? Second, while it occurs, how much will the natural world suffer? And third, will a portion of human beings survive into the new era? We believe that our Indigenous people

109

may have a better chance than Anglos of living into the post-industrial world—but only if we start now to revive the old ways." Listening to this, Paul thought, the discussions from the winter and spring have prepared us well.

James offered a follow-up thought: "Well, maybe the Amish would have a chance. I've seen their new outposts in Maine. They are very solid, good at self-reliance. Off the grid, attuned to the seasons, not rotting with individualism. They'll roll with the punches. But the rest of you—honestly, I think you're fucked. That's the best way I can put it."

The *New York Times* reporter replied to James, "Wouldn't that new world you foresee be a kind of hell, a Hobbesian war of all against all?"

"Myself, I think the capitalist industrial world already is on that path, how far we do not know." He warmed to his subject. "And that is why I suspect that we Indians eventually will withdraw from their madness."

The reporter looked puzzled. "Like how?"

James said, "I mean, split with the Worldburners. What they call 'civilization,' we call a suicide pact. It is a way of life that is going over a cliff. It may bring mass extinction, taking all the humans with it. But at least we can say that we tried. To the extent possible, we will not be a party to the destruction of the planet. We aim to live as much as we can as our ancestors did. In practical terms, that means we'll try to live in a close relationship with nature, as part of it, not as consumers of it."

Paul added, "Don't see it as a negative act. Think of it as stopping being selfish. If you put your people, your descendants, and most of all, the Earth, foremost, then perhaps you will find a different path. That is the path we are searching for, the one we hope to walk on."

The *Post* reporter's expression was skeptical. "Is that even possible?"

James shook his head. "For you? I very much doubt it. You and your tribe, these reporters here, you all worship information. That is your post-Enlightenment religion. You are the high priests of the swift collection and transmission of data. Your religious structures are cell phone towers. I've even seen them placed on top of churches, which I think leaves little question about your culture's priorities. You swim in a world of facts, figures, statistics. This is the context for which you have trained all your life, from elementary school onwards, and one in which you excel. And we think that world is coming to an end, probably sooner than anyone understands."

New York Times: "So we're doomed?"

"Honestly," James responded, gazing down at the plastic credentials hanging from the reporter's neck, "I think you guys are. I am sorry for you. Consider the home of your newspaper, Manhattan. It is an island in a swiftly rising sea. Will it even exist in a few decades?"

"So we'll build seawalls, or move to New Jersey," the *Times* reporter said a bit defensively.

"Good luck with that," said James. "You know what a New York newspaperman, Horace Greeley, said about Indians back in 1859?"

"No," said the reporter.

"He said, 'These people must die out—there is no help for them.'" James paused. "Well, we think the shoe's kind of on the other foot now. So, while you deal with that, we'll be in the mountains and forests, studying the changes, listening to the wind, sitting by streams and counting fish. We will try to learn from the crows, the deer, and the bears."

The reporter's face went blank. He was a hardworking striver, an excellent student, a brilliant reporter. He had moved up constantly in life, every few years, and had never until this moment thought of himself as perhaps one of life's losers.

Paul felt a pang of sympathy for someone who had never before encountered James in his prophetic mode and then got it full blast. Seeking to soften James's words, he added, "Perhaps you could join a wandering group of storytellers. There is always a need for good narrative. Human beings are narrative animals. It'll be wild." The word "wild" hung in the air. What did it really mean? Paul was conscious that none of them knew. The human was the least tamed of the animals, the only one that refused to be like others.

"So, what are your demands?" the *Times* reporter said.

James: "You know we Indian tribes have treaties with the United States, right?"

Reporter: "No, I didn't."

James: "Here in the eastern part of the country, the United States inherited many treaty obligations from the British when it kicked them out. Our interpretation of the treaties is that they require both sides to respect the environment."

"So?"

James: "We're saying that the United States, by burning fossil fuels at a reckless rate, has damaged the environment, and so has broken the treaty."

"What does that really mean?" asked the *Bangor* reporter.

"Well, we might have to invite you all to leave."

"Leave? Like leave this press conference?" asked the *Post* reporter.

"No, to leave the country."

"Is that a formal demand?" said the *Times* reporter, still looking for his lead.

"No, just a thought we're having, an issue we're pondering as we walk. The Anglos have been here a few hundred years. We think it's just not working out. We tried. So maybe it is time for you all to leave."

"Where should we go?" asked the *Times* person.

"Do we Indians have to take care of everything?" James said.

Ryan stood in the back of the crowd, watching all this. His cell phone rang. It was Bulster again from the Boston office, his boss's boss. Ryan turned away to listen to the call. "Agent Tapia, the president is talking about your Indian friends," he began. "We need to get out in front, be able to tell the director what he needs to know if the president asks. Remember, this is your chance to recover your career."

"I'm on it, sir," Ryan said. He didn't have much more to offer. After the conversation ended, he pondered this call and thought to himself, this is not going to end well. I am not going to be able to give the boss what he wants. In fact, I don't want to give him what he wants.

When the press conference ended, Ryan watched the Australian shepherd trotting along behind the parade.

27
MARCH DAY 5

JULY 9: THOUGHTS ABOUT PLAN B

In the morning, smoke from the annual Canadian wildfires that were burning a giant area of peat bog in that country made the sky hazy and the sun pale. Paul's pick for the pre-march speaker was Seaweeds, the young Malpense woman. She was short, sharp, and to the point, just like her highly styled black hair. "Yesterday I was looking around the march on the road, and I wondered, hey, where are all the women?" she said to the pre-march assembly. "I think I've counted three, so far. Why is this? I don't know. Let's go." That was it. Paul liked the brief, punchy nature of the morning speeches. But instead of moving immediately, James stood in place with his right hand curled behind his ear, his sign that he was considering what he had just heard.

They began the day on a quiet stretch of backroad that paralleled Route 1. There were no bystanders nor even any state police in sight. Paul and James appeared pretty much like two men talking and strolling on the country road, albeit with about forty people behind them.

James said, "Thinking about what you said a couple of days ago, when we were outside Machias."

Paul: "About me not making it?"

"Yes," James said quietly. "It made me think. First, if one of us gets attacked, I think it may well be me, cuz I'm easier to rile than you. Second, what's Plan B?"

They discussed that off and on for the rest of the day. By the time they came to that night's camping site, which was a meadow in the woods north of Route 1, they had decided on it. If either one of them were felled by violence, the march would end instantly. It would be the sign that their approach was not working, that the message was being rejected. Neither of them wanted any of their followers to become martyrs. But ending the march would not be the end of the movement. Rather, it would signal the beginning of another action. It likely would not be public, because it would start an actual separation, a move to leave behind the Burning World.

On the issue of timing, they agreed that whichever one was still around to carry on would need some time to recuperate and plan. So, they decided, three months to the day after any violent end of this march, its participants would meet at Site X. The group would be told by text what that spot was when the time approached.

But at the moment all was peaceful. News of the president's comments and the press conference had proven a powerful recruiting tool. Fifty new people joined the march that day. Rock was recording their contact information. A new marcher came up to Paul and James, a scrawny young man in a black T-shirt and black jeans. He introduced himself as "Blood." "Interesting name," James said. "How'd you get it?"

"I wanted to lose my Burner name," the young man, perhaps eighteen years old, said. "I don't have much, I thought. But I got my Indian blood, and I'm proud of it."

Paul reached out his hand. "Good man. Welcome to the march, Blood."

On this stretch of the coast there were no state parks and, because they were not yet at the part of the coast most desired by the wealthy, no big, empty mansions with inviting lawns. But Rock had noticed in his research that the area north of town was empty, with several small roads blocked by locked gates. Rock had found several big landowners listed, mainly paper and mining companies. They parked the two trucks on the grass before the gate, then loaded their backpacks with their sleeping bags and food and water for the night and the morning. About two miles in they found the lush meadow Rock had seen on Google maps, and there they camped. At the campfire that night, the Australian shepherd found a place in the group, squeezing between James and Paul. James put his hand on the animal's head. "I think you are Moolsem," he said, referring to a canine famous in Abenaki legend. And that became this dog's name on the march.

28
MARCH DAY 6

JULY 10: THE INDIES ARRIVE

The smoke was worse, reducing visibility to just a mile or so, and mixing with the coastal fog. So many marchers assembled in the dew-heavy meadow that Rock split them into two groups, which he dubbed "Mountain" and "Lake."

Foggy days have an odd effect on the sense of time on the coast. When skies are clear, the position of the sun constantly reminds everyone of the time of day. But the fog stretches time out and can even confuse the sense of direction. When the tops of the trees are obscured, there is almost no discernible difference in light or air temperature between dawn, noon, and dusk. On top of that, the fog pillows all sounds, making everything quiet.

James asked Paul for the morning speaker slot. He stood and addressed the assembled marchers. "Seaweeds's morning talk yesterday made me think," he began. He put his hand over his heart and said to her, "Thank you, Seaweeds."

"This is what she made me think. She asked, Where are all the women? Simple answer: Not here. Why? Because I am beginning to think that we, as a group, are like medieval monks."

Several faces expressed surprise and puzzlement. Even Moolsem, the march's new mascot, seemed to listen intently, turning his head a bit sideways.

"But, one big difference," James continued. "We're monks of the future. You see, during the early Middle Ages, when the climate cooled in Europe and wrecked the remains of the classical world, religious types created monasteries. Why? Monasteries were refuges for knowledge. I think that we're heading in that direction. Maybe we're going to create a sanctuary for humanity, like wildlife sanctuaries today. We're going to try to figure out how to live after the climate goes haywire and societies unravel. Hunker down like those monks did."

Seaweeds put up a hand and spoke. "But this isn't a monastery, it's a pilgrimage of sorts, a march. And those were often gender mixed. I've looked it up."

James said softly, "I don't know why. Seems to break down into gender separation, for reasons I don't understand."

Seaweeds crossed her arms, evidently in disagreement but not wanting to push it at this very moment. "I think we can agree that it's an area that needs work," she finally said.

"Yes," James said.

They walked out into the morning fog, wisps caught in the trees along the road. Rock the wrangler came to Paul and James at the front of the march. He effectively had become their chief of security. "Got four new ones, not on any tribal rolls, no ID cards," he told them. He was not pleased.

Paul: "Did you tell them to march in the rear, and no camping with us?"

"I did, and they, uh, *disagreed*."

"How?"

"Well, they said, 'Fuck that, you rezzie Redman.'"

James laughed. He was intrigued. "Why?"

"They say they are Indies," meaning independent Indians who are unaffiliated, living out by themselves, usually in backwoods areas, but proud in their heritage. "These ones are from Liberty Island. Said they stay up on their own salt creek, don't mix much. Have lived off hunting and fishing all their lives, like their fathers before them."

"Let's talk to them," said James.

The four came up and joined Paul and James. The tallest one, perhaps twenty years old, with black hair tied in a bun and a wispy beard, said, "You guys are talking about living in the future, but you're talking about the way we already live, right now. We're off the grid, always have been."

"And you're real Indians?" James said.

"Totes," the youth said. "People on our island know us. We're Skeejins—you know, Penobscots. But, you know, we never got corralled into the reservations and got our official Indian permits. We're old school."

"Well, welcome aboard, and glad to have you. What's your name?"

"Gutter."

"For, like, on houses?" Paul said, puzzled. "You work construction?"

"Nah, it's for how a few years ago, one morning after a big storm, I gutted a fisher cat that tried to take a big lobster from me on the shore, came straight at me, hissing and snarling." He patted the hunting knife in a sheath on his hip.

Paul was impressed. "Those fishers are mean," he said. "I had one come onto my island, chased me all around."

At the campsite that night, one of the Indies came in from the woods carrying a freshly killed deer, a big buck, over his shoulders. There also was a grouse hanging from his belt.

Rock: "How'd you get that deer? I didn't hear any shooting."

"Ropes and knife," the Indie said, offering nothing more but patting a loop on a rope on his shoulder. He was indicating that he had set up a snare on a deer path, captured the animal, and slit its throat.

"Well done," Rock said in genuine admiration. To himself he thought, makes me wonder what else they know. These guys have talent. He liked how they kept busy in the campsite. When they finished setting up, they went out hunting and fishing. Not only were they eager for fresh food, they also liked that much of the land the march went through had gone largely unhunted for decades. It was ripe for harvesting, rich with game that had grown fat and slow. Even when they sat resting by the campfire, they sharpened their knives, passing around a small black whetstone.

"You know, there's a lot of us out there in the woods," said another Indie. "Nobody pays us much attention, and we like it that way."

"How many, do you think?" Rock said.

"In the whole state? No idea. But in my part of my county, maybe thirty or forty in about five different families. Probably more than that in some of the eastern and northeastern counties."

29
MARCH DAY 7

JULY 11: SOLID LANDS

A t morning assembly, Paul called on Distant Thunder, who remained sitting cross-legged. He shook his broad head. "I got nothing," he said.

Paul knelt by him. "I believe everyone has something to contribute. I see it in you."

"You don't want to know what's in my head," the tall young Indian said. "Not kidding."

"I do," Paul said. Now others were watching.

Distant Thunder unfolded his long legs and stood. "Ooooohkay," he said slowly, as if to say, *You asked for it.* He cast his gaze around at the morning grouping. "My family—that's what you all feel like to me," he began. "I love this group, this march. But I have to tell you, one thing I miss: silence. I live in the woods, and I miss that.

"So," he said, "I am going to ask for a minute of silence. Sometimes I think we all need to shut up, including Paul and James."

They stood for sixty seconds. Then Distant Thunder clapped, and they began the day. "Good group discipline," James said approvingly.

Paul noticed Ryan in the crowd and waved him over. He explained that he had driven down from Bangor to catch up with the state of the march. Paul said, "You picked a good day. The governor's coming to visit us late this afternoon." Ryan raised his eyebrows, but said nothing.

At the campsite, they left a big area clear for the governor's helicopter. Paul was curious and asked Ryan why she would fly in. "It's a big state," Ryan said. "And the National Guard pilots need to get in their flying hours, so why not ferry the governor around on some weekends?"

Rock had set up a tent with a table and chairs. When Solid landed, Paul and James escorted her over. They offered her tea. "To begin," she said, "I'm in basic sympathy with you. The state of Maine is not hostile to your views. We also are concerned by global overheating."

"That's good to hear," said Paul. "What does it mean in practical terms?"

Solid had prepared. "We can offer state police escorts, but only if you need and want them."

"Okay, but no game wardens," James said.

"Why?" asked Solid, clearly puzzled.

James explained, "They're the authorities we always hated most, 'cause they would arrest our hunters, and that means Indian families would go hungry. That's what 'warden' means to us—empty stomachs."

"Got it," said Solid. "I'll take care of that. And I will make it clear that the state agrees to your unimpeded access to state parks, state land reserves. As long as you refrain from violence and really minimize property damage."

"We can do that, if your people can," James finally said. He cupped his hands together, a habit he had when he was mulling over something.

"Is there anything else you want or need?" she asked as she sipped her tea.

"No," said James. "Just stay in touch. The march changes from day to day."

She agreed to do so. "Finally," she said, "I have a personal question."

"Yes?" James said, curious.

"How are you guys doing on money?"

"We scrape by," Paul said. "We don't need much. Marching and camping is free, so our costs basically are two: Food to supplement whatever we hunt, and gas for the two trucks. We're running on a few hundred dollars a day."

"May I offer a personal donation?"

"Sure," said James.

Solid handed them an envelope with $5,000 in cash.

"That helps a lot," Paul said. "Thank you."

Ryan waited with the news media outside the tent. It would be the first time he had seen Solid since she dumped him. He introduced himself to Solid's National Guard pilot, Captain Bala, who was a dark-skinned woman with long black hair, almost certainly of South Asian background. He explained that he was keeping an eye on the march for the Bureau.

Bala said she had majored in aeronautical engineering in college and had served in the regular Army for five years, becoming a Black Hawk pilot, and a good one, she told him. "Left to do a

PhD at MIT, but found I really missed flying. The Massachusetts Guard couldn't guarantee me an aviation slot—they had a lot of applicants who flew out of Logan and Hartford—so I joined the Maine Guard." She gave him a business card that said DHIVYA BALA / DOCTORAL CANDIDATE IN BIOSECURITY / MASSACHUSETTS INSTITUTE OF TECHNOLOGY.

"What did you miss about flying?" Ryan asked.

"Immediate results," she said. "You don't pay attention, the aircraft can smell that. You make a mistake, you know it right away. In my academic work, you can make a mistake and not know it for years.

"Look," she added, "if you're here with the march a lot, you can be handy. Let us know that the landing zone is clear, stuff like that. Here's our freeks." She gave him a laminated card listing the radio frequencies for the air control net and the Maine National Guard command net.

❖

Coming out of the tent, Solid noticed Ryan. She gave him a nod and a small smile but didn't pause. Reporters were waiting. She strode to their cluster of microphones. "Hello," she said. "I am Solid Harrison, the governor of Maine. I think I know most of you. I want to begin by saying that I admire these marchers. They are seeking answers to problems that all of us face of climate change and environmental destruction. Basically, today I offered them the best wishes of their state and asked how we can help."

"What did you tell them about violating private property?" asked one reporter.

She had thought through this message. This is what she was here for, to lay down a clear distinction between the state's view and the messages coming out of the White House. "I thanked them for not destroying property. When they use someone's land, which they have been doing some nights, they do not take anything, they do not cause needless damage, they clean up in the morning and leave.

"I also invited them to use state property as needed. Maine is a mighty big state, with hundreds of thousands of acres of land in the north and northwest where almost no one lives. A lot of that land is owned by out-of-state real estate investment firms who snapped it up back when the pulp paper companies dumped it and moved south. A few people walking around on those lands, hunting and fishing, isn't going to hurt those investments.

"What's more, and I want to emphasize this, especially for those of you who don't know the state well. Maine has a long and honored tradition of public use of private lands, going back to colonial times. More than any other state, we encourage that use. As a lawyer, I can also tell you that tradition has a strong legal history. You should know that Maine law states that if there is no sign forbidding entry, then people have implied permission to use that land, even if it is private property."

Reporter: "What if violence breaks out?"

Solid put her hands on her hips. "They have not shown any indication of that. They should not be met with violence. For too long, that has been our national government's ultimate response to Native American demands. I think, and I hope, that there is another way."

Reporter: "What about the president's comments?"

Governor: "I intend to be part of the solution. Right now, he is sounding to me like part of the problem. Thank you."

And with that she walked to her waiting helicopter.

❖

Ryan watched the Black Hawk lift off toward the north. That was Solid, he thought, always on her way.

He walked to his truck and wrote a short report titled "ACTIVIST PROFILE/ MAINE-IND/ JAMES REVEUR." He emailed it to Jimmy Love and Bob Bulster. He summarized Reveur as "A meditative person, given to mysticism, of undoubted spirituality. His central belief is that American civilization, defined as the society based on fossil fuel consumption, is doomed. He expects it to begin showing signs of societal stress within our lifetimes—riots, shortages, epidemics, and so on. His dominant trait is an ability to observe and analyze intensely. With others he takes the stance of a skeptical visionary, one with his ear to the ground, listening for the rumblings of tectonic change.

"Parents: Deceased. No known siblings."

Five minutes later Bulster wrote back. "I don't need this puffy shit. I need to know where their pressure points are."

30
MARCH DAY 8

JULY 12: A SHERIFF LAYS DOWN THE LAW

News coverage of the governor's respectful visit led to an increasing number of young people showing up from around the country. On each one's first morning, they were told they had to help with the site trash sweep before they could march. After everyone had cleaned up their own campsites, there generally were odds and ends left around. Paul and James were determined to leave every site impeccably clean.

They were talking over plans for the day when they heard a skinny young man, perhaps seventeen years old, who was slowly picking up cans and napkins around the main campfire area, mutter, "This is such bullshit." As they got closer, his work pace slowed and his voice loudened. "BULLSHIT."

Paul strolled over to him. "You don't want to pick up trash?" he asked.

"Not what I came here for," the youth said. "Came here for the climate and for my people." He did not appear to know who Paul and James were.

"Okay, give me your bag and run along," Paul said.

The young man handed over the bag and sat down at a picnic table, his arms sprawled behind him on the table. He had nothing else to do but watch Paul and James clean the campsite. After about five minutes, he came over and gestured with his hand that he was ready to take back the bag.

"Nope." James shook his head. "Ours now."

"Please," the youth said.

"Okay," Paul said. Paul looked at the young man, skinny and intense, wearing black glasses that made his eyes seem bigger. He passed over the trash bag. "What's your name?"

"Red."

"Seriously?" James said.

"Yeah. My hair was reddish when I was a baby, my mom says."

"Okay, Red, why don't you clean up with us?"

Rock came over with the security questions of the day. "You two picking trash again?" he began skeptically.

"It's honest work," Paul said, a smile on his face.

Rock's report was pretty much as usual. "Police at the next three towns are notified, seem cool with the march. They want to know where we're staying tonight, but I told them that for security reasons, we couldn't tell them now. Didn't like it, but can live with it."

"Okay," said Paul.

"You got any special visitors coming in today?" Rock asked.

"No," James said. "But some ministers from New York want to join us for the day tomorrow."

Red listened nearby. By this point he had come to understand that these two trashpickers actually were the leaders of the march he had just joined, and of the movement it represented. He began to work faster. Paul noticed and thought to himself that this kid Red was a good observer and a fast learner.

At the morning assembly, Rock created a new group, "River," mainly made up of the newcomers, who were disproportionately young, mainly in their late teens. They designated Trout as their spokesman. Rock decided to keep a special eye on them. "First couple of days, I'm walking with them," he informed James.

James had noticed a Passamaquoddy named Alexis who had a good voice and sang as they marched. James pointed at him, and said, "You're up for today's pre-walk talk."

Alexis happily stood and sang a song that began, "Hey, hey, good lookin', what ya got got cookin'?" Some others joined in.

"That's a Hank Williams song," James observed when they concluded.

"What tribe is he?" Alexis said.

James smiled. "He's a white guy from Alabama. But you're right—he had the soul of an Indian, I think."

"Whateva," Alexis said nonchalantly. "My mom sang it sometimes when she was making supper. I always thought it was an Indian song."

"Maybe it is," James replied.

They marched through the little blueberry-picking town with the wishful name of Cherryfield, where they picked up Route 182, for a swing through the backcountry. The rural, winding road felt like the Maine interior, with boulder-strewn hills, rocky ridges, and shallow ponds between them. Also, it had more hardwoods—ash, maple, birch—than the coastal region generally did.

Late in the day, the road led them back to Route 1 on the eastern outskirts of Ellsworth. At that intersection, on the gravelly edge of town, four deputies of the Hancock County sheriff awaited them, blocking their way. These men were standoffish in the way that younger American police officers often are nowadays, expecting respect without earning it, and getting a little scratchy if respect was not offered quickly and freely.

The oldest, who also was the plumpest, walked toward James and Paul.

"Officer—" Paul began.

The deputy quickly held up the palm of his right hand. "Button it," he interrupted. "I'm not here to negotiate with you. I'm just here to halt your advance and babysit your group until the sheriff arrives."

And so they stood and waited for about fifteen minutes. When the sheriff appeared, he said, "You the Indian demonstrators?"

"Yes, sir, I guess we are," Paul said.

"I saw about you all on the TV news. You the ones gonna block Route 1?"

"No, sir, we did not ask to block Route 1, but we have applied for a march permit."

"If you don't have the paper, you can't march."

"Can we walk on the shoulder?"

"No."

"Why not?"

"I'll find a reason. Maybe public defecation."

James said, "Ain't got time," and walked around him. The other marchers followed. The sheriff and his deputies got in their black SUVs and drove ahead a few hundred yards to cut them off. The marchers again walked around them. It began to look foolish. Finally, a half hour later, in the parking lot of the town's Pizza Hut, the sheriff had a line of state troopers ready to cut them off and a school bus awaiting to transport them. He told them they were all under arrest. There were too many to take to the county jail's four cells, so he had the high school gym opened. As they walked into it, gazing at the wood floors and the stowed basketball nets, he said, "You will remain in custody, here, until further notice."

"We each get to make a phone call, don't we?" Paul asked.

"And what about our Miranda rights?" added James.

"And where's our dinner, man?" demanded Mook, a lanky young Malpense who had joined the march just hours earlier, appearing out of nowhere. He was tall, loose, and glib. He spoke loudly so that the other marchers could hear him. "I'm thinking pizza and beer, or maybe lobster rolls. None of that McDonald's trash—that's nasty." He got a laugh from the other marchers, and bowed in acknowledgment.

By 7 P.M., the marchers had seventeen lawyers calling the sheriff's office. By 10 P.M., two of those lawyers were being interviewed on CNN and MSNBC. "Indians Arrested for Peeing in Woods," read one chyron.

And by 11, the sheriff was sick of the whole thing. He went back to the gym. He found Paul and James, sitting on wrestling mats. They were talking about Gandhi, a subject that endlessly fascinated James. "You're free to go," the sheriff said.

"Nah, it's the middle of the night," Paul said sleepily. "We could get killed walking along the road."

"Will you leave in the morning?" the sheriff asked. He didn't want to plead.

"After a good breakfast," James said grumpily. "For our troubles."

31
MARCH DAY 9

JULY 13: A CONFRONTATION

Paul and James huddled with Rock at dawn over morning tea, standing outside the gym. "Let's call an audible," Paul said.

They decided that instead of continuing on Route 1, which the sheriff expected, they'd cut south to a big estate. "You got something like that, Rock?" Paul asked.

Rock opened his laptop to check his files of possible nearby campsites. He selected a waterfront mansion a few miles to the southwest of town. He pointed to the image on his screen of a rambling, green, twenty-five-room mansion with a thousand-foot-long greensward sloping down to the Atlantic, and a view of Mount Desert Island in the distance. "On the market for a year, just under nine million dollars," Rock said. "Eight miles from here." He noted that it also had a pond on the property that was of historical significance to Maine Indians.

"Good research," James said approvingly. "Tell me about the pond's history tonight, okay?"

"Before we go," Rock said, "another issue."

"Yeah?" Paul said.

"Indies want to form their own marching group," he said. "Okay with you?"

"Long as they stay friendly," James said, only half joking.

"Okay," Rock said.

At morning assembly, Paul said he wanted to speak, if that was okay. There was general agreement. "Last night, James was telling me about Gandhi's March to the Sea," he began. "You heard of that?" Some nods. "Well, back in 1930, in India, this guy Gandhi wants to get rid of the British colonialists. So he leads a march to the sea, and he breaks British law. James asked me, Did I know how many people were in that march. I said I thought maybe thousands. James said it was seventy-eight. Sure, there were big crowds that greeted them. But the marchers were a total of just seventy-eight. And that got the ball rolling for freeing India from British rule. I'm going to think on that while we walk today," Paul concluded.

Late that afternoon they found the long driveway of the estate Rock had selected, winding through birch groves planted before World War II. It was a spectacular summer day of the kind that Maine specializes in, with a brisk breeze of about ten knots coming from the southwest, carrying onshore the refreshing air of the Gulf of Maine, itself chilled by an Arctic current curling down from Labrador. The sun sparkled on the small whitecaps.

In his online studies over the winter and spring of the vacant estates for sale on the Maine coast, there was one factor Rock hadn't considered: The effect of the march itself on property holders. As the march became better known, some alarmed owners drove or flew to Maine to occupy their properties. Thus what had been accurate in April was not necessarily still true in July, after the march began to make news.

James and Rock were discussing the day when a red-faced, white-haired man of about fifty-five emerged from the mansion and began striding purposefully toward them. He was wearing pressed khakis, Topsider loafers, and a baby blue cashmere sweater over a pink Oxford dress shirt, the casual wear of an uncasual man. And the snarl on his face showed that something was on his mind.

"Hey, Rock, I thought you said this was unoccupied," James said warily, as he watched the man approach.

"It was last I checked," Rock replied. "Is that a pistol in his hand?"

"This is my land," the man said as he neared them. He was louder than he needed to be. He was both angry and nervous. "It belongs to me."

"Well, sir, we have a title problem," James said softly.

"Why?"

"Because we belong to the land. But we don't belong to you." As he said it, James thought back to last winter, when he and Paul had talked through this issue. "That's an interesting contradiction, don't you think?"

"I'm not playing games," the man said. "You can stuff that fancy talk."

"Nor am I, sir," James said. "I am stating a fundamental belief. Please don't dismiss it as wordplay."

"Anyway, you'll have to go," the man said.

"No," James said.

"What does that mean?"

"Don't you speak English?" James said, less patient now. "It means I am standing my ground. We"—he gestured to the hundred or so marchers now circled around them, watching this confrontation—"are going to stand our ground."

The man's resolve faltered. "I'm not going to shoot you," he said. He stared down at the Heckler & Koch 9-millimeter weapon in his hand as if an alien being had just pressed it into his palm. What was I thinking? he asked himself. He shifted from one foot to another, uneasily.

"No," James said, the contempt evident in his voice. "You're too rich for that. You'd get someone else to do it."

"What do you all want?"

"Well, I'll tell you what we're going to do," James said, clearly in charge of the situation. "We are going to stay right here overnight. We will do as little damage as possible to the land. That's not what we are about. At dawn, we are going to pray on the shore of the pond near here—"

"My pond," the man interrupted.

"The pond here where our ancestors were massacred in 1756," James continued.

"Oh." The man sagged. He was on the ropes, mentally.

"Yeah," James said flatly.

"Didn't know that," the man said.

"There's lots that people don't know," James said. "And after we pray and eat, we will leave you in peace."

"You have my permission," the man said.

We didn't ask for that, James thought to himself. But there was no need to say it aloud. The point had been made.

The man walked back to his house. The soothing gurgle of expensive whiskey pouring into a large glass loosened his taut back muscles. He thought to himself, unhappily, What good was being rich if poor people could push you around? He stared out the picture window of the house at the startling sight of tents being erected on his lawn. He picked up his cell phone and called the lawyer who handled his personal finances. "The damnedest thing is happening," he began. "It's like Fort Apache up here."

"Told you to buy in the Hamptons," the lawyer drily reminded him. "But no, you wanted the beauty of the wilds of Maine."

"Well, I've been trying to sell lately, but no takers," the owner said.

After that conversation, the lawyer called a former partner of his who now held a secondary position on the staff of the White House counsel. "Are your people paying attention to what's happening up on the Maine coast?" he asked.

"Tell me what you're hearing," the former partner said. Later that day he composed a memo on the subject for the president's political team.

❖

At the campfire, an Anglo man, perhaps thirty-five years old, came up to James and Paul. He looked and talked like a typical hardworking Mainer. "I'm Buddy Smith," he said. "And this is my son Lincoln." He indicated the boy, perhaps six or seven years old, standing by his side, a dazzled grin on his face. "Linc's a big fan of you guys. He's a smart kid, always reads the sports pages in the newspaper, following the Sox and the Pats. But nowadays, he also follows your march."

The boy held up a road map his father had given him. "Every morning, I mark where the march had gone the day before," he said proudly.

Paul smiled down at him. "Kids like you give me hope. We're marching for people like you."

James didn't quite agree with that—he was marching for Indians, he thought to himself, but he didn't say anything.

"Can we get a picture?" the father asked. He took out his cell phone. Paul nodded.

James edged away. He didn't feel like being photographed as if he were a roadside attraction. Moolsem, with no such qualms, and always looking for an opening near the fire, slipped into the space he left. The image on the father's cell phone showed Paul on the left, the boy on the right, the dog in the middle, all three illuminated by the warm glow of the campfire. "Would you send that to me?" Paul asked.

32
MARCH DAY 10

JULY 14: A MOTORCYCLE CHAT AND A PLANE BUZZING

In the morning, after quietly saluting the spirits of the ancestors hovering above the pond, Paul and James circled the grounds of the mansion, making sure no damage was done and that the place was being left in good shape. They saw Red supervising three new recruits, but not doing any trash picking himself. Paul and James went up and asked Red for a trash bag.

"You two," Red sighed. "Okay, what's the message I'm supposed to be getting now?"

"Leaders work twice as hard. And we lead by example." Red nodded and set to picking.

The march was heading northwest on Shore Road, back toward Route 1. As it curved northward, the lead group found their way blocked by three motorcycles. A man stood in front of one. His arms were crossed and his feet spread apart, as if he were ready to take or throw a punch. "Figured if you Indians can block roads, so can we," he said aggressively.

James began to argue. "Sir, we have a march permit application, and the permission of the state government. So I am telling you—"

Paul interrupted. "Hold on. Is that an early model panhead?" he said, pointing at the black motorcycle in the middle.

A frown crossed James's face. "Paul, please. This is not the time." He lowered his right hand slowly, his hunting sign for "cool it" or "back off."

"Oh yes, it is," Paul countered. "That motorcycle is a true work of art."

The man, hearing his response, was pleased. Paul had his attention.

"Is that yours?" Paul said.

"Sure is," the man said, a bit more relaxed.

"Must be a what, nineteen forty-nine or fifty?"

"You know your stuff, man. It's a fifty." His arms uncrossed.

"I was guessing by the telescope fork," Paul said. "I've never seen one that old. That's the first year of the Hydra-Glide, right?"

"Yep," the man said, pride evident in his voice.

"You rebuilt it yourself?"

"Yeah, I did. Well, me and my cousin, Vincent, he helped a lot."

"Vincent Black, down to York?"

"You know him?"

Paul beamed. "Sort of. About ten years ago, I went down to take his one-day course on restoration. Learned a lot. Can I look over your machine?"

The man walked him over. Paul began inquiring about the long dual exhaust pipes, how hot they got, and how they had handled the suspension problems. "I've never seen hubcaps like that," Paul observed, pointing at the big steel things the size of dinner plates.

"We took them off a junked Hudson car," the man said.

"Nice touch," Paul said.

After about five minutes of this, Paul stuck out his hand. "I'm Paul. I need to get back to my march. Can you walk with me a bit?"

"I'm Randy," the man said, shaking Paul's hand. To James's surprise, the man agreed to come along for a spell. He rolled his bike over to the side of the road, put up the kickstand, and fell in stride between Paul and James. His friends remained with the bikes.

"Where'd you find it?" Paul asked.

"In a barn outside Skowhegan. Guy said his grandfather owned it, no one in the family wanted it, just sat there for years, like thirty or so. Me and Vincent, we took it down to parts, cleaned every one, put it all back. Great way to spend a Maine winter, you know, put on Metallica and work on a classic bike? The carburetor and gas tank alone took about a week." Randy and Paul talked motorcycles some more, a subject that bored James, especially when they began to discuss the beauties of the classic 1948 Harley Davidson service manual—"just essential for that kind of work," Randy said.

Paul agreed. "Oh yeah," he said, "that and the Palmer manual, you know—the edition that has the photos of where to route the wires and control cables."

"Couldn't have done the work without those," Randy said.

"I'm not sure I'd have the patience," Paul confessed.

"Well, it helped to have Vincent to talk to. Also, he's totally plugged into the parts network, and that sped things up. I think we got pieces from about twenty different states. Got to know all about the FedEx man's life."

After several more minutes of this, Randy said he should get back to his bike. But before he did, he offered a kind of apology. "I wasn't out to make trouble for you guys, I just wanted to make a point, about our rights and all that," he said.

Paul smiled. "I hear you, man. This march is all about our rights, and your rights, and your kids' rights. We gotta do some things different on this planet."

They shook hands again, and the man began walking back up the side of the road.

In this way the work of the march was done, in Paul's view. But James had his doubts. What would Paul do next time, when he didn't just happen to know everything there apparently was to know about vintage motorcycles? Yet he had to admit, Paul knew better than him how to connect with people, how to find common ground that could drain the tension out of a confrontation.

It was, indeed, a peaceful, sunny day. Less pressure than usual. The world seemed righter than it had for a long time. Ryan came up from the back of the march and strolled near them. Moolsem trotted out in front of them, leading the way.

As they walked, Paul said to James, knowing Ryan was listening, "I've been thinking about your monastery talk the other morning. Where would it be?"

James: "I dunno. The border seems right to me, but I don't know why. Maybe a strip up there one hundred miles long, ten miles wide on each side of the border."

"Two thousand square miles? That's larger than some states. You're thinking big." Paul could pivot with surprising swiftness, in part because he had come to trust James's instincts. He embraced the idea, saying, "I think you're on to something. Maybe that's the next step we've been searching for."

❖

As they walked through the old paper mill town of Bucksport, Ryan noticed the fourth group in back, the Indies. They weren't flashy. They resembled a group of frontiersmen, with a distinctive shaggy appearance, yet also giving off a quiet confidence. Among themselves, they didn't talk a lot. With others, they were almost shy. They kept busy. Ryan made a note to himself to find out later who this rough-looking fourth group was, where they came from, and why they stood out so much.

Ryan had turned to gaze back at the end of the march when he heard a buzzing like a chainsaw. Mook, marching nearby, shouted, "It's coming right at us."

"Get down," Rock yelled even louder. As he did he reached out with both hands to push Paul and James to the ground. Then, lying between them, he threw his arms over their heads protectively.

The aircraft came in low, the two wheels of its landing gear passing only about twenty feet over their heads. Ryan rolled onto his back to watch it. The fuselage, white with a blue line, flashed over his head. He wrote down the tail number.

When the plane had droned into the distance, Ryan checked with Paul. "Did that plane look familiar?" he asked.

"Yeah, I think so," Paul said. "At least they didn't drop anything on us this time."

Ryan walked a mile back to where he had left his truck by the side of the highway. He sat in the cab and tapped into federal databases to get the history of that troublesome aircraft. It was a Cessna 182 that had been registered to a man in Voorheesville, New York, a prosperous suburb of Albany. With a few more keystrokes, Ryan learned that the owner, a dentist, had reported the aircraft missing two years ago, apparently stolen from the little private airport he used. Someone had flown the aircraft out of Plattsburgh at least three times in the last year. A Google image search showed that the plane for some reason had been parked lately in Manchester, New Hampshire. No one had even tried to repaint the thing.

Ryan called Phyllis Ames, down in Kittery. "Let me run some traps on that," she said. Good to her word, she called back in fifteen minutes. "Here are more pieces of the puzzle," she began. "It looks like the plane was brought to Manchester by the Plattsburgh dealers. They're smart and careful. So I think they got rid of it after using it a few times. It looks like they sold it, or gave it to, some guys over there. You need to talk to Pete Martin over in Concord. He's the lead guy in New Hampshire law enforcement for intel on drugs and habitual offenders."

He dialed the number she gave him. "After Phyl Ames called, I pulled their files," Officer Martin said. "She mentioned you might call me. I'm sitting here with them on my screen."

"Which files?" Ryan said, feeling a step behind in the conversation.

"Oh, I thought she told you. The Sullivans. A couple of our local knuckleheads."

"A gang?"

"No, just brothers, and real jerks. Peddle drugs, tap their own supply. Steal some cars."

"What's their background, and why would they have a beef with Indians marching in Maine?" Ryan asked, even more puzzled.

"Wellll, that is interesting," Martin said slowly. "The Sullivans are broken Pennacooks."

"What does that mean?"

"They were kicked out of that tribe, their names stricken from the list of members. It's just a small grouping, not formally recognized by the federal government or even the big Maine tribes."

"Why'd they get stricken?"

"I don't know what they did, but after that expulsion, they kind of drifted around, wound up in Manchester. They became some of our usual suspects. Did a lot of small-time crime. Their specialty became car thefts on assignment. They'd go down into the rich suburbs of Boston like Andover and steal foreign sports cars, German SUVs. But happy to sell meth, crack, oxy, whatever."

"How'd they get in with the Plattsburgh people?"

"Probably the usual way. There are two or three places in Manchester and Nashua where the lowlifes gravitate to around here—bars, chop shops, pawn shops. And while the Sullivans may not be smart, they probably turned out to be good utility men for minor jobs." Martin paused. "You know what bothers me most about criminals? The lack of imagination. Just think of the most predictable course, and nine times out of ten, that's what they do."

"So what do you think the Sullivans are going to do next with that airplane?"

"If we let them, the same damn thing they just did to your march today, is my guess. Want me to call down to Manchester and get that aircraft impounded?"

"That would be great," Ryan said.

33
A CONVERSATION AT THE WHITE HOUSE

The White House press secretary told a pliable reporter from Fox News that if she would ask the president about "this Indian march up in Maine," the president might call on her.

She asked exactly that question. In off-the-cuff but on-the-record remarks after a White House bill-signing ceremony, the president responded, "I see where these Indians are camping out on the property of people up on the Maine coast. I don't like that, not one little bit. You try to have a hot dog roast on my land without permission, you're gonna be sorry!"

He added, "This country was founded on respect for private property. I'm not seeing that new governor up there, with her big Harvard law degree, remembering that. Some people are so smart they're stupid, you know?" He was letting his resentments flow forth, something he always enjoyed. "Don't they have any police up there?"

"Are you going to do something about it?" another reporter asked.

"I just might," he said. "I think someone should stop them." That became the next day's headline about the march. As the *New York Post* put it: PREXY: "SOMEONE STOP THEM."

34
MARCH DAYS 11 AND 12

JULY 15 AND 16: SEASIDE THEATER

R yan was at home with his morning coffee when Pete Martin called him back. "No luck with the Manchester airport," he said. "That Cessna's not parked there."

Ryan called the FAA in Boston to put out an alert on the aircraft with that tail number. The law enforcement liaison there transferred him to a clerk who didn't seem much interested in helping him. He turned on the local cable news and saw a reporter eagerly covering the Indian march.

On that day, the marchers finally had reached the wealthy section of the Maine coast. The zone of prosperity didn't extend far inland, perhaps just a few miles, but oceanfront land had grown exceedingly expensive in recent years. "This is where we begin to make our point," James told Paul that morning.

The president's "stop them" remarks had elevated the march to a running national story. The number of reporters doubled, with a small caravan of TV trucks following the marchers, and at times threatening to dwarf the actual march.

"Hey, man, why so many trucks?" Distant Thunder asked a TV crew member.

"Cuz we all compete with each other," the woman said.

"You better watch out, James might put you all on a school bus together," Distant Thunder replied.

A side effect of the increased media attention was a minor gold rush for hotel desk clerks along Route 1, who suddenly found themselves receiving "tips" of several hundred dollars from TV fixers to persuade them to cancel existing room reservations. The rooms were then given instead to the TV on-air talent, who needed their regular sleep to look good on the air.

The newcomers among the reporters still wanted to know what this was all about. Mook, who had been hanging around with the TV stars and local talent, suggested to Paul and James that they hold a press conference that evening when they camped. The chosen site that night was the property of Seaside Cottages, a motel complex that was indeed on the water but had been closed and on the market for two years, with an asking price of $5 million.

This time, James began. His face was illuminated from below by the campfire at his feet. The cameramen liked that. It made for great theater. James's young face now looked old and serious in the flickering firelight.

"Who are we, and what are we doing?" he said. "From my perspective, it's not that hard. First, you should ask: Who are the people trying to get you to ignore what's going on with the planet heating up? They're the people who want you to focus on distractions like drag shows. They're the rich, the authoritarians. We call those people the Worldburners.

"Who are the people in this march trying to get you to pay attention? They're the poor, the small, those who actually have to deal with what is going on. They don't have the money to insulate themselves from reality."

Writer from *The Atlantic*: "Isn't this just romanticism, going 'back to the land' like the hippies did decades ago? And what happened to all that?"

James: "It may appear that way to you. But consider that word, 'romanticism.' It usually means someone who is being sentimental about something. By contrast, I think we are taking a logical, rational view at global overheating—I would say, probably more than you are. So I don't see that as romantic at all. What seems to me to be delusional, to use a more precise word, is to know that your way of life is burning up the planet yet you do nothing to really change the way you live."

Wire service reporter: "But your position seems to be radical, out of step with the environmental organizations. Are you against sustainable approaches, all the steps being taken to slow down climate change?"

James: "Yes, I am. Major crises require radical responses. So things that slow down the coming of crisis, maybe, or make people feel better about climate change, no, I don't like them. All they do is prolong the agony, help us avoid dealing with the inevitable. Being for small fixes is like claiming to be an abolitionist by trying to make slavery more humane. How many species will go extinct while we pretend to address the problem? Life is not sustainable for them if they're gone, is it?"

Plzzz online magazine reporter: "So planting vegetables is the answer?"

Paul: "Well, that depends on what the question is. If your question is, what does a thoughtful person do when he or she sees the world is burning, yes, I think that is a fine first step."

James, always slightly edgier, added to the reporter, "What's yours?"

The *Plzzz* man said, "I plan to go to the grocery store."

James replied, "And one day, what if it has been stripped by rioters, or burned? Or what if the vegetable truck can't get through because the roads have been flooded by another anomalous storm? Or, most likely, the farmers can't grow them because they can't get water for irrigation?"

But no one would starve that night. As the conference ended, a caravan of pickup trucks and Priuses arrived, driven by those same aging "back to the land" hippies who made up a good part of the local population on this part of the coast. One had a huge pot of Hungarian cream of mushroom soup. Another brought zucchini pies rich with gouda cheese and onions. A third offered hash brownies. And still they came. The marchers feasted, even the Indies.

In the morning, Paul and James decided they should stay another day on the site. It would give them a rest—and keep opposition off-balance, if the president's urging was indeed stirring that up.

In the afternoon, there was a slight ruckus at the main campfire, a bit of shouting. Rock went off to investigate. "It was the Indies," he reported back to Paul and James. He was smiling. "They don't have a lot of tolerance for wannabes. Some guys appeared, said they were 'part Indian,' didn't have anything more than that, started sucking up to the Indies."

"And?" Paul said.

"Indies took out their knives, began sharpening them, recommended the wannabes leave. That big Indie muttered, 'Get your own culture,' which I know is a line in a song by the Dead Pioneers. They're a punk Indian band."

"And?" James asked.

"What would you do?" Rock smiled. "Indies don't fuck around. Problem solved—wannabes left."

35
MARCH DAY 13

JULY 17: CO-OPTED

As they prepared to get back on the road, the morning talk was delivered by Moosecollar. His friends on the march knew that his name was a misspelling, ratified by time, of his great-grandfather's ability to summon moose. He stood, said, "This is what I was thinking yesterday as we walked," and looked around. He chanted:

> *We've always been treated as a ghost of America's past*
> *But what if we hold the key to its future?*
> *There's a power in that to be tapped.*

There were general nods all around. That was a good one, a thought that could fuel you through the day, people agreed. Paul stood with his hand curled behind his right ear, a signal he had learned from James.

As the group slung on their daypacks, Panhead Randy appeared on his Harley with some of his friends. He said to Paul, "Me and the boys would like to ride up in front, give you all an escort, if that's okay with you."

"It is indeed," Paul said. "Thanks for asking."

James, always a bit grumpier, added, "But try to keep the revving down. People in the march need to talk, you know?"

"I've got someone who wants to meet you," Randy continued. He gestured to a bearded man standing nearby to join them.

The man was another Harley rider. "I was real big for Trump back in the day," he began, "but I think you guys are onto something."

"What are we onto?" Paul asked, interested in the man's take. "I ask because we're trying to figure that out ourselves."

"These big empty rich peoples' houses where you're camping," the man said. "I see it myself. I work for a cable company. Half my job is disconnecting those houses in the fall, reconnecting them in June. Those big houses are empty most of the year, nine or ten months. But what really bugs me is that the towns down on the coast, they're just wastelands most of the year, no one there. It's downright creepy. Whole downtowns with not one car parked, only thing open is the post office. What I'm saying is, I don't know the answers. But you're pointing out the problem. And that's good."

"Thanks," said Paul. "We don't have the answers either. We're hoping this march might help us all find some."

"Anyway," the man said, "anything I can do, lemme know. I'll be up front with Randy." The two rumbled off, revving their big Harley engines.

James sighed. "Well, at least we can get cable service now," he said skeptically.

As they approached the first village of the day, they were surprised to see locals lined up along the highway through town.

Wary of violence, Distant Thunder, the leader of the Mountain, the first group marching, braced his people. "Keep your dignity and discipline, keep going," he admonished.

But instead, they heard applause. "Shoulda been done long ago," someone shouted.

"Keep it up," said the man next to him.

"Stick it to the Massholes," shouted a bearded man in his twenties. At that, there were grins all around. His friends high-fived him. He was a clammer who repeatedly had lost access to mudflats where he harvested when out-of-staters put up fences and signs across trails that had been used to walk down to the shore for hundreds of years.

But there was indeed trouble on the horizon. The real estate industry was worried. Prices on inland lakes continued to rise, as they had for years, because people were becoming more concerned about finding refuges on a heating planet. But since the March to the Future had commenced, out of staters had become wary of buying big parcels along the coast. Prices for big estates there had dropped by 5 percent in recent weeks. Rich people take money even more seriously than most, because their identities tend to get tied up in it.

By the time they had left the town, some fifty people were walking along behind the regular groups of Mountain, Lake, River, and Indies. "Will you check out the newcomers?" James said to Rock. "Also remind them that when people hand them money, that should go in the bucket at night to help pay for food and gas."

On their noon break, a man came to see Paul and James with a formal invitation. "The people of Lincolnville have prepared a party for you this evening," he said. "And we have roped off half the beach as a campsite for you."

That evening, Paul and James sat at a picnic table with a party going on around them. They split a bottle of Beaujolais that had been handed to them on arrival. The Islesboro Ferry tooted its horn and docked, its last trip of the day finished. A cormorant, black and pointy-beaked, stretched out its wings to dry them, waited, then flew away. The small waves rolled in quietly, twice a minute, making a sound like "shush" on the gravelly beach. Rock stood nearby, arms crossed, quietly watching over the scene.

James: "Paul, I'm worried about being co-opted by these welcomes."

"So, what should we do?" Paul replied.

"Maybe make more of a point about picking our own places to camp. Rich peoples' empty mansions, remember that sort of thing?"

"It's all in Rock's files."

"Let's surprise them tomorrow night."

Over at the campfire, fart jokes and dick pokes were the subject of the evening. Seaweeds listened for a while, then said, "Yet another reason why there are hardly any women on this march. Listen to you guys!" She stood up and walked down to the waterside for some peace and clear air. The jokes continued. And the farts.

36
MARCH DAYS 14 THROUGH 17

JULY 18–21: THE MESSAGE OF MOOK'S CHAMPAGNE

A t morning assembly, Paul, on a hunch, picked out Daylights, a
Passamaquoddy in his twenties who didn't say much but had
a thoughtful face.

Daylights stood. "Here's what I was thinking last night. For
years, it seemed like every time I saw something on TV news
about us Indians nowadays, it said we were 'demoralized,' like we
were dragging our asses through history, you know? I feel like I
was always taught that we were the losers. Poor old noble Indians,
now jobless alcoholics. Well, fuck that. On this march, at these
morning assemblies, you know, I'm beginning to feel like we're
the winners. I don't really know what that means yet. But I like it.
Standing here this morning, I feel *re-moralized*. Like we are leading
the way." This brought a general shout of approval.

Daylights held up his right hand, flat, meaning that he wasn't
quite finished speaking. "We're like the stars. They're always there,

but you can't see them sometimes when it's cloudy. But you know, they were always up there, bright as ever. Now, as capitalism burns out, the Worldburners' lights aren't so strong. And the stars are becoming much brighter every night. Let's go!" Daylights shouted.

"GO!" the marchers shouted back. They took to the road with a new energy in their steps.

Paul turned to James. "I think that's what this march is all about," he said. "Trust these kids, let them speak their minds, and we'll see the way forward."

James nodded. "I know what you mean. Every morning, I wonder what I'm gonna hear at morning assembly. And every morning, I'm pleasantly surprised. 'Re-moralized,' you might say."

Paul: "The secret is, I think, that these kids really are in charge, not us. We just direct the flow."

James: "I agree. And that's a good thing. 'Cause when the white power structure reacts, it's going to come after us two."

"And?"

James: "That will be our task, to catch that reaction. Shield the others as much as we can." He blew out a puff of air and then turned to look up at the sky. He was wondering if he would be up to that task, and at the same time, praying that he would be.

Paul's face fell as he listened to those words. They began walking. After a few minutes, Paul said, "You know, you can be a real downer, man."

James didn't disagree. "And that's my task, sometimes."

Daylights's observation pointed to something they all were beginning to notice: They themselves were being changed by the march. Their lives felt full. Being with the same group of people every day and night, carrying out a public action, and experiencing an array of interactions—all that made each day feel like a week of their lives.

Next on the road was the town of Camden, which thought of itself as distinguished, and wanted to welcome the marchers in a way that stood out. At an informal town meeting, a small but significant percentage of the faculty of Harvard University who were up there for the summer, plus several who had retired there, contributed suggestions, outlines, and even concept papers about how to best greet "this meaningful new manifestation of Native American consciousness," as one of them put it. The entire downtown was closed to traffic. A banner flew across Main Street from the Lord Camden Inn to the Once a Tree gift shop: "Welcome Indigenous Protesters."

Just to the left was the land set apart by the town for the marchers to camp that night, below the town's library, and above the docks of the schooners that took tourists for cruises out on Penobscot Bay. Under a circus-like striped tent, a feast awaited the marchers and their hosts, two hundred leading summer residents. There were lobster rolls, shrimp wrapped in bacon, iced oysters on the half shell, chilled salmon with dill and sour cream sauce, and puff pastries with cheese and spinach. There were waiters in summery uniforms prepared to serve red wine, white wine, and seltzer. There were the waiting two hundred summer people, who looked forward to talking to these marchers and then being able to relate for the rest of the reason that they had talked personally to these marchers who were making waves and provoking the president.

Indeed, everything was in place—except for the marchers. Paul and James had decided that it was high time to make the point that they were not directable Indians. They marched straight past the reception, through the town center, and took a left, one they had mulled months ago, toward a vacant mansion on the water. It was for sale for $6.5 million, and had the solid feel of being worth every penny. Their two pickup trucks already were parked outside.

Paul and James led the way, hopping over the chain across the driveway, and across the long field that led down to an ocean cove where two sleek Concordia yawls and a ketch were moored.

They liked it so much they decided that evening to remain for several days and nights. They were not going to be predictable. This time, no outsiders were permitted to be with them, not even the news media. For the first time, Rock posted guards at the gate, saying they needed peace while holding meetings and recovering from their walking.

But they hadn't counted on the yachting world being so interested. The protesters had become a kind of magnet for the floating party that the Maine coast becomes in high summer. By their third evening more than a dozen powerboats and yachts were anchoring just offshore. Paul and James sat on the overlook, surveying the scene, as they watched a young woman rowing in a dinghy from a motor yacht that must have been sixty feet long. They saw Mook meet it on the beach. He accepted the woman's extended offer of two bulbous green bottles of champagne and led her to the campfire.

James shook his head as he watched. "I think we're still way off message," he said.

"Yep. How do we correct course?"

They agreed to sleep on it and talk in the morning.

After their long rest, they were preparing to march again. Over morning tea, James said, "You remember the sheriff in Ellsworth, the one who said we were going to block Route 1?"

"Yeah, I do," Paul said.

"I think he was right."

"How?"

"We should be more aggressive. From now on, I think we should stick to Route 1. And block it."

"Because?" asked Paul. Not disagreeing, just wanting to understand the rationale.

"We need to drive home the point," James said. "We are not doing this to amuse them. We are doing this to awaken them, to say that things have to change, including their presumption that they can drive down Route 1 and get to the store for more sauvignon blanc anytime they want.

"And a big change," James added. "No more marching on the shoulder anymore. We take the entire road."

"Yes," Paul agreed.

When Ryan Tapia appeared, Paul greeted him. "You might want to stick around for a full day, even two," he suggested. "The tone of the march is going to change some," he said.

"Will do," Ryan said. He welcomed the invitation. His supervisor, Jimmy Love, had told him simply to keep an eye on the march. But Ryan wanted to do more than observe. He wanted to understand the march, and the thoughts and motivations of its leaders and participants. He wanted to be seen by them as someone who understood them.

Ryan spent the night sleeping in the bed of his truck, and then joined the group for morning assembly. Unusually, James picked himself to speak. As James stood, everyone paid a bit more than the usual attention.

"Here's what I thought about the last couple of days," James said. "There was an English poet named W. H. Auden. We'd call him a shaman. As World War II began, he wrote that, 'We must love one another or die.' Later he decided that was incorrect. But I think he actually had been close to the truth. And that truth,

I think, is that we must love the planet or we will surely die. We must live in ways that show that love."

He looked around. "That's what I'm thinking about. Let's hit the road."

River, the youngest of the three groups, tended to be on average, a bit wilder. They were the last to go to sleep at night and the last to wake up. They often talked and sang until two or three in the morning. Rock kept a special eye on them.

That afternoon Rock asked Paul and James if they'd seen what the River group was up to. It was in the rear that day. "They've developed a new way of marching," he reported. "They're going very slow, very stylized, moving at half speed." He showed them how slowly they moved one arm, and then another, and next did the same with each leg.

"Any special reason?" Paul asked.

"Trout says it is because speed is not the answer, not the way to the future."

"That's a good take," James said. "I like giving physical expression of a thought."

Paul stepped to the side of the highway and waited for the River section to come by. They were singing a new tune by a Yankton Sioux rapper out of northwest Iowa who called himself L'il Bad Wolf:

> *My people, people, they're marching down the coast*
> *Lifting their feet and dancing with ghosts*
> *Leaving behind theft and sorrow*
> *Bye-bye you Burners, we're dancing tomorrow*
> (Chorus)
> *March, march, march, my brothers*
> *March, march, march, my sisters*

Marching in Maine like there's no tomorrow
Cuz without us . . . [spoken with a mic drop] *there ain't*

Paul applauded, and they waved back in delight, their bodies and limbs moving with slow, elaborate motions. Moolsem had joined the River, spending the majority of the day with them, in part because they had purchased treats for him. They tried to teach him to march slowly but the dog declined. Instead he circled the group, working at herding the River marchers along the road.

But as he stood there, Moolsem splayed out on the ground, cowering. Paul, next to the dog, knelt down. "What's bothering you, boy?" he asked.

In the next moment he heard what the dog's more sensitive ears had picked up first: a distant buzzing. That flying chainsaw sound, that's what had worried Moolsem. Paul saw a flying dot in the distance and shouted, "That plane's coming in again."

This time everyone reacted swiftly. Almost the entire march dropped down as one, throwing themselves to the asphalt, some landing on top of each other. The Cessna came in just as low as before, and this time a little slower, perhaps doing seventy mph. But this time it had a nasty surprise. The pilot was venting the plane's reserve tank of gas, dousing the marchers with a stinging mist.

One marcher, Tallfellow, froze in place. Mook, who had been walking alongside him, looked up, tugged at his leg, and said, "Down, get down." He did not. The rubber right wheel of the plane's nonretractable landing gear hit Tallfellow squarely in the face, killing him instantly. The impact pulled down the right side of the plane. The tip of the right wing fell. With the Cessna's low altitude and slow speed, it had no margin for error. Losing lift, the tip of the right wing snagged on the asphalt of the highway. The plane hit the ground hard, spinning around once and then, fifty feet beyond the prone marchers, flipping forward and upside down. Those who looked up from the ground could see two people in the plane, unconscious from the impact, hanging upside down in the cockpit, held in place by seatbelts.

With the reserve tank cracked open, gasoline trickled down the sides of the capsized aircraft. The fuel soon reached down to the red-hot steel of the plane's exhaust pipe. The Cessna exploded in a tall fireball.

"Instant justice," muttered Mook, who had been marching next to Tallfellow and was still on the ground. As people stood up, some yelled at the plane and its dead occupants. Mook would repeat the phrase in each of the several television interviews he did later in the day. One of the journalists identified him as "a fast-rising new leader of the Indian protesters."

Ryan called Pete Martin over in New Hampshire. "I think we found your Sullivan brothers. And their plane. They, uh, won't be a problem anymore."

The marchers walked down into the nearby ocean to wash themselves of the gasoline. By the time they got back to the highway and began to walk again, the fiery crash was on cable news channels. In a speech that night, the president talked about the Indian protesters. "That plane wouldn't have been there if the marchers hadn't been there," he said. "So to my mind, these Indian protesters invited the violence. And when a tragic accident occurred, they responded really nasty, like savages. I mean, how did that plane catch on fire so quickly? I have some questions about this whole incident. Maybe the plane was sabotaged. Some people think that."

Ryan, watching a clip of the president, recoiled at the word "savages." His back muscles tightened. These were fighting words.

Tallfellow's body was shipped by ambulance back to his family. That night, James and Paul led a memorial ceremony for him. "We do not respond with violence," James reminded them. "If you can't stick to that discipline, you need to leave. Tonight." No one did. At the end, the marchers lined up and filed past the campfire, each sprinkling a handful of tobacco on the flames. Then they sat in silence and breathed in the rich smoke.

37
MARCH DAY 18

JULY 22: AN OFFERING FROM SATAN

The next morning, Paul stood at assembly and said, "No words today, just memories of Tallfellow. March today with him in mind. Honor him by keeping our discipline."

When the local police met them at the Rockport town line, Rock told them the marchers would be taking the entire road today. This provoked some chin-stroking among the knot of law enforcement officials who greeted them. The police officers' hearts generally were with the president, but their heads reminded them that they worked for the state or the county or the town.

That afternoon, Paul turned and looked down the length of the march. He didn't see any Indies marching. "Indies gone?" he asked Rock. He was worried that they had decided that violence was indeed the answer.

"They said they're going hunting and fishing for a few hours," Rock said. "After yesterday, they said, they needed it for their spirits."

That evening, Rock found Paul and James at the campfire, where they were talking over the plane attack and Tallfellow's death with several anxious members of the River group. The security chief was escorting a white man in a suit and tie clutching a big brown envelope. "The guy won't give it to me," Rock said. "Only to one of you." Rock turned to the messenger. "These are the guys you want, James and Paul."

"I've been hunting around for you guys all day," the suit said. "I'm a big fan. But I'm here to give you this." He handed over the envelope. On the outside it said, in an elegant handwritten black ink, "To the Leaders of the Indian Protest/ONLY." Inside was a note from a relative of the Rockefeller family, which still owned considerable land on Mount Desert Island. "Keep up the good work," it read. "Please keep this gift anonymous." The gift was a cashier's check for $1,000,000.

Paul stroked his cheek in thought, then handed the note and check to James. He said to the messenger, "Can you wait for a minute?"

James said nothing for a while. Finally, he softly said, "A million, that's a lot of dollars." A moment later: "We could do a lot of good work with it."

"You know the history of that money?" Paul said.

"Yeah, Standard Oil. Rockefellers created the oil business in this country, monopolized it, made probably the biggest fortune in American history on it."

"And we accept it?" Paul said.

"We could think of it as reparations." He didn't mean that, but he wanted to explore the situation before they arrived at a decision.

"And would anyone buy that?"

James shook his head. "I know I wouldn't. This is a test from the Devil. He doesn't come at you with a pitchfork. He offers something very appealing. But here's what I think." Instead of speaking, he did a circular wave of the hand, with the index finger high for emphasis, his hunter's sign for "fuck it, I'm outta here."

"It is tempting," Paul conceded.

"That's how he works. Feels different when he's coming for you, don't it? Makes sense."

"All right," Paul said. "Let's say no." He lifted one end of the check between a thumb and finger. He pointed the other end of it at James. "Take hold," he said. Together, a hand at either end, they dropped the check onto the campfire.

James wrote on the back of the Rockefeller note, "No thanks," slipped it into the express envelope, and handed it back to the man in the suit.

"One lesson here, I think," James said, "is, never accept a gift so big that in the future you couldn't live without it."

Rock and Paul got up and walked around the camp. The Indies, who were roasting two dozen breasts of freshly killed doves, invited them to sit. "Next up, grilled salmon," promised Gutter. The rich gray smoke from the fish curled high into the air. In an iron pan, hazelnuts they'd gathered that day in the woods and just shelled were roasting, giving off a warm, inviting odor.

One of the younger Indies stood to chant a rap he'd just composed:

> *Indies eat good (CLAP)*
> *That's the reason why (CLAP)*
> *Indies gonna live (CLAP)*
> *When Worldburners die (CLAP-STOMP-CLAP)*

"Harsh but fair," Rock judged, his arms crossed.

Paul asked, "Could you make it, '*Indians* gonna live'?"

"I'll think about it," the rapper said. "Not sure it's true. Everyone got to skin their own skunk, man."

Perhaps, Rock thought to himself, there is a needed wisdom in the hardness of the Indies. He saw James nodding in agreement.

Paul got a bottle of wine from Mook, and then sat alone against a pine tree. James kept half an eye on him, in the distance. An hour later, as the campfire burned down, James went to check on him. He found Paul, drunk and stoned, and quietly weeping.

"Paul?" James asked, sitting down next to him. "You're not okay."

Paul looked up, the tears streaming down his face. "I don't want to die out on that highway. I want to go on, to live, to see what happens."

James threw an arm around Paul's shoulders. He could feel them heaving. "You're carrying a lot, I know," he said. "You hold it in. Let it out."

"I still fear it," Paul finally said.

"We all do," James said. "And Rock and I will do our best for you." And, James thought to himself, I hope that will be enough. They sat in silence for an hour.

38
MARCH DAY 19

JULY 23: RYAN IS SOLD OUT

Ryan arrived just before the march's morning assembly. James stood up. "Just a heads-up," he told the group in a voice softer than usual. "I know a lot of you saw Paul having a hard time last night. He's carrying a lot of weight, mentally, especially after the death of Tallfellow. Let's all—"

Ryan didn't hear the rest because his cell phone buzzed in his pocket. When he saw it was a call coming from Bulster in Boston, he turned away from the assembly to take it.

"Agent Tapia, what are you seeing with this march?" Bulster began.

"Sir, as you know, the Bureau has a troubled history with the Indigenous peoples of this nation," Ryan began. "Wounded Knee, things like that."

"The Indig what?" Bulster said. "Son, you don't need to be PC with me. You mean Indians, right?"

"Affirmative, sir," Ryan said.

"In the Bureau, we call that 'Indian Country,'" Bulster reminded him. Indeed, he was correct—that was the official title for Bureau operations on nearly three hundred reservations across the country. Mainly they investigated child abuse and other domestic violence cases, drugs, and gangs, and tried to aid tribal police as needed.

Ryan told Bulster that he believed he was winning the confidence of Paul. "This is our chance for the Bureau to do right by, uh, Indigenous people. I think a different path is called for here. Find ways to discourage attacks on them. Deconfliction. Sir, I have sat several times at their campfire as a guest. They talk to me." But as he spoke, he had the sense that Bulster was not interested in any of this. What Bulster wanted was inside information on the vulnerabilities of the marchers, and any dirt Ryan could find on their leaders.

Bulster said, "Stick with it, and report to me directly. And frequently."

Ryan said he would.

Following his instructions, Bulster then called the director. "Sir, I just talked to our man in the field. Not only is he all over them, he's inside their tent, metaphorically speaking. He knows their moves. We are way ahead of any other law enforcement agency on this. You can tell the president that."

When the director talked to the president later that day, Ryan's role as an insider was further embellished. "Sir, without getting into sources or methods, I can assure you we are plugged into the very top of this Indian thing. Basically we know their every move. Got it wired. We have an agent who has listened to their plans."

Taking up Paul's invitation, Ryan came to the campsite that night. He settled down next to Paul and asked how the day went. As Paul began to speak, someone said, "Hey, the president's holding another press conference." Someone else began streaming a news channel on a cell phone.

About five minutes in, a reporter asked the president to expound on his objections to the Indians marching in Maine. "Glad you asked that," President Maloney responded. He returned to one of his favorite themes. "I have got some real problems with them. This country was built on respect for private property, and they are just walking all over like they own the place."

"Well, they used to," the reporter said.

"Attitudes like that will get them in trouble," the president admonished. "I am a tolerant man"—in fact, he was anything but—"but even my very, very big patience has a limit. If the state government won't act to protect its citizens, well, maybe the federal government will have to intervene."

Another reporter: "That sounds like you are contemplating action. What do you have in mind?"

"I'm not gonna give away the playbook," the president said. "But I can assure you that we are watching this closely. In fact, the FBI tells me that we have sources at the very top of this Indian movement. These protesters don't make a move without us knowing about it. We have it wired. So I would advise them to be very, very careful."

With that, Paul and James both looked at Ryan, their faces questioning. "That doesn't sound good," Paul said.

Ryan was speechless. "I don't know what to say," he said, shaking his head. "I have reported what I am doing, what I am seeing, but I have *not* worked against you."

Paul believed him, wanting to trust their shared history. James, however, was always more skeptical, and shook his head. "This is a bad piece of business," he said. "You should go. Even if it were okay with me, it is not going to be safe for you to be here anymore. The

Indies don't play that game." He turned to Rock, who was not upset to see Ryan made unwelcome. "Rock, make sure he gets out okay."

Ryan got up and left without a word, led by Rock and trailed by Moolsem, who didn't want Ryan to leave.

Ryan had just been entirely sold out by his chain of command, right up to the president. Now what? At his truck, Rock said, "I'm sorry for that." He pointed at the driver's door, where somebody had keyed "SNIT," apparently running away before having the chance to finish it with a C and H. Ryan looked at the vandalism and realized James was right.

The world seemed very dark to Ryan. He had tried to do the right thing by the march and even by the FBI. But he had somehow fallen between the two. And he was worried that the march would not end well, that there were threats out there that he perhaps had a better sense of than did Paul or James. They had rattled America, and there were people who could try to retaliate.

39
MARCH DAYS 20 AND 21

JULY 24–25: SHAG AND RED TAKE A WALK

The marchers camped in Thomaston on the grounds of the old state prison, which was now a bare field with a group of roofed picnic shelters. The day dawned dark and gray, with lowering clouds. It was a welcome break from the incessant sunshine.

"Is this really where *Shawshank Redemption* took place?" a marcher asked Paul over breakfast tea. It was Pigtoe, the kid with the unibrow whose morning statement had been about his hatred of mosquitoes.

"Absolutely," he said.

With that, the heavens opened. Driving rain came raking in off the coast, pouring in the abundant cold moisture of the gray North Atlantic. Given the large picnic shelters, they decided to spend the day and another night there. Thunder rumbled to the east. One of the Penobscots looked in the direction of the rumble and said, as he had been taught as a child, "Hurry along, grandfather."

Rock came by with his morning report. "Mook's letting in a lot of phony Indians, especially if they bring a bag of grass."

Paul and James took Mook aside later that day, suggesting that he tighten up on enrollments and lighten up on the marijuana. Mook frowned but said he would do so.

"We can do good work even if we're not marching," James said to Paul. He put out the word to the groups that he would be holding an afternoon meeting around the big firepit in one of the shelters.

"Now there's a lot of people here who are new to each other," James began. "So we're gonna do something different today." He randomly pointed out two people, one on either side of the fire. "You two, take a ten-minute walk. Tell the other person about what led you to join this march."

When the two returned, James said to the older, taller one, named Shag, "Tell me about the other guy's life."

Shag was taken aback. He hadn't expected that. "Uh, his name is Red. He's, uh, from somewhere in New York, some town I've never heard of. He's into rap music. I, uh, can't remember which rappers he said. I'd never heard of them."

"Why'd he come here, for this march?" James said.

Shag shrugged. "I don't know."

Red pulled a long face, frowning behind his big glasses. He felt he deserved a better accounting.

James turned to him. "Okay, Red, you tell me about Shag."

Red dove in. "All right. Born in upstate Maine, near Caribou. Moved to his mother's family's place on the res, in Indian Township, when he was about five or six."

"You don't remember which year?" James persisted.

"Nah, he don't," Red shot back. "I remember everything he told me."

"Continue," James said.

"He got older, built himself a little wigwam camp on Big Black Island, on a lake. When he was a teenager he would stay there by himself, hunting and fishing. You can paddle right up into Canada from there, he said. His uncles sometimes let him use one of their snowmobiles in the winter. He chased deers out onto the ice where they lost their footing, then cut their throats. Saved a bullet and kept the game wardens from hearing.

"Anyway, last summer he heard about your Tides protest, thought it made sense. He also likes how you are finding a different way to send a message that we Indians are thinking, that the Anglo way of life, their whole approach, is pretty much 'doomed.' That's the word he used. I remembered it cuz it made me think of the Marvel movies."

"What does Shag think of the march so far."

"Pretty good," Red said. "He says you and Paul mean well."

"But?"

"You want the whole thing?" Red asked warily. Shag winced.

"Yes," James said.

"But sometimes, and this is Shag talking, not me, right, sometimes you two are like schoolteachers. I think he said, 'a couple of old wet socks.'"

Shag's sour expression said that he felt like he'd been ratted out. But he didn't dispute the account.

James's eyes surveyed the gathering. "Now Red here, he's a good listener. That's what we all got to be if this march is going to mean anything."

He turned to Shag, whose shoulders were slumped. "Shag, you get a free pass tonight, cuz you didn't know what was coming at you, with having to tell the other person's story. Next guy has no excuse. We got to learn to trust each other. And to do that, we have to know each other. Without trust, we have nothing. With it, we have almost everything." Then he selected ten more marchers to go out and take walks in pairs, telling each other their stories.

When the walks were done, they all walked down to the river just behind their camping area. The Indies fished it for all it was worth, and even lent hooks and lines to others who asked to learn.

40
MARCH DAY 22

JULY 26: BLOCKING ROUTE 1 IN MID-SUMMER

The day broke sunny and clear. "It's St. Anne's Day," Paul mentioned to James over breakfast.

"Catholic holiday?" James asked.

"For them, yes, but she's also the patron saint of the Mikmaks. They go up to the cathedral near Quebec City for it. For my tribe it has always been the annual day of healing, of remembering to lean toward generosity. It is kind of the height of the summer. Last week of July, first week of August, are almost the hottest weeks of the year. Time to get together, embrace each other, and begin working together toward surviving the winter."

James considered that as he chewed his fry bread. "Well, let's hope we do," he said.

"Survive?" Paul asked, thinking back to his wine-driven weeping the other night.

"Yeah," Paul grunted. "Remember the president called us 'savages.'"

At the morning assembly, James said, "We're going to march on the road today. You all ready for that?"

"Yeah," the marchers shouted.

Trout, the spokesman for the River, held up a hand. "I'd like to speak this morning, cuz it's a special day," he said. Trout stood in front of a wolf pine and proclaimed:

> *Anglos speak a language of nouns*
> *Which makes them a people of possessions*
> *We were born to a language of verbs*
> *Which makes us a people of action*
> *Let's go*

They walked a block and immediately filled both lanes. Within a few minutes, the highway, the major route along Maine's coast, was one long, hot traffic jam. The late morning news reports out of Portland, Bangor, and even Boston were dominated by tourist complaints about the march.

As the column walked, their two pickup trucks rolled just behind with blinkers on. Near midday, the marchers sat in a field by the side of the highway for their lunch break. Cars that had been stuck in the huge backup slowly rolled by. A man in a car with New York plates shouted, "Ya dumb motherfuckers."

Then a Massachusetts car: "Assholes!"

Then Connecticut, always slightly more polite: "Stupid Indians!"

Then another Massachusetts plate: "Get lost."

A pickup truck from Ohio slid by, and from it a half-empty can of Diet Coke came arcing over its cab. The soda splashed at the feet of Paul. "Now we're getting somewhere," he said.

"Feel that negative energy?" James agreed. "It's just sparking. Haven't had that before."

"Yes, I do," Paul said. "I sense it, too."

"We need to capture that energy, recycle it into something positive. Ride it somehow."

Rock came up from the rear. "They say on the radio that Route 1 is a parking lot down to Damariscotta," he reported.

"What do you think of that?" Paul asked.

"That we're getting their attention," Rock said. "Good."

A Camry stopped next to them. A woman in her thirties opened the front passenger window. "You ruined our vacation!" she screamed.

"You ruined our planet," James replied evenly.

Mook, sitting nearby, playfully said to James, "Oh, you a bad Indian!"—a reference to a song by the Dead Pioneers that plays with the notion of "the only good Indian."

Paul waved at the two children, perhaps five and ten years old, in the backseat. They returned the salutation eagerly. "At least your kids get to see real live Indians," he said to the woman. The older boy at the rear window pointed an index finger at them, curled back the other three fingers, and made "pew-pew" sounds, as if shooting at them.

Rock appeared with a cell phone and handed it to Paul. "Governor's office is asking for you," he said.

Solid came on the line. She said she needed them to cut back a bit. "Can you limit your time on Route 1 to two hours a day?" she asked. Paul said he would discuss it with the others in the evening.

He convened a general meeting of the march that night. Rock counted 156 attendees. "Governor wants us to cut back to marching on Route 1 to two hours each day. She's an ally, but that's a de-escalation. It lets some air out of the bag, some energy out of the action. So what do we all think?"

River members were for escalation. "I say we camp out tomorrow right on Route 1," one suggested.

Distant Thunder, from the Mountain, was alarmed by that idea. "You know what that is? It's an invitation for some drunk Mainer to come rolling over us in his pickup truck at two in the morning doing eighty miles an hour."

Another member of Mountain: "Pissing off the governor, who has been an ally, doesn't sound like a smart move to me."

The Indies kind of liked the idea of more direct physical confrontation. "How about slashing tires? Or refusing arrest, just not going along, running away, even fighting police?" Several members of River nodded.

James emphatically rejected those suggestions. "No violence, for strategic reasons. That is not what we are about. And all you do when you use violence is speak the language of the opposition. They are fluent in that. They have used it against us for four centuries. What they don't understand is peaceful but aggressive confrontational nonviolence. That approach is what keeps us a step ahead of them. They don't know what to do with it."

A voice came in from behind them: "The president's about to come in on the radio." They all got up and walked to the nearest pickup truck and turned the radio up loud. They had heard the scratchy, irritable voice of President Maloney before. But this time there was a new note of anger in his voice. It was clear that he took the blocking of Route 1 personally, as a pointed response to his previous comments.

"Today's immature and irresponsible Indian demonstration demands a response," he began, reading aloud from a prepared statement. "Hardworking Americans deserve a decent vacation. These Indians, out carousing on the highways, high on drugs, are getting in their way. If the state government will not do its duty, the federal government will step in. These illegal and outlandish demonstrations must be stopped."

After the president finished, James stood again. "We've got his attention. We are provoking powerful forces. Let's sleep on it. If you are going to wrestle with the Devil, it is worth putting some thought into it first."

41
MARCH DAY 23

JULY 27: THE DIMMING OF AN AURA

They were in a kind of strategic pause. As an unspoken com-
promise with the governor, they marched cautiously, trying
the two-hour plan, but not announcing any change. Mook spent
much of the day with the media. A joke went around: Q: What's
the most dangerous place on the march? A: Between Mook and
a TV camera. But they had to admit that the camera loved him,
his expressive face and gestures, his quick wit. He was becoming
a celebrity, at least for the moment.

That night they camped on Salt Bay, two miles north of
Route 1, on private land Rock knew about. Rock had three other
properties on his list for potential campsites that night, but one
was occupied and the other two were adjacent to major roads,
which made them too vulnerable, given the rising tensions. So
he went down his list of places that had been offered to them
and chose the remoter acreage on Salt Bay.

James and Paul were talking near the fire. They could hear Mook regaling some newcomers and a couple of print reporters with stories of the early days of the March. "Just a little bunch of us up in the Down East, almost got carried away by the black flies and mosquitoes. Man, we was *rough.*"

James's natural face was a frown, but now it deepened into an actual scowl. Paul noticed and asked, "Are you worried about Mook?"

James: "Yes and no. On the one hand, I don't think he is going, ultimately, where we are going. On the other, I think this moment, in this march, right now, is perfect for him. Some of us are crows, others are finches. We all have roles to play, and the one he has taken on here fits him well. He is built for it. But it also tells me he is of this world, not another one that you and I are both seeking."

Paul: "So where does that lead?" Paul trusted James's judgment implicitly, but especially on the question of the roles people could play in the protests.

James: "At some point, Mook's path will diverge from ours. That's not bad. That's the way of things. But not yet."

They turned back to the subject at hand, which was where the march was going. Paul said, "I heard someone say today we're just naïve people trying to get back to the Garden of Eden."

James considered that. "Here's where that's wrong: That's an Anglo dream. We're Indians. We didn't come from a garden. We came from the forest."

Paul: "So that's what we need to get back to?"

James: "I think so. Have you heard that song the River section sings? It ends, 'Bye bye to the Burners.' That's where I'm at now. Time to go."

"Maybe you," Paul said. "I'm not sure I'm going to make it."

James said nothing, just stared at Paul for a long time. He feared Paul had somehow discerned a looming catastrophe. Paul's aura was low and dark orange.

That dimming color spurred James to stand and go find Rock. "About Plan B," he reminded the security chief, "if Paul or I get killed, or both of us, or if there is mass violence against the march, at that moment, the march ends. Poof. No announcement, no press conference. We disappear, go to ground. Don't meet. Don't call each other. Exactly three months to the day later, we meet at Spot X."

"Where's that?"

"Between us, the Fat Frog, a bar I know near Augusta. But keep that to yourself."

Rock left to spread the word to the leaders of the four groups—Mountain, Lake, River, and Indies: "If there's any killing, the march stops instantly. Just disappear. Poof. We'll meet up exactly three months later."

"Where?"

"It's a place in Maine. We'll let you know specifics."

42
MARCH DAY 24

JULY 28: RED'S DOUBTS

A t morning assembly, Paul noticed an eager face on a marcher named King Turtle, who at the age of sixteen was the youngest person in the march. The kid had something he wanted to say. Paul pointed to him.

The kid sprang to his feet. "Okay!" he practically shouted. He lifted the Red Sox hat from his head and waved it in time.

> *Look with me down the stream of time*
> *Tell you what you'll see*
> *Moose to mouse, all heading for the woods*
> *And here comes—little me*

He was so enthusiastic, so delighted to be addressing the assembly, that even his weak rhyming game won a round of applause and appreciative grunts.

Red caught up with Paul later that day on the highway. "You're worried," Paul said. "Walk with me."

They walked in silence until Paul said, "Red, you've always been straight with me. What's on your mind?"

"To be honest, I'm not sure that this march is the right thing," Red ventured. "I've been thinking about what King Turtle said in morning assembly. And who made him a 'king' anyway?"

"The turtles, I guess," Paul said lightly. "But tell me more about why you're worried about the march."

"Like where does it go?" Red said. "How does it end? Will it mean anything? Isn't the answer to get away from Anglo society?"

"You mean decouple our life from theirs?"

"Yeah, unplug, that's it."

Paul nodded. "I hear you. Half of me feels the same way, and I think James, he's more than half."

"So why are we doing it?"

"To ask questions like yours and think about what the answers might be. You're asking the right ones. I think the best way to meditate on this is, we are taking the first step in a long journey. It may be a journey longer than our own lives. It even could take several generations. With luck, our great-grandchildren will say, 'They didn't know where they were going, but they got started, and here we are now, thanks to them.' I hope. I don't know. It's a pilgrimage into the future."

"I hear you," Red said with feeling. "It's like you're riding on a train. Someone tells you it's going to go over a cliff in a few minutes. Do you want to argue that the train should go slower, or do you want to figure out how to jump off the damn train?"

"Exactly," Paul said. "And right now, the damn train is accelerating. Let me know if you see somewhere we can get off."

43
MARCH DAYS 25 AND 26

JULY 29–30: A COMMUNAL FEAST

A t morning assembly, Paul pointed to Red. "What are you thinking, Red?" he said.

Red, a bit surprised to be asked to unburden his mind, rose slowly and looked around. "Okay," he said. "I used to think we were on the right road. But every day I worry more that I don't know where it leads. I hope that makes sense." It was a somber way to begin the day's walk.

As they headed out, James said to Paul, "I just realized something."

"What?"

"We've marched longer than Gandhi did. The Salt March lasted twenty-four days. We're on day twenty-five."

"What do you think that means?" Paul asked.

James looked up at the sky. "I think we should be alert to truths emerging."

"Is that good or bad?"

James, almost in a whisper, said, "We'll see." He had another thought about Gandhi. "You know what Gandhi called his autobiography? *Experiments with the Truth.* What he meant was, he tried different ways to find the truth, the reality of things, and tried different sorts of actions to show that to others. But he knew he was playing with fire. People like their myths and will kill to preserve them."

"Okay," Paul said, hearing the concern in James's voice. "Let's give them a break." He and James were both assessing the fatigue and uncertainty of many marchers. Between the plane buzzings and the president's verbal attacks, many of the marchers were tense. If something was coming at them, they needed to be in a good frame of mind, rested and ready.

The day's march cut away from Route 1 to camp on a large, lush estate overlooking the Sheepscot River. It was a spectacular property, isolated, with the river in front and a lake in the evergreen woods behind it. "Been on the market for fourteen months, but they asked too much for it, and interest rates crept up some," said Rock, who over the winter had become surprisingly knowledgeable about the intricacies of Maine's high-end coastal properties.

Paul and James watched as the marchers set up camp in a meadow between the river and the lake. An older white man, dressed in the neat, fresh clothes of a wealthy from-away, walked up to them. James thought to himself, what do they do, wear the clothes once and throw them away? To Mainers, a sweater wasn't really yours until it had a hole or two in it.

"This is my land now," the stranger said. He had a distinct squint, both in his eyes and in his pinched voice. His neck was long and his head bulbous and bald, giving him the aspect of a light bulb. "I just closed on it yesterday."

James looked around as if seeing the meadow and river for the first time. "Hmm," he responded. "You know what I see? I see here, this beautiful grassy spot, this is one of my tribe's traditional places for camping and fishing in mid-summer. They came here for maybe two or three thousand years." Paul wasn't sure if James was making this up.

"That's your belief," the man said. His entire face was now crunched inward.

James scrutinized the man's face for a moment, then said, aggressively, "Do you believe in God? I mean, really believe, with every fiber of your being?"

"Yes," the man said, wondering where this quick change of subject was going.

"I'd like to buy your God. How much? Name your price."

The man's eyes opened wide. Whether of incredulity or outrage, it wasn't clear. "That's ridiculous. I can't sell my God. Even if I could, I wouldn't. It would be a sin, a very great sin."

James nodded. "My point exactly. You think you bought my God. But we're not going anywhere. But I promise you we will treat this land well. It is sacred to us."

The man turned to leave. As he retreated, James said, "Walk gently. Your feet are treading on the graves of my ancestors." Paul, listening to this, wondered where James found such powerful language.

When the man was gone up the slope, James looked up at the full moon sailing across a clear evening sky. It was as if everything good about the summer in Maine had been brought together in one fine evening. At the campfire, a member of River stood. He began to do the section's trademark purposely slow walk back and forth through the cloud of marijuana smoke that drifted above the fire, then clapped and sang:

Yeah, Mountain, Lake, they're marching down the coast
But hey! River people, we be walking the most

Whistling down the road with cardinal and jay
New day bring us Wiscasset way

Someone from Mountain got up on the far side of the fire:

River people singing lots of shit
But to rhyme like Mountain you gotta have wit
River bringing up the rear, and we ALL know why
L'il baby marchers, they gonna cry cry cry

With this last line, he rubbed his knuckles against his closed eyes, as a wailing child might. Several people were looking at James, who was taking it all in. Would he let these insults fly back and forth without comment? King Turtle stood and challenged James to respond:

Heads up, my homies, and you might hear
The midnight rap of James Reveur
Hardly a man is now alive
Who can match this cat in climate jive

As Turtle finished, he thrust both his arms with open hands toward James, literally extending an invitation. James stood and made a show of considering his next move, measuring the mood of the crowd around the fire, mulling the moment.

Then he began walking slowly and clapping to set an equally deliberate pace—one (long pause), two (long pause)—and began to sing in a surprisingly strong baritone voice:

All us Indians marching with a song
Whatever we do, gotta get along

Mountain, Lake, River, they all flow sweetly
But Indies lead the way, pretty completely

That last line surprised people. James was sending a message. The marchers would have applauded the effort anyway, but the reminder against division and the shout-out to the Indies made the applause even stronger for James. The Indies high-fived each other in delight.

James had been planning ahead. Later that evening, he walked over and suggested to the beaming Indies that in the morning they offer more fishing lessons to other groups. They agreed.

The next morning, he asked the Indian running the food truck to buy several gallons of peanut oil, a twenty-pound bag of cornmeal, some eggs and milk, and some big jars of hot pepper sauce. "We're gonna have a full moon fish fry," he announced.

That afternoon, alongside the stream that ran from the lake down to the river, two Indies gave a demonstration to the other marchers of how to catch eels, elusive animals with a flavor prized by many tribes. They had been out in the woods gathering poke-berry roots and jack-in-the-pulpit leaves. They put the pile in a pot and used long stones to crush them. They pulled on long, black rubber boots that would protect their legs from the potent mixture, then strode out to rocks in the stream and poured the mix into an area where they had seen eels swimming. "I have a lot of respect for eels," the lead Indie told his audience, gathered on the shore, as he waited for the mixture to take effect. "They are tough, elusive, and strong. Sometimes you see them tucked way down into the cracks between rocks, hiding where you don't think they could even fit."

As he spoke a long brown eel rose to the surface, stunned by the intoxicating mixture and gasping for breath. Within minutes he and the other Indie had dip-netted a dozen big eels, some as long as three feet. Their watching students applauded, Paul among them. The Indies bowed. "That's how you do it," said one of them.

Just before sunset, the entire march sat down to a communal feast, consuming the salmon they'd speared and striped bass they'd hooked. The most prized catch was the eels, which the Indies had skinned, wrapped in onion grass, and roasted on sticks. "Indian bacon," one said with a smile as he took a bite from the roasted eel and passed it along. They pulled roasted potatoes from the coals of the fire. A good time was had by all. By the time the moon was high, they had gathered their strength.

As the evening ended, Rock came to Paul and James. He had an expression of deep concern, shaking his head as he walked. "You know that hurricane down off North Carolina?" he said. "They say it's turned, gonna hit the Maine coast in four days. Fishermen already are hauling their boats." In recent years, as hurricanes had become more common in New England, the drill of bracing for their high winds and water surges had grown familiar. It was as if Louisiana or Florida had moved two thousand miles north.

Paul stared into the campfire. He was brooding again.

"What's on your mind now?" James asked.

"Fire," Paul said. "About how we gather around it every night."

"Man is the fire animal," James said. "I read a book about that at McGill."

"What does that mean?"

"At some point, humans began to control fire. No other animal does. We burn, we shoot, we explode things. Just us."

Paul meditated on this. "It reminds me of something from the class I took on twentieth-century literature. A poem that said, 'In my beginning is my end.'"

"That's T. S. Eliot," James said. "Great poet. Why does thinking about fire make you say that?"

"I just feel that's the way my life ends, somewhere on Route 1. In flames."

❖

Meanwhile, on this full moon evening, Ryan Tapia was at home. But he was not at rest. Having been made unwelcome at the march, he was spending a lot of time at his kitchen table, going through the internet, idly searching, reading discussion groups on the march. One long "anti" thread had lots of commentary about how Indians need to be contained, the president is right. He paged through it, hardly reading it.

Then he saw a rant from "Rocket Man," saying it was time to stop talking, time for action.

"Libtears" wrote back: "More words words words. That's all you got?"

Rocket Man, clearly provoked, shot back, "Fuck you, I'm gonna do something about it."

Ryan did some research on "Rocket Man." There was someone in central Florida who used that handle, a retiree who had worked for decades for an aerospace firm in Melbourne. He was active in supporting a local right-wing paramilitary group. But there was no indication in federal databases that he ever had done something that would get him a second look from law enforcement.

Still, Ryan worried. He called Rock's number and saw that his phone was blocked. He really was unwelcome.

He paced the kitchen.

44
MARCH DAY 27

JULY 31: WISCASSET

I n the morning, Ryan again checked on "Rocket Man." He had
posted just one word, all in capitals: "SHOWTIME!"

An alarm went off in Ryan's head. He called James's phone,
then Paul's. He was blocked by both of them as well. He called
the Wiscasset Police Department and got a voicemail: "All our
officers, including our harbormasters and the shellfish warden, are
out working on march security today. Please leave a message and
we will get back to you. If this is an emergency, please call the state
police." Ryan got a similar message there.

Ryan ran to his truck and sped south on Route 27. He turned
on the radio to the NPR station, which he knew would interrupt
its talk shows if there were any urgent news.

Meanwhile, at morning assembly, Paul saw that Trout had his
hand up. He pointed over to the young tribal poet, who scrambled
to his feet. "Red's moment yesterday morning led me to this
thought," Trout said. "I am not saying he is wrong. I am saying

this is the other side of the coin: *We march today on deathless feet.* Meaning, however it ends, that ain't the end, it's the beginning of something else, the next phase in our journey."

They set out. The man with the light-bulb head stood by the side of the dirt road that led out to the highway, his arms crossed, his face grim. "You guys are pissing a lot of people off," he shouted when he saw James. James looked at him and nodded in agreement.

One issue was still hanging fire: They had not decided how long to march on Route 1 that day, once they were through Wiscasset. For the first part of the day's route, they had no choice. There was just the one road into town ahead of them, the long bridge that took Route 1 over the mile-wide Sheepscot River estuary and then up the hill into the town. There was no river crossing to the south, while any course northward would require a long and useless detour, with few places available for an overnight stop.

And so they funneled onto the bridge across the Sheepscot that led over to Wiscasset, which billed itself as "the prettiest town in Maine." With its streets lined by well-kept brick and wooden houses displaying the best of Federalist architecture, that boast got few arguments. It was another festive day. Children especially had been intrigued by the march, and encouraged their parents to come out and support them, even to press dollar bills into the hands of marchers.

Lincoln Smith, the boy who had been marking the march's progress on a road map of Maine, was there by the side of the road. Today, for his seventh birthday, his father drove him over from their home in Lewiston to see the march. Lincoln had brought a little flag he had made with his mother that said, "March to the Future." He and his father dined on lobster rolls, French fries and blueberry pie at Red's Eats before crossing the street to sit on the curb and await the Indian marchers, who were still out on the bridge.

Paul saw Linc Smith and waved to him. Linc knelt to pat Moolsem, who had trotted up to the front to investigate why they were moving slowly. At the street at the bridge's western end, just past the railroad tracks, there was a car parked at the corner on the left, a little red Fiat 500. Paul noticed it because he thought it was odd that it was facing in the wrong direction, with its trunk toward Route 1. And it also was sagging down in the back.

Just as he noticed the heavy trunk, nearly two hundred pounds of high-velocity HMX explosives in the trunk of the Fiat detonated. The body of Lincoln's father blew sideways up the hill, coming apart as it did. Lincoln's own small head, just two feet away from the car, detached from his neck and rocketed across the road. His skull, by now fleshless, hit Paul solidly in the chest, stopping Paul's heart and killing him instantly. Red's Eats collapsed in a cloud of dust, bread rolls, tubs of melted butter, and cold lobster meat. Most of the leaves on the big old elm tree shading it were blown across the town's roofs. The shock wave snapped Red's flagstaff, dropping the American flag in a heap on the road. The six blue Pepsi canopies over the tables on the grass sailed out into the river, along with several of the people who had been eating at the tables. Arm and leg parts floated in the water, along with the body of Moolsem the dog, who was either unconscious or dead. East-facing windows up the hill and across the town shattered.

James, next to Paul, had been studying the road up the hill toward the town green where the marchers had been invited to make camp for the night. The town's select board had offered to throw a picnic for them and the townspeople—burgers, franks, beans, and lobsters. When the bomb detonated, James's world flashed into bright white, hot screaming light. Next the world went silent. James fell sideways to the right, a movement that seemed to take hours but in fact was just a second. By the time his body hit the asphalt he was barely conscious. He had no sense of time or hearing. His eyesight was hazy or worse. Eventually he began hearing sounds again, pulsing loud and soft. Sirens. Screams. Cries. People shouting names as they searched for friends and family, howling sometimes in despair when they found them.

Paul's body had shielded James from most of the blast. But James's left side had been exposed and had been hit with hundreds of bits of shrapnel, as if a giant shotgun had peppered it with buckshot. He rolled his head sideways on the wet asphalt to check on Paul, hoping his friend would awaken. But one glance told him that Paul was gone. Eyes go cold fast. Death looks like nothing else. For the first time that James could remember, Paul had no aura. James thought to himself, You are walking the Ghost Road now, my friend.

Paul's body was sprawled across the old railroad tracks. Paramedics were working on him, but James realized they were just going through the motions. James lifted his right hand. It was wet. Sticky. Red. Blood was everywhere. His. Paul's. Lincoln's. Just a kid. How many more? he wondered.

Another first responder knelt by James. She listened to his breathing for a moment, then his heart. Both were functioning. "Can you hear me?" she said.

James tried to speak but his jaw refused to move. He tried to move his head to nod yes. As he did the first wave of pain hit him. He screamed and that hurt even more. The paramedic cut off his shirt and ran the knife up the left leg of James's pants. "You're hit," she said. "No arteries cut. Bleeding's not too bad. I'm going to give you a shot for that pain." She patted him on the shoulder.

As the drug hit, James relaxed back onto the wet road. He felt he was melting into the sticky, warm black asphalt. She took out a grease pen and wrote on James's forehead: "M/I," indicating that he had received morphine and was considered to be triage class one, likely to live, care needed but not urgently. She moved on to the next victim.

Rock ran up with Mook. The two, who had been at the rear of the march, stood above their two leaders lying supine on the asphalt, one deathly still, the other in an otherworldly state. Rock was steady and expressionless, while Mook's face ran through a series of changes, as his lips trembled and his eyes cried and his head shook.

James felt eerily at peace. He knew he wasn't going to die, so he figured that he was somehow being given a chance to do what needed to be done. James wiggled his fingers to indicate to Rock to kneel next to him. "Rock, you know it is time for Plan B, right?" he whispered into Rock's ear.

Rock said, "Got it. I'll put the word out." It meant, go home and come to Site X exactly three months from today. James wondered hazily why he and Paul had decided on three months. Maybe that was a good mourning period. Or time to regroup, reevaluate, and move on. Now, it would give him time to recuperate.

"Mook, start a memorial fund for Paul online, okay? We're going to need some money."

"All over it," the young man said softly.

James closed his eyes. The sirens seemed to get quieter. He woke up when someone shook his shoulder. It was an ambulance driver. "Gonna move you over to the medevac landing site," he said. Red, the kid he had taught to pick trash as a form of service, came and sat in the blood by his side. Red wept silently, his head on his crossed arms.

There were two parking lots just south of the blast zone. The first became the staging area for medevacs. Another hundred yards down was the Wiscasset Yacht Club parking lot, which became the landing zone for the helicopters that started coming in every few minutes. The urgent cases were being shuttled to Portland by Medstar helicopters. James was placed in the line for the less critical ones who could wait, and were being flown to Bangor by a mixture of smaller green-and-white Maine Forest Service helicopters and larger dark green Army National Guard Black Hawks.

Ryan, hurtling down Route 27, heard a newsflash that the Indian march had been bombed in Wiscasset and there were mass casualties of both marchers and bystanders. He roared through Pittston and Dresden. He turned his FBI radio to the National Guard's frequency and heard that the governor had dispatched the two National Guard helicopters that often transported her to be used now for supporting the medical evacuations.

In Wiscasset, he parked on a side street and ran to the medevac zone, seeing a line of stretchers holding casualties to be flown out. He recognized James lying on one and squatted next to him. "James, Paul is dead," he said. "I heard it on the National Guard radio. I'm sorry."

James winced and whispered, "I don't talk to white people anymore." He lifted his right hand and circled it weakly in the air, the index finger extended, his sign that he was outta here. He closed his eyes as a blue cloud of morphine expanded inside his brain.

Ryan let him be and walked over to the site of the bombing. He saw that Mook, one of the Indians he had met visiting the march, was speaking to reporters. "Who do you think might have done this?" one journalist asked. Mook's T-shirt was soaked in blood.

Mook responded, "I already know who did it: Some dumbass who took the president's words literally. President Maloney called us 'savages,' and someone should 'stop us.' Someone did. The bomb did that and a lot more besides. Did you see that kid's head that got blown off? He was a little kid, damn it. The actual name of that pathetic person who put the bomb there is more or less irrelevant. He was doing the bidding of the president. What more do you need to know?"

Mook wept, wiped his eyes, and continued: "But know this: The killings today didn't stop this action. They started a new one. You will see. It's bigger than us now." The striking photograph of his wet face, sad eyes, and bloody shirt flew electronically to news sites around the world.

Ryan stepped away and called Jimmy Love's number at the Portland office. "I am on the scene and will begin investigative work immediately," he reported.

"You can stand down," Love said in a murmured monotone. "I just got off the phone with Bulster. He says they're sending in what he calls 'the A Team,' a bomb forensics squad from DC along with the security squad they usually work with."

"So what do I do?" Ryan asked.

"They request that you take as many photos as you can. Collect names and contact information for witnesses. But they say don't mess with the scene. Make sure the local uniforms have it secure. Our guys will be there in a couple of hours. They're flying on the director's Gulfstream to Brunswick."

Ryan tried to be professional. He thought, At least they're not kicking me off the case.

"Oh, and they also asked that you find a place for them to bed down. Hotels are going to be full, so maybe a house or something. Beds for twelve. They'll also be emailing you a shopping list."

Ryan said, "So, I'm the gofer?"

Love urged him to go along. "Walk a mile in my moccasins," he told Ryan. "Neither you nor I are on the good side of the director. Bulster thinks of us as his wayward children. They're not going to give us any slack here."

Ryan walked across the street to where Red's Eats had collapsed and gazed across the wide river. He looked down at the shoreline. A state trooper stood there on the sand, unholstering a pistol. Ryan's immediate thought was that the last thing we need right now is more violence.

He saw that the officer was standing over a dog lying at his feet, half in the water, half out. The dog was alive, but just barely, its breathing ragged. Ryan realized it was Moolsem, the stray that had become the mascot of the march. The trooper clearly was about to put the animal out of its misery. "Wait!" Ryan shouted.

The officer looked up, a bit irritated. Ryan rushed down to him. "This dog has multiple wounds, and two front legs are broken," the officer said. "Not just broken, smashed. Look, his left eye is gone. And we have lots of human casualties."

Ryan said, "This dog means a lot to some people here."

"You want responsibility for him?"

"Yes, I do," Ryan said.

"All yours," the officer said, holstering his weapon. The man clambered up the bank to the road to deal with other tasks waiting there.

Ryan gently scooped up Moolsem. "I will take care of you," he said. "I promise." The dog whimpered and passed out. Ryan took the limp animal to his truck and placed him on the passenger seat. He reached back for the down jacket he kept in the truck and draped it over Moolsem. He checked his phone and found a vet located on the highway down to Bath.

Fifteen minutes later, the vet looked over the wounded dog. "This animal is dying," she said.

Ryan said, "I'm desperate. Can you try?"

"No," the vet said.

"For a thousand dollar bonus?"

The vet looked at him, her eyes big. "No. Why?"

"Okay, for five thousand?" In his mind, what had happened to Moolsem was somehow connected to the death of the family dog, along with his wife and children, years ago. Let one dog's death help another one live. It made him feel a little better about the millions of dollars in settlement money he had put in the bank and tried to forget about.

She winced and said, "Plus expenses."

"Agreed," he said.

"I will try," she continued. "But you need to understand, even if this dog does live, it is never going to walk normally again. The best I can do is basically put in rods the whole way. And those rods aren't cheap."

A week later, Ryan drove back down to collect Moolsem. The dog's front legs were both encased entirely in casts. "The joints were destroyed," the vet said. "The dog will never be able to run. The best he will be able to do is a kind of hop. That will put a lot of wear and tear on his front shoulders. So at the top of the rods, where they meet his shoulders, I put in little shock absorbers, and where the ankle joints were, little industrial springs."

"Expensive?"

"For each leg, just that set of gear costs twelve thousand. Lots of titanium, along with some very strong nylon."

"Okay," said Ryan. He had made a promise, if only to himself and to Moolsem. He carried the dog, still half-conscious from painkillers, to his truck.

PART III

WOODS

45
A VISIT WITH THE GOVERNOR

MID-SEPTEMBER

T he wind was cool and dry from the northwest, bringing the first day of fall weather. Ryan drove the hour down to Augusta and parked outside the statehouse. Inside, the governor's confidential secretary said it would be just a moment.

After several minutes, Ryan was ushered in. Solid rose from behind her desk. She appeared different, he thought. Still tall and cool, still alluring. But she was older, too. When they were a couple, she had dressed perhaps a decade younger than her age, favoring tight jeans and leather jackets, and she could pull it off. Now, operating as a powerful public figure, she dressed a decade older than she really was. It was as if she had leapt a full generation ahead of him. Somehow she had transitioned into a grand dame, an elegant person holding a position of power and prominence. She was dressed conservatively, in a knee-length gray wool skirt and matching jacket, with a blue blouse and a small red carnation as a boutonnière. Her hair was piled up in a fluffy, Gibson Girl–style bouffant. That, along with her high heels, made her appear well over six feet tall.

The governor's office, with its old woods and mirrors, and big crystal chandelier, fit her new style. They sat in two green leather armchairs that stood before a cold fireplace.

"You wear it well, ma'am," he said. That last word was intended to remind him and her both that this was not a social call.

"You wanted to see me?" she responded, equally formal.

"There's a place you should know about," he began. "I am not supposed to know this, but I do." He told her the curious tale of Camp Cripple, the secret CIA installation up on the Maine border with Quebec, and especially how it became so useful in the post–9/11 environment of omni-surveillance.

"Interesting," she said evenly. "But where does the state of Maine come in?"

"Here's the good part: You actually own it."

"I do? That seems unlikely."

"Well, the state of Maine does," he said. "Blame it on government secrecy. During World War Two, the existence of this particular POW camp had been kept undisclosed by the Army. After the war, the backwoods acreage devolved to the Maine National Guard. No one much cared, and no one ever expected to use it. It was just a handful of acres lost in the million square miles of uninhabited backwoods up there. When CIA took it over, they continued the secrecy by not formally taking ownership. So, officially, Camp Cripple is still the property of the Maine National Guard."

"And this means?"

"I think it means there is a potential refuge for the marchers. From my conversations with Paul and James before Wiscasset, I think the survivors will be looking for one."

Ryan unrolled a paper copy of the US Geological Survey contour map of the area and pointed to a large oval marked by dozens of small brushy symbols. He said, "The actual site of Camp Cripple was marked, misleadingly, on this map as a freshwater swamp, in order to deter hunters. And on satellite images, it is blurred. But I went to the FBI's own database of imagery within fifty miles of the US border." He handed her a printout he'd made. It showed the camp tucked in a valley below the high ridge the border ran along. "See," he said, pointing to parts of it. "There's a helicopter landing pad. That's a residence with bedrooms, a small dormitory for staff, a large kitchen and office space. Behind it, this is a storage shed for equipment and fuel." The closest major land feature on the map was Hardhead Mountain, a few miles to the east. The map also showed a border gate two miles to the northwest of the camp, with notations indicating that it was locked and had no scheduled service by Customs or Border officials.

In a nation never known for discretion, this was an extremely discreet location. The prime minister of a NATO nation had once been invited there, on a "day of rest" between his visits to Ottawa and Toronto, to be shown filmed and audio evidence of his several meetings with two different KGB officers involving kinky sex and bags of cash money. After that review, he went home and behaved himself, stepping down quietly a few months later.

She stood and thanked him. They shook hands. He left her office thinking she was already looking ten steps ahead of where they were even right then. Maybe she saw a way forward after the bombing that he didn't. Or a cabinet post. He honestly didn't know. He wondered if that freckle he had loved was still there just above her heart.

46
JAMES AND PAIN

James's convalescence was uneven. He was young and fit, so his broken left leg and arm knit quickly. He did not realize until he woke up in a hospital bed that he had lost the use of his left eye. The eyeball itself was uninjured, but some of the shrapnel had lodged against the front of the optic nerve, cutting off its sight.

And few medical situations move as slowly as recovery from shrapnel wounds. The big metal pieces, while destructive of tissue, were relatively easy for surgeons to map and remove. But James's left side, from his left ankle up to his earlobe, also was peppered with hundreds of specks of dirt, asphalt, threads, and bone fragments. These demanded patience. His body would work diligently but slowly to expel them. Eventually the bits would emerge on the surface of his skin as angry purple and red pimples, usually oozing pus. Once they were in that state, a nurse could scrape and suction them out and dress the remaining wound. With perhaps four hundred such spots on his left leg, torso, arm, and face, it was a long and laborious process. James had a lot of time to think and adjust to his diminished eyesight and his post-bombing world.

For the first week, he tried to follow what the doctors called his "pain management regime." Essentially, he could have a dose of morphine every three hours. The first hour after each dose was bliss—no pain at all. The second hour was edgy, as the agony slowly mounted, and with his knowledge that it would only get worse. And the third hour was just a matter of gritting his teeth, pouring out sweat, and waiting it out as his mind filled with the static of pain. Each piece of dirt, asphalt, metal, and bone that had blasted into the side of his body began to writhe inside his skin. At one point he wondered if the spirit of Paul had been blown into his side and was clawing to get out. He dismissed the thought: Paul's spirit was benign. By the end of each day, these three-hour-long roller-coaster rides through Hell had worn him out.

On the second Tuesday, he woke up and said aloud, "Fuck it." Instead of chasing the peace of morphine, he decided to stop all painkillers. He would take meds for health, yes, but nothing more to make him feel better.

"You sure of this?" the nurse asked him twice. She arched an eyebrow.

"I am," he said. "I suspect it would be better to live with the pain than to lie here bracing for the shock of it to hit me every three hours."

"I'll check back," she said.

"When you do, please bring me a sponge or leather belt I can bite on when I need to," James said.

"Damn, you're serious," the nurse said, reassessing the man's resolve.

It took him a full week to adjust. Oddly, he found the time went fast. Instead of waiting for the pain to find and catch him and beat him, he learned to live with it. He would mentally hunt it, figure out where the shrapnel and debris might emerge next. With the deep shrapnel moving, even if it was minute, all he really could do was scream and bite the old leather belt the nurse had given him.

If he was going to feel pain, he decided, he might as well benefit from it. When a piece began pressing from inside against his skin, he would wedge it out with a scalpel, then apply a tiny vacuum cleaner, and finally daub the ensuing wound with antiseptic. The medical attendants frowned, but it kept him busy.

After a few hours of this, he would sleep, unaided by narcotics. When he awakened he would eat from the food supply kept in his bedside refrigerator—small amounts of meat, nuts, eggs, dark green vegetables, berries and other fruit. Then he would go back to work. His goal was to ride the pain instead of it riding him. Most of the time he succeeded. But sometimes his internal pain needle went past five, and all he could do was bite the leather belt and sweat. The worst was when the pain hit seven or eight, just stabbing shocks, one after another. It felt like a maddened weasel was trapped inside his damaged left calf and clawing to get out. He tried to talk to it, but it came out as a scream, "HELLO, UNCLE WEASEL, I WILL FIGHT YOU!" The nurse came in to look at him. He swung the belt into the bedding.

47
SOLID VISITS JAMES

Solid called ahead and asked James if she could visit. He told her he didn't talk to white people anymore. "That's okay, you can just listen," she said briskly. She had taken well to being the highest official of the state.

She sat down in the chair next to his bed. "How are you doing?" she asked.

"A man must learn to carry his grief," he said simply but perhaps obscurely.

"I hear you," she replied, taking him to mean he was still adjusting to what had happened in Wiscasset. "Both personally, and as governor of this state, I want to express regret for the attack. It was a crime and an outrage. I am sorry for your losses."

It seemed petty to him to remain silent, so he broke his vow and quietly said, "Thank you." He felt she was reaching out to him, and she deserved a response. Being resentful of what happened was human, but so was trying to be decent despite what happened.

"It is the least we can do," Governor Harrison continued. "Another thing: I hear the FBI is about to detain a suspect, a retired aeronautical worker down in Florida who says he was just doing what the president told him to do."

"Doesn't matter," he said dully. "Won't bring back Paul. Or that kid, or anyone else."

Solid pressed on. "But I came today with another reason. I have something for you, some information that might be helpful."

"Yes?"

"I understand you are interested in a refuge in the woods, far from population centers, the remoter the better. I think I have something for you." She told him about Camp Cripple and its strange, hidden history. She handed him a slip of paper, saying, "Here are the GPS coordinates." It was, she added, a fully equipped facility, but extraordinarily isolated. It even had a reliable, year-round spring with clean, flowing water. That intrigued James, who believed that every spring harbored a small and benevolent god. Make your peace with that local god, and that small deity will watch out for you.

"The president's not gonna like us going into a CIA facility," he said.

"A state property, borrowed by the CIA," she corrected. "And I can deploy a National Guard unit nearby to deter any funny business by the feds."

He nodded.

After she left, James asked Rock to come see him. James told him about this odd base deep in the Maine woods. "It sounds perfect," Rock said. Together, they planned a reconnaissance mission for early October. They picked three of the steadiest Indies. Rock left to brief them on their task.

The scouts reported back in late October. Rock brought Gutter to see James. "It was pretty low-key," Gutter said, his beard thicker now than it had been in the summer. "Just a locked gate on a gravel road that leads to the border gate. No perimeter fence. Great location—tucked on the south side of a hardwood ridge that's covered with birch, ash, and maple, and a big fresh spring halfway up toward the border. That ridge would keep a lot of cold wind off your back in the winter. And all the deer and moose you'd want for fresh meat. Area hasn't been hunted much for years, maybe decades.

"We walked in, checked out the place. Broke into the main building through a back window. Found dormitory beds for twenty, a big kitchen for feeding that many. In storage, enough canned food and basic staples—salt, sugar, flour, beans, coffee, tea, UHT milk—to feed a group for weeks, especially if we supplement it by hunting and fishing. A big Generac generator, powered by natural gas. A backup generator, too. But we could keep warm with wood, pretty easy. There's a large and well-equipped tool shed, everything from chainsaws to bear traps. Ammunition for hunting, too.

"Here's the thing that surprised us," Gutter continued. "No surveillance cameras, anywhere. We know how to find them. We searched high and low."

"Are you sure? Maybe in trees?" James said.

"Pretty sure. They may have micro-cameras or ground sensors somewhere. But we're used to keeping an eye out, when we're hunting on land the Burners claim. But there was no sign of anything. It was kind of weird. Maybe ground sensors, but without some imagery, those won't tell you much. Bear makes pretty much the same impact as a man."

"I'm not surprised," James said. "Cameras would defeat the entire purpose of the camp. It may be the last place on Earth that isn't surveilled." Only the US government could afford such a luxury, he thought.

James thanked Gutter and asked him to take the scout team back into the camp. "Lay low, report any activity." To do that, they decided to use a variety of ways—"maybe hike out to where there's cell coverage one day, or if sending someone out to the highway for supplies, have them mail a letter. Or even bring a message down. Mix it up," James admonished. "As little electronics as possible. Watch your signals."

On a Tuesday morning three weeks later James opened his eyes to a gray afternoon. Something was missing. There was no pain—yes, a heavy ache, but that was different. His left ankle, leg, torso, arm, and neck were not sending agonizing signals. He felt almost like a group of friends had decamped without bidding him farewell. He thought to himself: Okay, it's time to go.

James was discharged on the condition that he stay near Bangor to attend daily physical therapy sessions in order to rebuild his shriveled and strained muscles. A friend of Paul's lent him a cabin on Lost Pond, a few miles northwest of the town. James had no knowledge that the FBI man, Ryan Tapia, also lived there. One day he was out doing his daily five miles of walking on the dirt road, back and forth several times, when he encountered Ryan. Both looked startled. James shook his head coldly and continued on his way. James wondered: Is the FBI surveilling? He called Rock for advice. The march's security chief said that to the best of his knowledge, the Bureau wasn't—but that James inadvertently was staying in the rural area near Lost Pond where Ryan Tapia made his home.

"Probably just a weird coincidence," Rock said. "But keep one eye peeled."

"That's all I have," James reminded him.

Nearly three months after the bombing, texts went out to the leaders of Mountain, Lake, River, and the Indies. It stated, "Let your people know that Spot X is the Fat Frog bar in Hallowell on December 1." It didn't say what time. That was on purpose. James and Rock had a plan.

48
A DAY AT THE FAT FROG

J ames and Rock waited outside the Fat Frog, a low-key bar á few
miles south of Augusta. At noon, when the bartender unlocked
the door, Rock took a stool at the bar. James moved to a table in
a dark corner where he would not be seen by most people. He
passed the time by reading a book titled *Confessions of a Recovering
Environmentalist* and slowly eating a kofta kebab, one of the joint's
specialties. These days his body, rebuilding muscle that had been
surgically debrided, craved protein. He ordered a second plate.

The veterans of the summer march arrived in ones and twos,
hurrying to close the door against the cold winter gusts. Rock had
before him about two hundred sealed envelopes, divided into two
uneven piles. The larger group of envelopes contained the GPS
coordinates of the Massachusetts statehouse in Boston. The smaller
one listed the GPS location of Camp Cripple.

The Farewell Movement was about to begin. It would be phase III,
following the Tide Is High and the March to the Future.

Only veterans of the march had been invited to come on this
day. James would glance up from his book as each person entered
and would touch either his right temple or his left. Touching his

right temple told Rock to give the person an envelope with the Camp Cripple location. Touching his left temple, which he did more often, meant the person got the larger envelope and should meet up in Boston in a month.

On just a few occasions, Rock pushed back on James's decision because he knew or sensed something about the person that made him think he was not right for the Camp Cripple operation. Most often when Rock shook his head, James would acquiesce. When Red, the kid who had knelt next to James after the bombing, came in, James tapped right. Rock shook his head. James tapped right again, and Rock shrugged and gave him a Camp Cripple envelope. Afterwards, James yelled over to Rock, "Kid's got spirit."

"Needs discipline," Rock said.

"He'll get it," James replied. "Fast learner. Good listener. Watches well."

Mook arrived. James pointed left, but also waved Mook to come over to him. Mook stood in front of James. He clearly was surprised as he took in James's thinned face and pockmarked left cheek. "You been through the mill, man," Mook observed.

"Sit, please," James said. Mook did. James leaned forward and said, "I have an assignment for you. I would like you to take the lead in our next action. It will be down in Boston, at the Massachusetts State House. You need to get down there, do your reconnaissance. Decide how to proceed."

Mook was interested but apprehensive. "And I hold the fort until you appear?" he asked.

James shook his head. "You won't see me there. I am going in a different direction."

Mook's face clouded. "I don't think I'm ready to lead an action."

James said, "Well, I think you are. What I need you to do is make a splash. You only have to make it happen for a week or so.

Here's the key: Don't try to do it all yourself. I've made sure you have some good leaders in your group. Pick out the ones you think will be good to run security, logistics, communications, things like that. You remember our planning sessions? Follow what we did in those, and you won't go far wrong. Distant Thunder might make a good strategic advisor, someone to talk to at night about how things went, how to do better. But you're the leader, so you decide who fills what role."

Mook considered those parameters. "I can do that," he said. He paused. "What's the 'different direction' you're going?"

"Still unfolding," James said obscurely.

Mook stood, still assimilating the new assignment. "You know," he said, marveling, "all the time we were on the march, I thought you didn't like me."

James stared at him evenly. "Didn't say I did."

Mook shook his head in perplexity. "But you put me in charge of an action. Of all the marchers from last summer, more than one hundred, you picked me. Not an Indie. Not Rock. Me. Why?"

"You're perfect for this action," James said evenly. "You know a lot about the world, probably more than me, I'd say." Had Mook been a man of colder judgment, he might have grasped that James was effectively saying that Mook was best used working in the Burners' world. Given James's belief that the Burners were corrupt and doomed, that was not a compliment. But Mook was not a contemplative person. He was a man of the moment. James had seen that and was using it.

After Mook was out the door, Rock came over to James, arms folded, square face skeptical. "Seriously, you're putting him in charge of an action?"

James said, "Mook's made for this, for the media and the bright lights. He can do that dance, and better than we can. Where we're going, into the woods, he'd shrivel up. So I am giving him his chance to shine and run with it. He can make of it what he can. The movement can take different forms."

"And us?"

"You, me, the other right taps—we're heading for the hills. I really, truly believe the Burners' world is heading for collapse. So I want to split off from it, find a different way."

"Does Mook understand that?"

"You know, I think he has a sense of it. Or at least he knows that where you and I are going, he wouldn't last a week."

Rock mulled all that, then said, "James, you're throwing away most of the movement. Why?"

"Because in our next stage, quality matters more than quantity. Anyone can march on a summer day in Maine. But not many will make it through a hard winter in the Maine mountains."

Rock's eyebrows lifted slightly. "Hard words," he observed.

James didn't dispute that. Instead, he said, "Words are stones. You can throw them, and you can build with them. The harder they are, the longer they last."

Through the day, he tapped left and right. James and Rock chose to direct sixty people to the remote Cripple location. He figured that maybe two-thirds would try and actually make it to the camp. The difficulty of getting there was the point. He wanted only those who were determined and resourceful enough to figure out how to navigate ninety miles of deep forest in the wintertime to join him.

The last person to arrive was Seaweeds. James didn't tap either side of his head. Instead he went over and greeted her with an extended hand. They shook. "We need to speak," he said. "We're planning a couple of actions, but I want you to think about something different."

"What?" she asked.

"You're smart, and I trust you," James said by way of introduction. "Would you be willing to spend this winter organizing a women's march for next year?"

"Where?"

"I'm thinking from the mountains to the sea."

"Alongside men, or just by ourselves?"

"You tell me. That's a good question to begin with."

Seaweeds paused to ponder. "Okay," she said. "I remember: You said, the beginning of strategy is figuring out who you are."

"Let's talk in the spring," James said. "You can let me know then. I'm gonna be out of touch most of the winter. Let Rock know where you'll be." She nodded and stood.

At closing time, James stood up and patted Rock on the back. "Let's go," he said. Rock left two $100 bills for the bartender. She thanked them. They headed out into the cold night.

"Lots of Indies in your picks for the woods," Rock observed.

"Yeah, I noticed that. They're better prepared for where we're going. We are going to have a long visit with the god of winter, and he can be a tough host."

Rock said, "We'll need them."

"I see it this way," James said. "If American society falls apart the way I expect, having a refuge far away from it will be a real advantage in the cold months, when people get desperate for food and shelter. There will come a time when distance could be an advantage."

49
JAMES TIPS OFF THE FBI

James missed Paul, most of all his advice and insights. Together, they had helped each other see the way forward. Now he was on his own, making him one-eyed both physically and spiritually. He tried to remember the steps they had taken to prepare for their first march: Educate yourself about the situation, study it, get the facts. Figure out who you are—that was a hard one—and what you wanted to do. Next, consider how you are going to do it. With that in mind, decide what sort of people you need to carry out those tactics. And how to train them to do that. Train them up, intensely, building trust and common understanding.

And then get out there and do it. At the end of each day, review your activities carefully and coldly. What could you have done better? What has to be changed so that you are not predictable? Who needs more training, more education?

He tried to do it all himself, thinking it over as he did his walking. He was stronger, doing fifteen miles a day, completing it in the time that initially it had taken him to walk five miles. As he walked one day in early December, he realized that he'd forgotten an early step that Gandhi had said was essential: self-purification.

To that end, he decided that instead of walking to Camp Cripple with others, he would make the journey solo. He spent his evenings studying satellite images and topographical maps. He planned his route. He figured he could make it most of the way on snowmobile trails.

In mid-December, he spent the late afternoon of a quiet day putting food and other gear in his backpack. When he finished, he saw the lights on in Ryan's house, across the pond. He walked the driveway around the pond and knocked. Ryan came to the door, opened it, looked James up and down and said, "I thought you didn't talk—"

James held up his hand. "Making an exception this one goddamn time," James said. "I thought you should know we're going to have an action down in Boston soon. End of next week, maybe. Gonna occupy the State House, issue a set of demands."

"Why there?"

"Because that's where the treaties that gave away our land were signed. Even has a gilded pine cone on top of the dome, celebrating everything they took when Maine was part of Massachusetts."

"You're telling me this because why?"

"Because you were a friend of Paul's, I guess. You knew him before I did."

That didn't strike Ryan as James's way. But he didn't want to look a gift horse in the mouth. "Can I use this information?"

"You can do anything with it you want," James said, and turned away into the darkness.

That green light was enough for Ryan. He wondered for a moment about where James and the movement were going. With Paul gone, it felt to him like it had taken on a harder, even more cynical tone. He put away that thought and, doing his duty, phoned Bulster in Boston and filled him in.

The Boston SAC was ecstatic. He felt his long-tested patience had been rewarded: Tapia had produced something. "Good work," he said. "You're finally earning that big paycheck." He called the FBI director, who offered to reinforce the Boston office. The director called the president to inform him that the Bureau was all over the case. "We know their next step, and we will be there to meet them."

The president was pleased. These "rogue Indians," as he thought of them, had begun to bug him personally. "None of this would have happened if they had just stopped their marching," he said. He instructed the FBI chief: "This time, no mollycoddling. I want the law enforced."

"Sir, you're right, of course," the director said as unctuously as possible. He considered asking the president to tone down his rhetoric, but decided on second thought that he liked his job.

50
THE ORDEAL OF JAMES REVEUR

James was ready at dawn the next morning. Rock drove him up into northwest Maine, dropping him in a parking lot for snowmobilers. "See you there," Rock said, turning the truck around.

James swung on his pack and began his solitary trek. The trail had been packed by the snowmobilers, and the walking was easy. By sundown he had made twelve miles. Only another eighty to go, he thought, as he prepared for the night. He'd found a spot where there was a lot of dry wood nearby. He made a fire, melted snow over it in his sole pot, and put in a packet of military spaghetti with meatballs. After that was warmed, he put a teabag in the pot and added honey, making a warming drink to get through the night. While he sat, he took off the day's socks and dried them near the fire while wearing the other pair. It was the only change of clothes he brought. He wrapped a plastic tarp around his gigantic winter sleeping bag, good to 25 degrees below zero, and slid into it.

He was up before dawn, which came at about eight o'clock in early December in the mountains of Maine. He breakfasted on chocolate-covered crackers and tea. He put two carrots in his inside jacket pocket to defrost them and then ate them while walking.

He also kept his handheld GPS device in that inner coat pocket to keep the batteries warm, which maintained their power better. Once or twice a day he turned on the device to review his walking progress and plans. When the sun neared the western horizon, at about three thirty in the afternoon, he would gather another pile of wood, make a roaring fire, and have another meal. Sometimes he had the sense that something was trailing him in the air, some kind of benign spirit hovering over him.

He was no expert woodsman, but he began to feel comfortable. He even awakened earlier and began walking under the stars and moonlight. He made about ten to twelve miles a day, depending on the terrain and the quality of the packing on the snowmobile trails. On the third afternoon, he made camp beside a little frozen woods pond. A curious deer walked across the ice to inspect him from just a few feet away. It felt like a good omen to James.

On the fourth day, overcast and windy, the temperature never getting above 15 degrees, the ground began to steepen. The snowmobile paths petered out and ended. The territory felt genuinely remote. The going got harder, overland through the woods, often in two or three feet of crusty snow. Each step was laborious—lift the foot, move it forward, push it down through the snow again. Lift the other foot and do the same. He couldn't swing his foot forward because of the snow, so the walking was slow and difficult. Occasionally his boot would hit a rock or branch hidden underneath the snow, stressing his ankles. But, he told himself, with every step, he was getting closer. Again, something seemed to be hovering near him, monitoring him. Perhaps a snowy owl, he thought. As long as it wasn't a federal drone.

He came to a steep mountain, and on the GPS device saw two possible routes. He could either climb it, which would be slow and exhausting, and slippery on the rocks, or he could go around the mountain, taking a longer route to the east that followed the bank of a stream up to a swamp.

He chose the bank. For about a mile it went well. After that, the cliffs on either side were coming closer, narrowing down rapidly. He came to a beaver dam that spanned the stream, its sticks piled with mud about three feet high and twenty feet wide. It touched the base of the cliff on either side. The narrowness made the place feel dark and gloomy. Before him was a small canyon, perhaps one hundred yards long. Beyond it he could see from the light that the swamp began. He had not wanted to walk on the ice of streams, but thought he could chance it this once, for just a short stretch of a hundred yards. All he needed to do was make it through this one narrow stretch, the canyon walls so close he could almost touch each side at once, and he would be up on the flats of the swamp, where the walking would be easier. He trod carefully, halting after each few steps to listen to the ice that he could not see underneath the snow. He heard no cracking. Stopping to listen, he thought he could hear water rushing below. But there was no cracking, so he took another step—and his boot hit a honeycombed section of ice and plunged through into the water. With most of his weight then shifted to fall on the other foot, it too went in.

In just a moment, he was up to his shoulders in rushing ice water that caught his backpack and spun him around. The cold was shocking, taking his breath away. He gasped for air. As he did, the backpack filled with water, pulling him under. He was trapped under the ice. He was on his back, his face a few inches from the bottom of the ice. He sensed through the dark water some gray light.

He came to a hard stop as his feet and then his backpack hit a sieve of boulders. He used the respite to slip out of the pack. He tried to get back to the hole he had made when falling in. The water was only four feet deep, but he could make little progress upstream against the swift current. He could take only a few steps each minute. That put the hole four or five minutes away. He didn't have enough air to make it.

He was aware that within a minute or so, he would need to breathe or he would die. He stopped trying to move upstream. Instead he slammed an elbow upwards against the ice. It didn't budge. He braced his legs and pushed with his shoulder. He thought he felt a little movement, but not enough to begin to make a difference soon enough. He felt with his leg for a loose rock, about the size of his head, and knelt down through the icy water to lift it. Pushing off the bottom with his legs and holding it above him, he slammed it upward. The ice cracked. He did it again and again, panicking now, knowing that between the freezing water and the lack of oxygen, he soon would be dead. He was about to pass out. The black was closing in from either side of his eyes. The ice cracked and opened slightly. He pushed his head up through the fractured section and took a breath, deep and sweet and long. He had never appreciated air so much in his life.

The cold stabbed his lungs, overcoming the adrenaline surge that had momentarily warmed him. He was standing shoulder deep in freezing water. He flopped sideways onto the ice, getting his arms out and reaching for something, anything, to grab. There was nothing. He pushed off the bottom and gained a few inches. He kicked his legs in the water and gained another inch. He kicked again and was able to grab with one hand a cedar root sticking out from the strip of bank at the base of the cliff. He pulled, fearing it would snap, but cedar roots are surprisingly strong. He was able to get his other hand on it. He pulled again, got his legs out of the water. He rolled sideways onto the ice. Again he was exhausted.

Lying on his back, gazing at the sky, he realized that his survival depended on his backpack, which was still down there under the ice. Without it, he could not make fire, and without fire, he would be dead within an hour or two.

His sense of time stretched as the adrenaline again surged through his body. There was so much of it pumping through his body that he did not feel the cold. Moments earlier, trapped under the ice, he had known he had only seconds to live before he would pass out and die there. Now he knew he had at least fifteen minutes before frostbite set in, and another fifteen before hypothermia began to shut down his brain, heart, and lungs. Thirty minutes, that seemed a luxurious amount of time to someone whose life had just been measured by seconds.

He rolled over and eased himself down into the hole he had just made emerging from the ice. With one hand he held the edge of it. With the other he groped for his backpack, still held by the current against the boulder sieve. With an effort, he wrapped a hand around a back strap of the pack and pulled it toward him. He pivoted, propped up the pack on the floor of the stream, and stepped up on it to heave himself out of the ice hole, holding on to the strap as he did. Once he was out of the water, he lifted the pack and heaved it up across the ice toward the narrow bank, just a few inches wide. He crept across the ice, spread-eagled to distribute his weight, and pulling the backpack alongside him, crawled on all fours along the ice at the side of the stream back to the beaver dam. He dropped down across it and climbed up the bank, now wider, with a small meadow of swamp sedge beyond. In mid-winter the grass stood out of the snow, knee-high, brown and dry. If he were going to be saved, he knew, it would be by this dead grass.

James flexed his fingers. They were not responding well. He was beginning to lose control of his muscles. His mind drifted. He idly wondered what would happen to his corpse: Would animals gnaw the frozen body, or would they wait for him to thaw out in the spring? And what kind of animal would eat him? Probably an eagle or owl, he thought—something big enough to fight off other comers. He hoped it wasn't a fisher cat. They were mean.

He shook himself, told himself to focus. Don't give up, he thought, and then said it again out loud. Figure out what to do, and get it done. He kneeled next to the waterlogged backpack. He had been careful always to store his wooden kitchen matches back in the same spot in the backpack, the lower left pocket, and kept them there inside a plastic zip bag. He opened the pocket and saw it was filled with water. The plastic bag too was awash, perhaps jostled in there by his fall or by tossing the backpack to the bank. The matches were sodden and useless. He shook his head.

But James, when packing for this journey, had known that anyone going into the woods alone in winter should bring two sources of fire. Just below the bag of matches was a plastic cigarette lighter. It too was full of water. He turned it upside down, shook out a few drops of water, and tried it, but there was no spark. His motions were slowing and his brain was fogging, two signs that he was running out of time. He waved the yellow lighter in the air, put it in his mouth and blew on it, knocked it on his palm. He tried it again. No luck.

He stared into the lowering gray sky and said, "Please." He wasn't sure who the word was aimed at. "Please," he said again. A barred owl swooped down over him, perhaps curious at the clatter coming from the streambank. James felt in that bird the presence of Paul's spirit. He tried the lighter a third time. A small flame flickered.

"Thank you," he said. Grateful in a way he had never been before, flooded with the feeling, which actually warmed his chest, he lit a tuft of dry grass in front of him. As the flame caught, he pulled up more grass and piled it around it. He piled on more. The flame grew higher. His hands were so cold that for a moment he thought the fire was giving off no heat. The smoky warmth hit the blood in his fingers. The fire began to spread across the field, driven by the light wind coming across the swamp and funneled down the little canyon. The flames grew to three or four feet.

James stripped off all his clothes, put his sockless feet back into the cold boots, and stepped into the flames. The iciness in his legs began to dissipate. He held his hands over his genitals. As the flames consumed the meadow grass, he followed them, letting them lick his legs. He began to warm. He moved with the flames until they arrived at the base of the cliff, now two hundred feet from the stream. There was a kind of cleft there, protected from the wind. There, he knelt and piled together small dry sticks, and grabbed some of the burning grass and lit the pile. Still naked but for his boots, he ran back to the beaver dam and gathered every birch twig he could find, because their bark would ignite quickly and help keep the fire going. He piled them on and dashed back again for more. Then a third and fourth time. The fire began to roar.

By this point he was sweating, though still naked in the frozen Maine winter. He retrieved his backpack and brought it near the fire. He emptied it and draped his wet clothes on the sides of the cleft. Even his sleeping bag was half soaked. There would be no rest in that for many hours. He stood in front of the fire and spooned out mouthfuls from his plastic jar of honey. When it was gone, and beginning to warm his stomach, he finally felt safe. Great energy now was followed by an overwhelming wave of fatigue.

He knew he could not let himself close his eyes. He kept the fire going for hours, making trips back to the beaver dam as needed, filling his backpack with the driest, choicest sticks and short logs.

By about 4 A.M., after dozens of trips back to the dwindling dam, he was nearly asleep on his feet. He reached up for the sleeping bag and felt that it was dry. He laid it near the embers, slipped into it, and slept for hours.

When he awoke, he turned to the stream and said, "Brother River, I failed to respect you. I hope I have learned my lesson. You taught me well."

Then he stood and went over to his coat, hanging on the rock wall. In his fatigue he had forgotten about his GPS device. He took it out of the inner coat pocket. It was a wet mess. He took out the batteries, dried them in his shirt, dried the insides of the device as best as possible. Tried it again. It was dead. The topo map printouts he kept with it were even worse, soaked and blurred badly. The ink he had used to mark the location of Camp Cripple had turned into a kind of black teardrop.

He packed up, sighed, and set out hiking again. His elbow and shoulder ached where he had slammed them upward into the icecap of the stream. He began by backtracking to where he had opted the previous day for the easy route following the stream. This time he took the long and hard way, trudging up the mountain and down the other side, sweaty work even in mid-winter. He kept going, aiming for where he guessed the camp was. The day went by and evening came up. He ate most of the rest of his food and curled into his sleeping bag in a near-comatose sleep.

In the morning he continued on, hardly noticing where he was going. The walk now was almost all uphill. The final paragraphs of Gandhi's autobiography came to his mind. "The path of self-purification is hard and steep," the great man had written. "I have still before me a difficult path to traverse. I must reduce myself to zero." When he first had read those words, James had taken them to be metaphoric. Now, as he put one foot in front of the other up the slope, the great one's words seemed to James to be absolutely true and literal. He was just a body walking along, out of energy. Slowly. Slowly. Nearing zero.

After several hours he saw something in front of him but couldn't quite comprehend it. Lines in the way, crisscrossing, blocking his path. Some blue lights below them, still in the distance. His mind resisted recognizing what it was—and what that meant. In his daze, he stared at it and came to understand, after taking it all in for some time, that he had arrived at the fencing of the border between the United States and Canada.

He was dumbstruck. A horrible realization crashed through. Somehow he had missed the camp. He was standing on a remote section of the border. But he didn't know just where he was on that border. He was alone and exhausted. He had no means of communication. For food, only two carrots and half a salami sausage remained. He hadn't packed for a round-trip. He was dependent for heat—and snowmelt water—on a little cigarette lighter that might give out at any time. In his planning, he had never seriously considered that he might miss the camp altogether, because GPS is so accurate that a complete miss would be impossible.

Until he didn't have GPS. And his backup printouts also were useless.

Snowflakes began to fall. It was quiet. He leaned his shoulder against a big hemlock. He wept, quietly. He was numb with cold. Everything in his tired brain and muscles told him that his journey was over, and with it his life. He felt soaked with failure. The pain in his calf, which lately had been just a dull ache, lunged back to life with an explosive stab. Hello, Uncle Weasel, James thought to himself. I guess you win.

His mind, ambling blindly, roamed back through this long, strange year he had experienced. It had begun with those astonishing discussions with Paul about ideas for the march and for the future. They had been exploring something new and different and volatile, and they did their best to honor it by following it where it led them. Then came the march itself, beginning in the fog on the remote coast, and next the heady, sunny days of summer when at times it seemed like one long party. The unexpected success of it, the crowds coming out to cheer, and more importantly, the discussions of new ways to address global overheating. The crash of Paul's death, and the little boy's as well. Blood on the asphalt. The dog in the water. Lying wounded in the middle of Route 1. Falling back to regroup. Figuring out who might form the core of the next step.

"Sorry, Paul," he said aloud. "I shouldn't have let it all end like this." He studied the gray, lowering sky. He saw nothing that gave him hope.

All of that, just to come to this, being lost and alone deep in the woods, leaning against the dark bark of the big hemlock, perhaps miles from anyone who could help him. The year had started with talk about the Earth on fire, but now it seemed likely that it would end with him encased in ice. He had underestimated nature, just as humans always do, he thought. With that bitter regret in mind, he put his head against the hemlock and, still standing, fell asleep. Snow began to accumulate on his head and shoulders. The pain subsided. Now all he felt was cold, penetrating dark blue cold. It was wrapping him for his journey to the afterlife.

51
LIBERATING A SMALL GOD

As James had observed, Red was a good listener. Now, standing outside the main house at Camp Cripple, two things struck his ear. First, he thought he heard a kind of crunching sound in the distance, slow, uneven, like a man or bear struggling through the deep snow. He stood and focused. The second thing he noticed was that the chickadees had stopped singing. They were either watching or hiding from something.

Red cut west toward the sound. He came across fresh tracks in the snow, the boot prints of a man walking alone up toward the border. Red followed them up the slope. He saw something in the distance, either a man or bear, leaning against a hemlock.

"James?" he shouted. He began to run as fast as he could through the snow.

He arrived and shook James by both shoulders. James opened his eyes. The first thing he saw were those big black glasses. "Red?" he said. The young man was wearing a big Alaskan parka.

"Damn, it is you," Red said. "I hardly recognized you." Indeed, snow covered James's head and shoulders. But what was most striking was his face. The right side was blackened with what looked like soot. The left side was bright red. Stress and exhaustion had caused dozens of his shrapnel wounds to reopen. It was so cold that the leaking blood froze before it oxidized, so it remained red. "You in a forest fire, man?" Red asked.

"Sort of."

Red led him down the hill, James's good arm flung over his shoulder, his bad left leg kind of half dragging, half walking.

One of the great advantages of youth is resilience. After a day in bed sleeping and sipping chicken broth whenever he awakened, James emerged from a bedroom and took an hours-long warm bath. After that he seemed almost his old self, just moving at half speed and speaking only when necessary. He wanted someplace to sit and write. He had some ideas about a statement they could issue.

Two days after that, late in the afternoon, he walked outside for the first time since Red had brought him in. He slowly made his way up the hill behind the camp. He wanted to see the spring. He was dismayed to find it contained—to his mind, imprisoned—in a cement box with a brass pipe emerging from the downhill side. The water was flowing, cheerful and fast. He knelt before the outlet and cupped his hands. He drank from the spring's water. He took a cigarette from his coat pocket and laid it on the ground, the best approximation he could make of the old tradition of leaving some tobacco to thank the spirit of the spring.

This reliable, constantly flowing spring was the original reason the POW camp had been located there. To the CIA, it had been a convenience. To Indian hunters for hundreds of years before that, it had been a landmark and a rendezvous point. To them, and to James and his followers, the spring was a sign that the place was holy.

James sat. The outflow of the spring, emerging at a steady 55 degrees, formed a small pool that didn't freeze. It caught and magnified the brilliant orange and yellow light of the lowering sun, and also reflected some of the spruce and fir trees on the far side. He sat on a black rock and contemplated it. He thought about how he'd almost died, not once but twice, in the previous days. He felt like a different person after the two ordeals—not better, not worse, but altered, and perhaps harder. Maybe that was the necessary step for entry into this new phase of the movement. He decided he would change his name to Winter Owl, in thanks for the moment that the flame had sparked and lit the dry swamp grass, giving him life.

Two days later, he led the forty people in the camp up the hill to the spring. He began with a few lines of poetry that had been rattling around in his head. "These are some words from an English shaman," he said, and recited:

A cold coming we had of it
Just the worst time of the year
For a journey, and such a long journey:
The ways deep and the weather sharp,
The very dead of winter.

He looked around at their faces. "Welcome. That English shaman knew that in every ending is a new beginning. We here today, our little band, we are becoming a strange people. By that, I mean alien to the old world we knew. We are saying farewell to the Anglo world, to the ways of Worldburners. I now declare this camp the First Human Refuge of the Farewell Movement," James said. There were grunts of approval all around.

"Farewell," Gutter shouted.

James took up a sledgehammer and handed it to Red. "You saved me the other day," he said. "How about you strike the first blow to liberate the god of our spring?" Red did so, with a mighty swing. Then James struck it several times. The hammer was passed along the line. By the time it got to the end, the spring house was gone. None of them knew a Homeland Security surveillance drone was silently circling high overhead, capturing every moment of their destruction of the spring house.

After the ceremony they walked down the hill and went back to work, preparing for their new lives deep in the woods. There were snares to prepare, meat smokers to construct, curing racks for beaver pelts and deer skins, trails to learn, beaver lodges and deer yards to scout.

Even harder was the thinking that the group was trying to do. There were adjustments to consider: If you plan to live off the land, what happens to your way of life as the climate warms and animals and plants begin moving northward? And as you change, how much modern technology do you keep? Indeed, how much would be available? Would there come a time when ammunition for hunting was unavailable? If so, how to obtain and preserve knowledge of making and using bows and arrows? And how about putting in a store of buckwheat seeds? The old hands knew that crop grows fast, so if a hurricane takes out your regular planting, you can get in buckwheat fast and harvest it before the first snows, and that might get you through the hungry winter that would follow. Knowledge like that could make the difference between success and failure, between life and death.

52
THE STATE HOUSE SIT-IN

Meanwhile, two hundred miles to the south, following Mook's instructions, protesters began arriving one morning at the Massachusetts State House in ones and twos. All ninety-eight were veterans of the summer's march. They greeted each other quietly, familiar comrades joining together in a new action, with shoulder taps and fist bumps. They strolled through, gazing at the portraits on the walls, and trudged up the grand stairs toward the upper chamber. There they gathered before the long mural of "John Eliot Preaching to the Indians."

At precisely noon, all ninety-eight sat down under that insulting painting. Today they were responding to John Eliot, giving his unenlightened descendants a sermon on global heating. "Worldburners, Repent!" began the manifesto they distributed. Mook read aloud their demands, which were reported in Boston as front-page news under the headline: WHAT THE INDIAN ACTIVISTS WANT. They said they would not stop demonstrating until the state of Massachusetts took radical steps to curtail the heating trend. They wanted a 10 percent annual reduction in the use of fossil fuels, to be enforced by the police. They demanded that private vehicles be banned in large cities. Cars running on fossil fuels would only be allowed to operate anywhere else on Tuesdays and Thursdays. Gasoline would only be sold on those days. Gas stations violating those rules would be shuttered immediately. Persistent violators would have their stations closed down and razed.

Most notably, they also wanted large swaths of land set aside for people pursuing post-environmental strategies. These they called not "reservations" but "conservations." The residents would determine who could come on the land. Their focus would be how to live after the societal collapse caused by global overheating. Within fifteen years, these new "conservations" would amount to 20 percent of the land in the state.

The demands were more strident than what the group heading north toward Camp Cripple had in mind, but the Boston contingent remained engaged in American society. There had been a national outpouring after the Wiscasset bombing. They had received vows of support and letters with cash from across the country. Mook carried with him a copy of that photograph of Paul and Lincoln on either side of Moolsem. They were not walking away from the system, they were seeking to change it, to move it toward a post-fossil-burning system. In this sense they were far more optimistic than what James was contemplating. Any optimism James had was left with all that blood on the asphalt of Route 1 in Wiscasset.

Mook had alerted his friends in the media, who photographed almost every move, as did FBI personnel. The agents were struck that they saw few familiar faces among the leaders. It was, they noted, almost as if a new generation had taken over since the killing of Paul Soco the previous summer.

As cable news shows and radio talk shows spread news of the sit-in, people from around the area began bringing them food and sleeping bags. Mook was on the news every night. He enjoyed it thoroughly, but his instructions from James were to sit in for a week, and then get up and leave one day, with no explanation. He followed the instructions to the T.

After exactly seven days, the demonstrators dispersed. Mook put out the word that the next action was under consideration.

"They just evaporated," a puzzled FBI agent reported to his boss, Bulster. "I don't know why."

Later that day, Bulster found out why. It did not make him happy.

53

AGENT BULSTER'S VERY BAD, HORRIBLE DAY

In his Boston office, Bulster bit his lip and, after stalling through two cups of coffee, rehearsing his lines, finally lifted his secure office telephone and called the FBI director. He was dreading this conversation. He had three big, steaming pieces of bad news that he needed to place in the hands of his boss.

"Bottom line up front, sir," he began. "The state house sit-in here? Turns out, that's a diversion." That was the first one off his chest.

"What do you mean?"

"There's a smaller but more important effort we didn't know about. They got another group that has occupied a CIA base up in Maine."

"Hold up," the director sputtered. "A CIA base, *where*?"

"The mountains of Maine, near the Canadian border."

"Do we know why it is there?"

"Long story short, it's been useful in recent years to conduct unsurveilled border crossings, sometimes meetings with foreign officials. Been kept secret for obvious reasons."

"And how did these Indians wandering around the woods happen to find this secret base?"

This was the second moment Bulster had been dreading. "Sir, it appears that we told them, indirectly."

"Repeat that, please."

"What?"

"You heard me. Repeat what you just said."

"Uh, it appears we told them."

"'We told them'? *We?* No, son. There is no 'we' in this occurrence. I know *I* didn't tell them. Did you?"

"No, sir, I did not."

"Well, please stop tap dancing and enlighten me."

Bulster's throat tightened. "We believe, sir, that it was, uh, Ryan Tapia, our agent in the Bangor sub-office. He seems to have informed the governor of the existence of the base, who in turn told the marchers."

"Has this agent been taken into custody?"

"No, sir."

"Why the hell not?"

Now came the third dreaded bit. "Sir, it appears that he hasn't violated any law. Also, if we arrest him, we identify ourselves as the source, which could be, uh, embarrassing to the Bureau."

"Why do you see no cause for legal action against him?"

"It's complicated." Bulster sighed.

"Son, I feel like I'm pulling teeth here," warned the director. "Get on with it."

"Because, uh, the base doesn't formally belong to the Agency. It's on land they've been using since just after World War II. But in fact, it was the property of the state of Maine, and remains so."

"Oh?"

"The Agency liked it that way, keeping it off the books. And the issue of ownership hasn't come up until now."

"And there's something more you're not telling me?"

"I was about to get to that," Bulster said. "We made inquiries with the office of the governor of Maine. They inform us that she, that is, Governor Harrison, invited them to use the property. And that she considers them her guests."

"So we're fucked, completely and utterly? Special Agent Bulster, is that your message for me today? Because I am not enjoying this conversation, not one bit."

"Not quite, sir. There is one thing, one scrap of hope. Homeland Security has had drones overhead. And their imagery shows that a little bit of property destruction has occurred. Not much. Basically, for some unknown reason, they knocked down the housing for the spring on the northeast side of the camp. The camp also is well-stocked with food, and presumably they've been eating that, since there are no roads they could have used to truck goods in there in wintertime."

"So we can get them on destruction of federal property and the theft of food?"

"Yes, sir."

"Good. I can take that to the president." He paused. "We have a cause of action. Put a package of footage together for me to take over to the White House."

President Maloney's reaction to the drone video was immediate. "I don't care who it belongs to. They broke stuff, took it over. I want them out, and I want them charged."

The deputy attorney general, representing the Justice Department, asked the president how he wanted this mission done. "You tell me," the president said. "Form a task force—I don't know, Customs, federal marshals, whatever. The FBI, if they don't fuck it up any more. Just get in there and kick them out."

The White House counsel, sitting in, cleared his throat. "Sir, that takes time, effort, and coordination. That likely will be long and awkward. Consider: What if the Indians take off through the woods? Do we chase them? Not a good look—especially if we don't catch them. They're on turf they know and we don't. And what about the Maine National Guard troops the governor put up there to protect the Indians? Do we confront them? What if the Indians slip across the border? Do we pursue them? Canada won't like that—they are much softer on Indians than we are. It could turn into a monumental clusterfuck, an international incident. We don't need another Waco."

"You got a better idea?" the president asked.

"I think so. And one that will stick it to that pesky governor."

The president smiled. He was often in a truculent mood, but even more than usual today. "Tell me more," he ordered.

"Federalize the National Guard units she put up there to protect her Indian guests."

"I can do that? Just take the Maine Guard units away from her?"

"You can indeed. With the stroke of a pen. Good old Title Ten."

That afternoon, the federal government began to move as orders cascaded down the US military chain of command. Within hours, the commander of the Maine National Guard was radioing to Lieutenant Colonel Liza Chamberlain, the commander of the Maine Guard's 133rd Engineer Battalion. She was deep in the woods at the blocking position she had established about fifteen miles south of Camp Cripple, on the governor's orders to protect the Indians at Camp Cripple from being molested. Now the state's land component commander told her that her unit had been federalized. "Officially, you're in the Army chain of command," he added. "But in fact your orders will be coming from the White House situation room. I can provide you support, but you are no longer under my tactical or operational control."

"Let me get this straight, sir," said Chamberlain, who had a reputation as a smart, no-nonsense officer. "We were sent up here to protect the Indians in that camp, but now I'm going to detain them?"

"Pretty much."

"I don't like it, sir. Not one bit."

"Nor I. But that's the system we work under."

"Any advice?"

"Don't quit. You're smart and sober, and I need a commander with those skills."

"Okay. I won't leave my people, even if I hate the orders."

"Good," the Guard commander said. "Be careful, go slow, and try to avoid violence. And remember: Communicate, communicate, communicate."

54
RYAN IN THE WILDERNESS

The director's email to Bulster, the head of the Boston office, was labeled URGENT FOR IMMEDIATE ACTION. It was scathing.

"The single most important relationship the Bureau has is with the president," the director began. "Anything that erodes his confidence in the Bureau is of utmost concern. To have that damage inflicted from within the Bureau is unforgivable. It demands immediate action, swift and certain. Those who fail to comply with this directive will suffer the most severe consequences."

Bulster flushed as he read the note. It was clear that heads were going to roll. He didn't want his to be one of them. He quickly composed a note of reply and sent it to the director, CC'd to "FBI-Portland" and "FBI-Bangor." It read, in full, "Agent TAPIA (FBI-Bangor) is terminated immediately. It is concluded that said agent grossly mishandled his assignment in the MAINE-IND case. Whether TAPIA was criminally negligent remains to be determined. Pending the outcome of our inquiries, his immediate supervisor, Agent LOVE (FBI-Portland, Maine) is suspended. I will consult with the US Attorney on the legal steps going forward. I understand and emphasize that the utmost discretion is required in handling this situation. There will be no contact with the media or Congress about this situation. Nor will other law enforcement organizations be informed. We will keep this one inside the Bureau family."

Ryan was parking the truck at the federal building in Bangor when he decided to check his email. He read the note from Bulster. Hell of a thing to be fired by a CC'd email, he thought. He paused for a moment to mull his new state. He had thought he would be devastated, but in fact, he felt liberated. "It was time to go," he said out loud in the cab of the truck.

He turned to considering what his next moves should be. I'm a free man, at least for the moment, he thought. But what now? How do I keep faith? I am separated from the Bureau, so where does my duty lie now?

Perhaps because his immediate superior, Jimmy Love, had been suspended, or perhaps because Bulster was rattled and running scared, or perhaps because of Ryan's geographical distance from his bosses, or perhaps because of the exquisite difficulty of the situation—wanting to punish Ryan but not wanting to reveal why—no one had thought to order Ryan to turn in his government pickup truck, badge, and Glock. Or, even more important at the moment, his government radios. So, as Ryan considered the course ahead, he sat in the truck and listened to the National Guard command net. The commanders of two National Guard units were talking. "I only have half my company," said one. "Can you help, give me a squad or two?"

"What's the big emergency?"

"Oh, we just got told we're going in and detaining the Indian protesters at dawn. So we really need to get our troop numbers up. Can you fly some people here?"

"Not sure I'd want to be part of this next chapter of US Army versus the Indians, you know," said the second voice.

"Got no choice, we've been federalized," the first one replied. Ryan thought the man sounded a bit glum.

"The whole Maine Guard has been taken under federal command?" asked the second officer.

"No, just my unit and a couple of others already up there, the engineers."

Ryan sat up and thought about that. *They're going in*, he thought. In just a few minutes, he saw clearly what he had to do. He called a neighbor who lived out on the highway near his Lost Pond house and asked her to feed and walk Moolsem for a couple of days. Then he turned the key on his truck and sped northwest. When he saw a branch of the Bar Harbor Bank along the highway, he stopped at its cash machine and withdrew the maximum it would give him, $800. At a Bangor Savings outlet, he got another $500, the most that one would dispense.

The highway took him northwest into the snowy Maine woods. People here got through the long, dreary winter, lasting from early November to late March, or even early April, by snowmobiling. Their machines were parked in yards and outside bars and grocery stores. He was considering just knocking on a door and making an offer on one when he saw outside a mobile home a snowmobile with a sign propped against it, 4 SALE CHEAP, the orange paint sprayed on plywood. He parked in the muddy driveway and examined the oil-stained, scratched-up, aging black machine. The windshield had a big shatter mark but was still serviceable. It clearly had hauled more than one dead deer in its day. The fronts of the two skis had met their share of frozen rocks. It was likely at least twenty years old.

It would do. He knocked on the front door of the mobile home. A man with a gut bigger than his beard opened it. A rerun of a Patriots game blared on a television in the background. "Yeah," the man said.

Ryan said, "About the Firecat out front."

Guy said, "Thousand nine hundred."

"All I have is thirteen hundred."

"Cash?"

Ryan nodded.

"I'll take it."

Ryan reached into his pocket and handed the man sixty-five twenty-dollar bills, fresh from the ATMs. The man took the wad, but then had a fit of conscience. He looked Ryan up and down. "Mister, don't do it."

"Do what?"

"Do what you're thinking of. Making a run for the border."

"Why would you think—"

"You got that narrow look in your eyes, your pupils all determined. I've seen it before. Guys think getting to Canada, just crossing the border, will solve all your problems. I'm telling you, it won't. I know. They believe in law and order over there more than we ever did here. I got arrested up there once by the Mounties. I mean, they're fucking serious about it. None my business, but what you prolly needa do is go home, call a good lawyer or your minister, have them make an offer to the cops or the IRS or whatever. Saves a lot of trouble down the road. Fewer charges." The man gazed up at the night sky. "And also, it's mid-winter, gonna be about zero or less tonight. You could end up outta gas, outta food, and real dead out there. I've seen it happen."

"You're close, but it's different. I got to go there."

"Okay," the man said, giving up the effort and holding up a hand in resignation. "I tried. This is Maine. What you do is your business alone." The man turned to where coats and hats hung on a wooden pegboard. "But hey, if you're going up there on a night like this, take this snowmobile suit, okay? Free."

It was old, torn, and oil stained, a skid-row version of the Michelin Man. But Ryan appreciated the spirit. He threw it in his truck. "Thanks," he said.

Ryan backed the truck up to a small metal loading ramp. The man drove the Firecat up the ramp and into the bed of the truck. As he climbed down, he had a second twinge of conscience. "Also, you should know the title on this machine is kinda shifty," he said. "Truth be told, I took it from the dooryard of an asshole next town over who owes me money and won't cough up. I don't think he even knows it's gone yet. So maybe be careful about that."

There's always more to learn about life in Maine, Ryan thought as he drove away. When he saw the glowing orange sign of an Aubuchon hardware store a few miles down the road he parked. Using his credit card, he bought three red plastic jerry cans, three bungee cords, padded gloves, and a woolen ski mask. At the Irving station next door, he gassed up the cans and bought a handful of energy bars. He knew that the FBI would be able to track down the credit card usage within twenty-four hours, but by then it wouldn't matter. All that was important was what he did between now and tomorrow's sunrise.

In the parking lot, he called James's cell. There was no connection. He wasn't surprised. Even if James was in cell range, the federal government would be jamming his communications.

Next he called Solid Harrison on her private cell number. He hadn't used that number since she had dumped him. She picked up and said quickly, "Ryan, I don't have time right now—"

"Because they federalized the Guard?" he interrupted.

"Yes," she said. He told her about the plan he'd overheard to detain the Indian occupiers at dawn.

"Oh my," she said. "I need to think on that." She did for a moment, then said, "What are you going to do?"

"I'm going in," he said. "Not as anything official. I've been fired. I feel responsible. I think my telling you about the place up there got this situation started."

"They haven't federalized my aviation unit, last I checked. I will meet you there," she said.

❖

Solid made some calculations. Then she called her counterpart in Quebec. She wanted to know if the Indian marchers were welcome on his side of the border.

"Absolutely, Madame Governor," said the provincial premier. In fact, he told her, his ministry of Indigenous affairs had been monitoring the news of the marchers and already had located a place for them just on the Canadian side of the border. "There's a firefighters' base in the woods, Camp Levesque, about three kilometers northwest of the line. It is elementary, but has barracks there, stoves, running water." He added that he would dispatch an official from the ministry who would be waiting for her at the border gate. "Watching President Maloney, we expected this to come to crisis at some point," he explained. "He likes crisis, especially if it gives him a spotlight. He is a very crude man, I think."

"I agree," she said.

❖

In his truck, Ryan studied the official government maps. The Camp Cripple area on the map was quite blank, except for some swamp markings. The nearest feature listed was Hardhead Mountain, a few miles to the east. Ryan quickly traced out a route and headed northwest in the truck. After thirty miles more through deep woods, mainly flat, he turned off the tarmac onto a plowed gravel road. Fifteen minutes later it became dirt and was unplowed. He drove through the deepening snow until he came to a deep washout. The road had run out. He eased the pickup down the slope until its front fender came to rest at the bottom. He climbed out and checked that his back gate was close to the dirt. He lowered the gate and drove the old snowmobile onto the snow-covered dirt road. Then he put on the snowmobile suit and the other gear.

Aboard the Firecat, he turned northwest. The aging 700cc two-stroke engine gobbled up gas, especially on the uphill. For two hours he chugged along the track as it dwindled into a hunter's path. When he stopped to refuel, his handheld Garmin told him he was just fifteen miles from the border. He drove the wheezing machine up steepening slopes.

The Firecat jolted over a big root. On impact, the headlight went dark. Ryan stopped for a few minutes to let his eyes adjust to the night. Between the snow and the moon, he could see well enough to travel. But surprisingly soon, the snow buggy wanted more gas. He had just one can left.

It turned out not to matter because, when he was just three miles from the border, the old warhorse sputtered to a stop and gave out. It had fuel, but wouldn't restart. *Sorry, boss,* it seemed to say as it sagged and cooled. It was so still Ryan could hear the quiet hiss of its engine heat escaping into the cold night.

He dismounted and began walking. His GPS said it was three miles to the border. But the device didn't say how hard three miles through snow was, even if the deer and moose had packed it a bit. The wind out of the north was picking up. Yet after one mile of walking uphill through the snow, Ryan was sweating. After two he had taken off the wool hat, tied it to his chest. After three he had peeled off the entire top of the snowsuit and was wearing it flopping behind him.

The border was marked every two hundred yards by small solar-powered low blue lights, not unlike the ones that line the sides of airport runways. When he got there, he sat down below one to rest and think. He looked around and noticed that of all the damn things in the world, there were four rows of four gravestones. He flashed his cell phone light on them. The surnames it illuminated were German—"Horst," "Kafka," "Gauss" were the ones he could see. At the top of each stone was an iron cross with a swastika in the center. It was otherworldly. Where the hell was he?

He heard a beating sound above and turned toward the south. There was a light in the sky. The one light separated into two. It was two helicopters. They landed not near Camp Cripple but farther up, closer to the border, almost where the border gate was. He suspected that Solid had arrived.

55
SOLID AT THE GATE

S olid jumped down from her National Guard Black Hawk, its rotors still swinging slowly above her, and walked the two hundred yards to the border gate. It was an infernal scene. Helicopter engines gave off a low whine while on idle. Generators were grinding away to power National Guard communications. People in Humvees were revving motors and talking on radios. One Humvee had its front bumper up against the gate to prevent it from being pushed open from the Canadian side. A Canadian official, a dapper young man in his early thirties, stood just on the other side of that blocked gate, his face perplexed as he watched the Americans gather.

Solid surveyed the knot of people standing on the American side of the gate amid all the noise in the middle of the night. "I am Solid Harrison, the governor of the state of Maine. I believe I am the senior government official here," she said, as loudly as she could. They leaned their heads in to hear her. "I am asking—not ordering—that we begin by reducing the level of noise. Please." She turned to her pilot, standing at her side, and asked her to signal the crews of the two Black Hawks she had borrowed from the National Guard, "Moose 1" and "Moose 2," to cut their engines. She asked the Canadian official to have the generators and lights on his side cut off for a few minutes. He nodded in agreement. She asked the federalized National Guard officers, "Can you turn off your Humvees, at least for a few minutes?" Finally she asked the federal people—the Customs and Border Patrol officials now attached to the Guard unit—to do the same with their generators and lights.

In that moment, Solid had done something small but almost magical. She had reasserted human control of the moment, taking it back from the machines that had been creating an environment of high-pitched noise that made it difficult to think clearly. In that stillness, nature reemerged. The group stood there in near-silence. As their ears adjusted, they could hear the cold wind in the needles of the pine trees—and, to be sure, a few miles down the hill, the faint whine of the National Guard generators and trucks encircling Camp Cripple. Above they could see a stunning array of stars, with more light than darkness, the Milky Way flung across the sky like a blanket of hope. Solid hoped to herself that they now could deal with each other as humans.

She asked the officials present to gather around the still-warm hood of the Humvee blocking the gate. "Whatever happens," she said in a normal voice, "let's remember we are all comrades or allies, all essentially on the same side." They all agreed in various ways. "Now," she continued, surprising even herself, "let's join hands in prayer." The Canadian representative, hiding his surprise, reached through the wire of the American gate and took her hand. The Americans were so different, he thought—plump, informal, and surprisingly religious.

Heads turned to watch her. She was making it up as she went along. She had not been raised in a religious household and didn't know a lot of prayers. But she remembered the beginning of one: "Our Father, who art in heaven, hallowed be thy name," she began.

The others joined in, their voices a low rumble. "Thy kingdom come, thy will be done, on Earth as it is in Heaven."

The voice of Colonel Chamberlain, the National Guard commander, led the next phrase. She was being affected by the moment. "Give us this day, our daily bread," she said in a strong, clear voice. "And forgive us our trespasses, as we forgive those who trespass against us."

Solid looked at the circle of government officials and said even louder, "And lead us not into temptation, but deliver us from evil."

To her surprise, the Border Patrol official, a man in his late forties, joined in, saying in a thick, emotional voice, "For thine is the kingdom and the power and the glory, forever."

"Amen," said five voices.

"Now," Solid said, taking in the faces reset a bit by the prayer, "let's talk."

Into this quiet moment came the crunching of Ryan's footsteps, moving down the ridge, following the blue lights of the fence line.

They all turned to look at this ragged figure entering their colloquy. "Agent Tapia?" asked the official from Homeland Security. "I thought you were being detained."

"Apparently not." Ryan smiled, wiping the sweat from his face.

"Also I think FBI Boston BOLO'd you," Homeland Security added. "Stated we should be wary of erratic behavior."

"Bolo?" Solid asked, unfamiliar with the law enforcement habit of turning an abbreviation into a word.

"Be On the Look Out," Ryan explained. He turned to Homeland Security. "Last time I checked, it isn't a crime to be erratic."

"Well, you were fired, so you have no standing to be here," Homeland Security said.

Solid intervened. "In fact, you're talking to my new assistant commissioner for federal affairs," she said. And she smiled. Ryan did too. Solid took a step back to make a space for him in their circle around the hood of the Humvee. Once again, she was a mental step ahead of those around her.

Solid turned to Colonel Chamberlain, who stood ramrod straight with an expression of calm moderation on her face. Before Solid could speak, the colonel said, "Ma'am, to begin, I need just to remind you, my unit has been federalized. I currently report to the Army chain of command. That means I cannot legally take orders from you."

"Yes," Solid said. "I understand that. But do you know the aviation unit that flies me has not been federalized and remains under my command and control?"

"Yes, that is my understanding," the Guard officer acknowledged. "I also need to inform you that my unit, acting under orders, has surrounded the camp down the mountain held by the Indian occupiers. We have a one hundred percent perimeter. There is no way in or out for them."

"Thank you," Solid said softly. She turned to the Canadian official standing just on the other side of the gate. He was dressed, under his parka, in a gray business suit, a white dress shirt, and a knitted black wool tie. He appeared to be absolutely intrigued by this scene of American officials meeting in the middle of the night deep in the Maine woods. "And you are?" she asked in English.

"Madam, I am Christian St.-Georges, the Province of Quebec's deputy assistant minister for Indigenous affairs," he said. "My premier has instructed me to be at your service."

"Good," she said. "I have some questions." She switched to French, betting that none of the federal officials would speak it. Those who had learned foreign languages in college or the military likely would have Spanish, Arabic, Russian or, if very smart, Chinese.

"L'offre tient-elle touhours?" she asked. [Translation: Does the offer still stand?]

Monsieur St.-Georges nodded eagerly through the fencing wire. "Oui, l'amnistie, la terre et tous les privileges de chasse et de peche d'une bande honoree des Premieres Nations. Et nous voulons qu'ils participant au regard du gourvernement sur la voie a suirve face au réchauffément climatique." ["Yes—amnesty, land, and all the hunting and fishing privileges of an honored First Nation band. And we want them to participate in the government's examination of the way forward with global warming."]

"Est-ce que ca va si nous prenons l'avion pour le camp?" [Is it alright if we fly to your camp?]

"Comme vous voulez," he said with a smile and a small bow. He was impressed by her grasp of the situation and that she had already thought her way to a solution. He extended his smartphone. "Voici le GPS de l'aire d'atterrissage." [As you wish. Here is the GPS of the landing area.]

She gestured to her pilot, who took the phone and wrote down the coordinates. The federal officials eyed this all suspiciously. Solid turned to them. "Just being diplomatic," she explained to them.

She added, "I like these Canadians. Now I am going to fly down to our camp."

The Homeland Security man—Solid suspected he really was CIA—held up his hand. "Governor, I can't recommend that. In the strongest terms, my people think that is a bad idea."

Solid dismissed him quickly. "Thank you for your advice. But I'm the governor, and that camp is under my control. It still belongs to the state of Maine, I believe. Even if the Guard unit down there doesn't."

"You've been warned," he said haughtily. She understood that he was washing his hands of whatever mayhem ensued. She could almost see him rehearsing his testimony for a congressional committee. "Mister Chairman, I advised the governor in the strongest possible terms that it was unwise to go into the Indian encampment. She disregarded my warning and, in my professional opinion, didn't really even consider it."

Solid and Ryan climbed up into the lead Black Hawk, Moose 1. Moose 2 followed it into the air. The flight down the hillside to the besieged camp was a two-minute hop.

Solid was first out of the helicopter, followed by Ryan and the pilot, Captain Bala. They leaned forward to brace against the arctic wind whipping down the valley from due north. At the edge of the landing pad, Rock stood in their way, his big square face not welcoming at all. Behind him stood Red, who had learned to imitate Rock's habitual frown. Both of them held their arms crossed in front of them.

"Ma'am," Ryan said, standing at Solid's shoulder, "you remember Rock. He was chief of security in last summer's march."

Solid extended her hand. Rock did not take it. He was wondering if her telling James about this supposed refuge in the woods had been a setup after all. "You are not welcome here," he said. "You come here uninvited. This is not a place for you World-burners." He turned to Ryan: "The president says you spied on us." Then at Solid: "The soldiers you sent to protect us, they are now surrounding us and jamming our cell phones."

"We are not your enemy," Solid said.

Rock frowned, shook his head slowly, and said, "I see you are talking, yet all I hear is the hissing of snakes."

"Listen harder," Solid said sharply, almost as an order. "There are people nearby who would do you harm. They are going to take this camp by force. We need to see James."

"I can give him any message you have," Rock said.

"Right now, we don't have the time for that sort of back and forth," Solid said. "The Army is getting pushed to move. Soon."

Rock considered that. "I will bring you to him. But as prisoners." Rock waved his right hand and Red and another man came forward to wrap red yarn loosely around the wrists of Solid and Ryan, giving them symbolic handcuffs. They did not do so to the pilot, showing her deference because she was brown skinned.

Ryan cringed. "That's a mistake," he said. "You know they're watching us with night scopes and drones. They'll think you're taking us hostage. You're giving them an excuse to come in."

"So be it," Rock said coolly. He no longer trusted a word Ryan said.

Rock walked them over to the main house. Behind them, Red, heeding Rock's example of taking a hard line, hauled the end of a fifty-foot-long logging chain to the closest helicopter and looped it around the front left wheel strut. The other end was tethered to a park bench of concrete and wood at the end of the landing pad.

❖

Colonel Chamberlain, observing the drone video feed from inside her Humvee, discussed what she was seeing with her chain of command. "I'm worried," she said.

She didn't realize that President Maloney was in the White House situation room and monitoring the radio traffic. "So am I," Maloney said. "I think it's time to go in."

"Is that an order, sir?" the chairman of the Joint Chiefs asked.

"Yes, it is," the president said. "Take them."

"Yes, sir," Colonel Chamberlain confirmed. She turned toward her XO in the adjacent Humvee and circled an index finger in the air, signaling that it was time to mount up and move. Then she flashed her open right hand twice, signifying "ten." They would drive down the mountain and cross the line in that many minutes.

❖

At the camp, Solid, Ryan, and Captain Bala were taken inside the main house, where James sat, bleary-eyed. He ignored Solid and Ryan, his anger at them welling up as he considered everything that had happened that had led to this "refuge" in the woods that was now feeling like a trap. He addressed Bala, the pilot, and said, "I don't talk to white people. But I can talk to you." Looking over James's shoulder, Ryan noticed a frame on a small table that held the photograph of little Lincoln Smith sitting with Moolsem and Paul, when the boy's father had taken him to meet the march's leaders. It had only been last summer, but to Ryan it seemed an age ago. Next to the photo was a candle. He wondered if this was a kind of altar for James, to help him remember what the cause was about.

Captain Bala, speaking quickly, explained that the Army Guard units that Solid had assigned had been taken over by the federal government and were about to come in and detain them all. "I think we have about five minutes to get you and your people out of here," she concluded.

"To where?"

"The Canadian government has cleared you and your people for landing on the other side. We have the coordinates. The governor will ride along as a guarantor."

James understood the urgency, that a decision was required instantly. He closed his eyes, thought for a moment, and then nodded. He slipped the framed photograph into his coat pocket, then picked up a bullhorn and walked outside.

From somewhere outside the camp, the National Guard fired an illumination flare high into the air. It descended slowly toward the camp, bathing the entire area in a pale yellow light. It reminded

James of the aura that he had seen over Paul. Now it was cast over the entire camp, signifying a fateful moment. It was time to take a leap.

Whether that leap was off a cliff or into the future, James did not know. He made a decision and pulled the red "squeal" trigger on his bullhorn twice to get the attention of everyone in the camp, but most of them already were standing around the landing pad. "Everyone, into the helicopters," he ordered. They trotted to the waiting aircraft and jumped in, landing on top of each other, sorting out their seating as the rotors began turning overhead.

56
THE FLIGHT OF THE THIRTY-SEVEN

Captain Bala strapped in. Her copilot was wide-eyed as the Indians piled into the two Black Hawks. "This is a lot of people," the copilot said. "More than twenty pax in each bird? That's way over regulation."

Bala had weighed that. "It's just five minutes. And they have no gear. So it's not much heavier than an infantry squad going into combat with a full combat load"—that is, weapons, radios, water, food, medical gear, and ammunition. James, sitting behind the copilot, glanced over at Captain Bala. He saw a red aura glowing over her helmeted head. He relaxed and closed his eyes. Fate was with her.

"Moose 2, you go first," Bala said into her radio microphone. As she did, a tan National Guard bulldozer breached the wire on the south side of the camp near the landing pad. The other Black Hawk arose and flew northwest into the night. As with Moose 1, it was so crowded that people were sitting in the doorways, their feet sticking out into the cold night air.

Simultaneously, the Humvee pushed through the locked gate, followed by another that had four long antennas. In that second

Humvee, Colonel Chamberlain, the commander, reported on her command net, "We're in." Seven more Humvees were behind her.

The president, listening in from the White House's subterranean situation room, turned to the chairman of the Joint Chiefs and said, "Just who is that woman?"

"That's the task force commander, Colonel Chamberlain, Maine National Guard," said the chairman.

"Interesting," the president commented unhappily. It had never occurred to him that women were running things out there. He had liked it better when men had run everything. He didn't understand women, especially when they held power. That scared him.

Bala launched her own aircraft, Moose 1. Its tail rose and then its nose. It moved forward and upward to an altitude of about fifty feet. At that point, the logging chain on its left wheel snapped taut. In the hurry of the moment, no one had noticed it.

The aircraft pitched forward, dangerously. Its left side was being pulled over almost thirty degrees. To those inside the aircraft, it felt like it was capsizing. Eyes widened as hands grabbed for anything—the nylon mesh or the seats, the metal protuberances on the sides of the cabin, or just an arm or a leg next to them. Two of the men sitting in the port door, Pigtoe and Big Duck, tumbled out, so suddenly that they departed wordlessly. They barely had time to scream. They hit the frozen ground hard and died instantly.

Bala's years of training kicked in. She called for full military power from the two turboshaft engines to keep it moving forward. The Black Hawk, a well-designed machine, responded well. The full three thousand horsepower of the two engines wailed and roared. That burst of power hit the chain and then the bench. First the end of the bench that held the chain came flying loose from the earth, and then the other. The Black Hawk suddenly lurched forward and gained altitude as the entire cement bench rose into the air below the aircraft, swinging back and forth. Bala eased the throttle and the aircraft settled a bit, dragging the bench below and behind it, sometimes on the ground, sometimes a few feet in the air.

A jagged, careening sling load is a helicopter pilot's worst nightmare. Handle it wrong and it will hit blades, either the ones above the aircraft or the smaller ones on the tail. Either way, that would be the end of the story. Every atom of your brain screams at you to put the aircraft down—but do that too fast and the sling load could swing up or back.

Bala, struggling to maintain control, didn't look at where the aircraft was heading. In fact, it was flying toward the Army column coming down the mountain and through the camp's gate. The bench hanging from the helicopter sideswiped the lead Humvee, the one that had breached the gate. That impact set the bench spinning wildly. Next it hit the command vehicle's windshield sideways, breaking the glass but not penetrating the cab. The bench, shattering into chunks of concrete as it went, dragged over the top of the vehicle, scraping off most of its antennas. "We're hit," Colonel Chamberlain said. Her radio went silent.

Above Chamberlain's Humvee, the aircraft, stunned by the impact against the vehicle, stopped almost dead in the air, as if preparing to fall from the sky on its own volition. Bala tipped the nose forward and again pushed the throttle to full military power—not healthy for the engines, but absolutely required to keep the aircraft's six tons of metal and plastic aloft. The engines screamed and the aircraft began moving forward again. The remains of the cement bench hit the next Humvee, and again the Black Hawk paused in midair, as if again contemplating dropping from the sky. Again she tipped and powered the aircraft forward. It was more daunting than any simulation she ever had flown. Her copilot was staring at her wide-eyed, mouth agape.

On the ground, Colonel Chamberlain got out of the Humvee with her combat rucksack in hand. First she quickly made sure that the wounded were being tended to. She shouted to the commander of the following Humvee, "No shooting. Safeties on. Pass the word." The last thing she wanted was to kill American citizens. That was not what she had signed up for.

She took out her handheld radio, pressed transmit, and said, "Jane, this is Six Actual. Patch me through to the White House and ask for the situation room, would you?"

In that room, the president said, "What the hell just happened? Are they firing on our guys? No one told me that would happen!" His eyes widened and he gasped for air. He was close to panic, and looking for someone to blame.

The infrared imagery from the drone circling overhead showed the Humvees stopped, and people getting out to get medical help to their injured. "No one's shooting," Colonel Chamberlain responded over the radio.

With most of the concrete gone from the bench, and its wooden slats falling away willy-nilly, the Black Hawk suddenly gained altitude, shooting upward almost two hundred feet. Several passengers vomited. Someone in the back of the cabin wailed in fear.

Bala, flying on instinct and adrenaline, eased the power and calmed the stressed aircraft. She began to fly it up the mountain toward the border. As she did, the liberated chain came whipping up toward the aircraft. Its end lashed through the starboard door and wrapped itself around the head of Daylights, who was in the middle of the open door. Bloody and unconscious, he fell out. The flapping chain next whipped backward and knocked out a chunk of a horizontal flap on the tail. The Black Hawk rolled to the right. Bala, surprisingly softly, instructed her copilot to "Fly the stabilator manually, okay?" The copilot, wide-eyed and white-faced, croaked out, "Will do." He was not sure he was going to survive this flight.

Ryan, who had been sitting just behind the pilot, ventured a quick glance out the port side and saw the bloody chain waving in the cold air. He leaned back as it moved toward him. He watched a section of it fly through the open door. He grabbed it. Another man, seeing his effort, leaned in to help. Ryan wrapped the end of the chain around the aluminum tubing of the leg of the nearest seat. As he did, the chain snagged a tree branch and went taut, catching the thumb of Ryan's left hand between the chain and the seat leg. The seat leg snapped, its broken shard knife sharp. As the tree branch broke off, the chain went slack again, but still was tied to the bottom of the broken seat leg. Ryan pulled his hand away and saw, to his surprise, that the last joint of his thumb remained in the tangled metal mess of the chain and seat leg. It had been neatly and totally severed in the moment it took for the chain to tighten and loosen against the sharp broken seat leg. He felt no pain—yet. He stared as the little radial arteries on either side of his thumb began spurting small jets of blood. A man sitting next to him took off a scarf, bent Ryan's fingers forward over the stump of the thumb, and wrapped Ryan's left hand in the scarf. Below the aircraft, the blue lights of the border zipped by.

Bala saw the blinking red light marking the landing zone and came in fast. She wasn't sure where the logging chain was and didn't want it swinging up into the rotors or against the tail again. She brought the Black Hawk in quick and hard, almost dropping it down vertically from fifteen feet. It hit the frozen tarmac with a screech as the front struts snapped, bounced six feet in the air, and came to a sudden rest. As soon as it did, Bala cut the engines, unsnapped her aviation safety belt, jumped out the door, staggered a few steps, and sank to all fours in the snow. Despite the cold, she was covered in sweat. It dripped from her face as she vomited.

Ryan walked over to her. "You need help?"

She lifted her head and shook it. "That was not fun," she said.

Still on the helicopter, James opened his eyes, stood, and proceeded to make sure everyone was getting out. As the last one to exit, he was met by Monsieur St.-Georges, the Canadian official. They shook hands. "Welcome to Canada," St.-Georges said.

The crew chief of the other Black Hawk, acting as the senior noncommissioned officer present, counted the total number of passengers dismounting onto Canadian soil. He told the governor, "We have the aircrews, you and your aide, and—lemme see—thirty-seven arrivals."

Solid nodded. She thanked Monsieur St.-Georges then turned to James. Part of being a leader is sensing the right thing to say. "I think you lost two or three people on that flight," she said. "I am sorry."

"I don't think it was your fault," James said. "But thank you."

"I'll be in touch," Solid said. "And please, a thought to keep in mind, from a book I read: Isolation is not necessarily independence."

James gave a half smile, but his eyes brightened. "I read that same book—by Fergus Bordewich! But in this case, I think isolation might be the necessary first step, separating ourselves from an Anglo world that is in denial of the crisis it is facing. Our little band is just seeking shelter from the man-made storm."

Solid turned to Captain Bala. "How are we?"

Bala said, "My helo will need to stay here for repairs. So we can all ride in Moose 2."

"Okay," Solid said. "Let's go." Moose 2 lifted off for the quick trip back to the United States. Below the open port door, Ryan saw James, gathering his men together.

❖

When the helicopter clattered eastward over the ridge and the night grew quiet, James turned toward the moon and bowed his head to the spirit of Paul. "You did it," he said out loud. "You rode the thirty-seven horses." He turned back toward the group and led them on the next step in their journey—which in this case was just a few yards to the three-room building on the edge of the landing zone where they would be served hot potato leek soup. In the morning, they would turn to building their new world.

❖

In the air, Solid leaned forward and spoke to the pilot, who nodded. The Black Hawk landed at the Camp Cripple pad. Solid got out and found Colonel Chamberlain, who remained a bit wary, even grim-faced.

The colonel saluted her smartly, but quickly said, "Ma'am, I'm still on federal duty."

"Understood," Solid said. "I just wanted to check on you and your people. How are you doing?"

Chamberlain visibly relaxed. "Doing good," she said. "A bit roughed up. Nothing critical. But you know, we call that good combat training."

"Do you need anything? Medevac? Supplies?"

"So far, nothing urgent," said Chamberlain. But she got the message: The governor of Maine was not at all angry with her, or inclined to blame her for the confrontation. "Ma'am, for your situational awareness, we have informed the White House that the area is secured. My people witnessed three bodies fall from the

266

helicopter and are collecting the remains and will convey them to the county coroner."

"Call me when you get home, okay?" Solid said. She handed her a card. "This is my cell."

Chamberlain saluted again, and Solid climbed back into the waiting helicopter. While it flew to Augusta, most of the others on board slept. Solid took notes on a yellow legal pad. She was thinking through her next move. How would the president react, and what should she say?

57
SOLID'S PRESS CONFERENCE

When the governor's helicopter landed in Augusta, the sun was coming up to the east of the runway. Standing on the tarmac, Ryan asked Solid for a word. "Thanks for the quick help on the border, but I don't think it's the right time for me to move to another government job," he said. She shook his good hand. She was about to say something when an aide to the governor interrupted to give her a printout of a news story. She stood on the runway and read it.

❖

At the airport's little car rental office, Ryan got a car and began the drive north. He turned on the FM radio in the car and found the Maine NPR network. An announcer was saying that she expected the governor of Maine to begin a press conference in just a few moments and that it would be carried live. "We are hearing there was some kind of international incident on the Canadian border last night and that the governor was present at it," the NPR announcer said, a bit quizzically. "The White House a few minutes ago issued a statement denouncing her and her support for the Indian movement."

❖

Solid hadn't expected reporters and photographers to be waiting, but there were about twenty who had set up in the airport's passenger lounge, which was no bigger than a good-sized residential living room. Solid looked around at the waiting reporters, then spoke. "I've just returned from the Indian movement's camp near the border," she began. "There were three deaths by mishap there last night. Several National Guard soldiers suffered minor wounds. Everything there is now peaceful. I have met with the commander of the Maine National Guard Task Force, Colonel Chamberlain, and she has the situation well in hand. She was put in a difficult position and handled it with strength and grace. I think she is a fine commander. I also want to thank the government of the province of Quebec for acting with speed and prudence. And now, I am ready to answer any questions you may have."

The Maine NPR reporter began, "Governor, in your statement just now, you didn't mention President Maloney. He has just called you 'soft on Indians' and 'part of the problem, not part of the solution.' Do you have any comment on that?"

Solid: "I've been busy on the border and in the air, so I haven't seen the entire statement. But I would say that this country has been hard on Indians for too long. Just read the history. This movement isn't asking for the moon. They want to figure out a path to the future. I admire that. To my knowledge, the March to the Future hurt no one. Not a single person. It has violated some property rights. But to me, humans come before property. It was others against them who have caused deaths, both to the Indian marchers and to Mainers. Let us not forget that.

"At any rate, you know, maybe it is time to be soft on Indians. Hell, maybe it's time for us all to be softer on each other. Is kindness a bad thing?"

The *Portland Express* reporter shouted out, "What about the president's personal attack on you?"

Solid had thought about the White House problem during the flight. She had expected a personal attack and had decided to say what she really thought. "First, my feelings aren't really important in this context. Keep in mind, people died last night up on the border. My condolences go out to their families. Let's think first about their feelings, okay? And we have some wounded soldiers to tend to.

"But if you still want to know what I think of comments like the president made, well, it pisses me off, to be honest. This was not a violent situation until he made it one. There didn't need to be a physical confrontation. I put it on him."

"But he says you encouraged the Indians to act this way—" the reporter countered.

"To be clear, I don't agree with everything they do. But I think they generally are on the right track. They are asking the right questions. And by helping us seriously think through climate change they are doing more, so much more, than anything the president or his administration have done. So I would say it's the president who is being the problem."

A *Boston Globe* reporter looked up from her phone. "He also just tweeted, like about five seconds ago, that he is watching this press conference live and he thinks you are, I quote, 'a noisy lady who should shut up.'"

Solid shook her head slowly in dismay. The photographers' cameras whirred and their lights flared. This, they knew, was the shot that would be at the top of websites across the internet within minutes. She put her hands on her hips and said slowly, "Well, I have a lot of respect for the presidency, but not for the man currently holding the job. Comments like that make me think he's a big baby," Solid said. "But where does that get us?"

That was enough, she decided. She had said what she thought, and in the process had regained the narrative. Some of the headlines would be about the president being a "big baby," which was fine with her. Her phrase about being pissed off was red meat for the TV pundits, who could chew endlessly on whether such language was appropriate and what it meant and whether she was material for national politics. Together, she thought, her two sound bites should put the president on the back foot.

Ryan smiled to himself as he drove north on Interstate 95 past Waterville, listening to the radio. He had known her when. Sure, she had dumped him. But he was still a fan. The stump of the severed joint on his left thumb was throbbing harder. He parked at a "doc in the box" urgent care office at the next exit. After they stitched up his hand and gave him some painkillers, he walked over to a Dunkin' Donuts and ate four glazed donuts with a gigantic cup of sweetened, creamy coffee. It tasted like warm coffee ice cream and was the perfect thing to drink after the night he had just experienced.

Around kitchen tables in Indian homes across Maine that winter, stories began to circulate about a mysterious and powerful one-eyed

Indian named Winter Owl. When Mister Bear chased him onto a frozen lake, Winter Owl fell through the ice. There he hid out for a day and a night, breathing bubbles of air trapped under the surface. When Mister Bear gave up searching for him, Winter Owl climbed out of the lake, snuck up behind Mister Bear and jumped on him, then rode that big bear all the way to Canada. Children's eyes grew big at the tale. "Tell it again," they would say.

EPILOGUE

FOUR MONTHS LATER

R yan set up the coffee machine, then lit the candle at the altar to his dead family. "I think I handled a difficult situation as best I could," he said to them. "Marta, I think you'd be proud of me. At least I hope that."

He took his coffee to the kitchen table and turned on his laptop. He looked out the window at the gray surface of Lost Pond, where the long Maine winter's ice was finally beginning to break up. He opened up the site of the Portland newspaper. The top story caught his eye. It read:

> BANGOR (Wire story)—The leader of a breakaway group of Native Americans announced that he is claiming a strip of the U.S.-Canadian border as a "human refuge."
>
> In a press conference given over a computer system from an undisclosed location, James Reveur, who is known within his Farewell Movement as "Winter Owl," said that he and aides have entered discussions with the governments of Quebec and Maine about establishing a

new "international zone" of refuge as a place for Native Americans to experiment with ways of living with accelerating climate change. The name "Farewell" connotes the group's stated determination to no longer live as part of modern Industrial Age culture, which it considers doomed.

Reveur declined to disclose the size of the proposed strip but said it could be as big as two thousand square miles. At least initially, he said, all those allowed to move into the area and live there would be hand-picked by his organization.

Press secretaries for the governments of the province of Quebec and the state of Maine both acknowledged that they had entered into discussions with Reveur's group, but said that no conclusions had been reached.

In a statement, Maine Gov. Solid Harrison (D) said that she is open to new approaches to dealing with climate overheating, "because we certainly aren't going to get them from the cement head in the White House." Harrison has been outspoken in her criticism of President Maloney, spurring speculation that she is eyeing a move into national politics, although still in her first term as governor of Maine.

The Boston Globe also carried an op-ed piece under the byline "Winter Owl." In its most striking passage, the essay envisaged a return to seasonal migration.

We hope to revive the traditional cycle of movement with the seasons.

In winter, we will hunt deep in the woods for moose, deer, and beaver. In late winter, we will tap the maple trees for sugar. In the spring, we will plant beans, corn, and squash. Then we will camp by the waterfalls on the rivers to fish for alewives, shad, and salmon. If they are sparse, we can move south to the coast—wherever it is, as sea levels rise—and live on duck and goose eggs, as well as clams, mussels, oysters, and lobsters.

We plan to spend summers and autumns there on the coast, where the wind keeps down the bugs. There we will fish for porpoise, sturgeon, flounder, and halibut, and take some seals and the occasional whale, and hunt the coastal islands. In the summer we also will gather blueberries, raspberries, and blackberries. In August some of us will return to the waterfalls to harvest the vegetables and to collect the eels, rich with fat and also with skins good for making durable rope. In the woods we also will gather hazelnuts, beechnuts, walnuts, and acorns. Others of us will remain on the coast to collect ducks and geese for their meat and feathers, both of which will help us in the coming winter.

In every one of these instances, we will deal with the animals with gratitude and reverence. I believe, for example, that every single time a loon sings, it is praying—and I join it in doing so.

We hope that by the time Western society collapses under the stress of climate change, with flash floods, dust storms, algae blooms, massive wildfires throwing off suffocating smoke, and other physical reactions of the Earth leading to global epidemics, food shortages, mass migrations, and governmental breakdowns, we will have been able to establish a new mode of living that truly merits the use of the word "sustainable."

To give us space in which to establish these new modes of existence, we are asking that the state set aside ample land reserves for our band at selected spots among the mountains, rivers, lakes, and coast. We are suggesting that these areas will become known as the University of Maine's Centers for Surviving Global Heating. As for the remainder of the North Woods, we ask that we be given a stewardship role, monitoring the use of the entire area.

Aside from that affiliation, we want as little to do with the Anglo world as possible. We believe their world—honestly, your world—is dying. What our ancestors knew may save us, but it cannot save most of you. We want to focus on building the next world, one that has no place for most of you. Maybe in a generation, we can talk. But we can't save you. That's a harsh verdict, but I think it's a true one. It is not unlike what we have heard from you for the last four hundred years. We may be wrong. We ask you to respect our choice and our effort to find out.

Ryan walked out onto his back porch and looked northwest, toward the camp up on the border where James Winter Owl was seeking to blaze a new path. He came to attention, smiled, and saluted. "Good luck," he said.

Then he and Moolsem walked into the woods on a path Ryan only recently had discovered. Next to Ryan, the one-eyed dog hopped forward on its knee-less legs, a slight spring with each forward move. Ryan reached down and patted Moolsem's head. For the first time since the bombing, the dog wagged its tail.

ACKNOWLEDGMENTS

T his book is influenced throughout by the thoughtful writings of
Paul Kingsnorth, especially his collection of essays, *Confessions
of a Recovering Environmentalist* (Graywolf). I recommend it. I am
grateful to climate journalist Vernon Loeb, an old friend, for telling
me about it as we sat talking one afternoon in my backyard. But
be careful. While I sympathize with many of Kingsnorth's views,
and have some characters who echo them in this book, I do not
endorse them all. Indeed, I worry that there is a direct link from
nineteenth-century Romanticism to twentieth-century national-
istic fascism that should make us wary of placing too much faith
in ineffable qualities such as "culture" and what feels "natural" to
us. As the astute political commentator Anne Applebaum recently
put it, there is a danger in "a society in which superstition defeats
reason and logic. . . . There are no checks and balances in a world
where emotion defeats reason—only a void that anyone with a
shocking and compelling story can fill."

I also learned about global overheating from several sites, most
notably this one: https://history.aip.org/climate/index.htm.

I also recommend *Fossil Capital: The Rise of Steam Power and
the Roots of Global Warming* (Verso) by Andreas Malm. Again,

there is much I don't agree with. But it made me think about how capitalism and global overheating go hand-in-hand. I plan to go back and read it again.

While writing this book I also became a fan of several Native American blogs covering tribal affairs, both in Maine and elsewhere. Some of the language I use reflects that coverage. I have borrowed some phrases and points of view, but please keep in mind that this is a work of fiction and is not based on real people or events.

Several books about the Indians of Maine and of the region influenced my presentation of this story, including some of the sayings and phrases that appear in the text. Among them were *Still They Remember Me* (University of Massachusetts Press) by Carol Dana, Margo Lukens, and Conor Quinn; *The Algonquin Legends of New England* (Houghton, Mifflin) by Charles Leland; *The Old Man Told Us* (Nimbus) by Ruth Holmes Whitehead; and *Twelve Thousand Years* (University of Nebraska Press) by Bruce Bourque; and *An Upriver Passamaquoddy* (Tilbury House) by Allen Sockabasin. All these books came to me through the Blue Hill Library in Blue Hill, Maine, and through Maine's wonderful interlibrary loan system. I also was inspired by the sharp portrayal of characters in Morgan Talty's lively work of fiction, *Night of the Living Rez* (Tin House).

Also, several studies of Maine's rich history are reflected in the story, including *Behind Barbed Wire: POW's in Houlton, Maine, During WWII* (PrintWorks) by Milton Bailey; *When Revolution Came* (Ellsworth American) by Vernal Hutchinson; and *Deer Isle, Maine* (Penobscot Press) by Edith Spofford-Watts. For a helpful overview of Naziism within the German POW population held in the United States during World War II, I am indebted to William Geroux's *The Fifteen: Murder, Retribution and the Forgotten Story of*

Nazi POWs in America (Crown). Geroux's book was the source of the term "The Fritz Ritz."

More broadly, the portrayal of Native American history in this book also was influenced throughout by the works of Pekka Hämäläinen, especially his wonderful book *Indigenous Continent* (Liveright).

Again, I am grateful to the generous photographers of Maine landscapes and wildlife whose work inspires me daily as I write. It was Laura Zamfirescu's work that first made me pay attention. Among the others are Michelle Beckwith, Michele Bishop, Michele McKenna, Myrna Clifford, Kim Holman, Christine Shepard, Heather Harvey, Shirley Whitenack, Pat Tufts, Layne Stilwell, Rachel Dube, Jean Dube, Nancy Smith, Keith Smith, Andrea Paradiso, Corinne Pert, Kerry Nelson, Diane Phelon, Veronica Violette, Sarah Violette, Sarah Seaman, Sarah Plourde, Richard Plourde, Mary Gaudette, Laurie Chaurette, Tracy Oullette, Craig Ouellette, Mike Audette, Natalie Massé, Loriann Beaucage, Linda Theriault-Quirion, Autumn Pelletier, Rhoda Bilodeau, Jim Groleau, Lou Fournier, Wayne Fournier, Suzette Fournier, Cassie Larcombe, Chris Labbe, Warren LaBaire, Dwayne LaBelle, Cody Auclair, Carl DuDevoir, Steve Bart, Steve Deschaine, Todd Dechaine, Chris Michaud, Sean Michaud, Stacy Marchand, Trish Martin, Guy Mitchell, Gerry Monteux, Dave Mireault, David LaRue, Mike Poirier, Stephen Cyr, Janine Andrew, Janet Marie G. Cyr, Steve St. Lawrence, Christopher Lawrence, Kevin Vachon, Dave Gomeau, Tony Robichaud, Tony Gedaro, Tony Palumbo, Tyler Pascocello, Marty Saccone, Mark Milero, Matthew DiGennaro, Randy Kaldro, Phil Mace, Amy Carlson, Megan Thomas, Megan Lowell, Joseph Lowell, Melanie Libby, Jared Smelter, Kelly Delano, Dakoda Gerrish, Johnny Dallas, Jerre Scott, Jerry Jones, Mark Perry, Dusty Perry and Rusty Dustin.

Let us not forget Cindy Wade LeMoine, Anne Post Poole, Julie Chase Bailey, Sue Bailey, Cathy Sanborn Gilbert, Donna Dodge Baker, Sean Baker, Tricia Young-Chappie, Jennifer Cropley-Farr, Amy Lyons Chambers, Robin Elwell Moran, Lisa Jordan-James, Helen Webster Drake, Tori Lee Jackson (and her moose), Stacy Girardeau Roberts, Tina Philbrick Richard, Scott Richards, Scott Loring Davis, Scott Osmond, Marcy Pluznick-Marrin, Baerbel Bönisch LoSacco, Earlene Dyer Lawrence, Jan Broberg Carter, Diane Freeman Losier, Susan Renee Lammers, Gayle Goldrup Elliott, Kim Turner Hitchcock, Lori Denise, Betsy Headley, Debbie Gallant, Elin MacKinnon, Kari McDonald, Alice McDonald, Joseph McCarthy III, Earl McKenney, Lance Macmaster, Kay Mallory, Mark Gosline, Trina Burns, Becky Waters, Marc Estes, Walter East, Lovena West, Scott Parker, Rick Harder, Deb Boxer, Deb Johnson, Mary Ann McAlpine Baker, Dave Conley, Dave Higgins, Jack Coughlin, Jace Cohen, Julie Coan, Susannah Warner, Bob Warner, Tammy Black, Jim White, Michael Facik, Carl Walsh, Teri Hardy, A.G. Evans, Marge Winski, Cindy Wadsworth, Cindy Willigar, and Bumpa Hennigar (still a great name).

I am indebted to those who gave early drafts a critical reading. Jonathan Bratten cast his informed eye over the manuscript and made several helpful suggestions. Molly Ricks was another early and helpful reader. I followed forty-two of her forty-four suggestions for changes in the text, and rejected the other two only because Seamus Osborne argued that I should do so.

Most of all, Jessica Case gave this book a helpful, thorough, and intelligent edit. That is good to find these days. I appreciate it. I am also grateful for the help given me by others at Pegasus Books, most notably Meghan Jusczak. I also want to thank Susan McGrath for her thougtful copyediting.

The mistakes, and there always are some, are my own.